CAUSE FOR ALARM

Rosemary could not believe this was happening. She, normally so fearful of any man, was alone in a hayloft with Stephen Huntington.

Even more incredibly, she did not shrink away when his hand cupped her face. Nor when he said, with his eyes fixed on her face, "Someone is bound to come here soon."

He bent toward her then, his eyes still on hers. When their lips met, her eyes closed, and her arms, as though they belonged to someone else, reached out and curled around his neck.

Rosemary's heart was pounding, but not from fear. In fact, she felt no fear at all. That was what was truly frightening. . . .

BARBARA ALLISTER is a native Texan who enjoys reading and traveling. An English teacher, Ms. Allister began writing as a hobby after experimenting with techniques to use in her creative writing class.

SIGNET REGENCY ROMANCE
COMING IN SEPTEMBER 1991

Carol Proctor
A Dashing Widow

Melinda McRae
An Unlikely Attraction

Emma Lange
The Unmanageable Miss Marlowe

SIGNET REGENCY ROMANCE

A LOVE MATCH

by
Barbara Allister

A SIGNET BOOK

SIGNET
Published by the Penguin Group
Penguin Books USA Inc., 375 Hudson Street,
New York, New York, 10014, U.S.A.
Penguin Books Ltd, 27 Wrights Lane, London W8 5TZ, England
Penguin Books Australia Ltd, Ringwood, Victoria, Australia
Penguin Books Canada Ltd, 2801 John Street,
Markham, Ontario, Canada L3R 1B4
Penguin Books (N.Z.) Ltd, 182-190 Wairau Road,
Auckland 10, New Zealand

Penguin Books Ltd, Registered Offices:
Harmondsworth, Middlesex, England

First published by Signet, an imprint of New American Library,
a division of Penguin Books USA Inc.

First Printing, August, 1991

10 9 8 7 6 5 4 3 2 1

BOOKS ARE AVAILABLE AT QUANTITY DISCOUNTS WHEN USED TO PROMOTE
PRODUCTS OR SERVICES. FOR INFORMATION PLEASE WRITE TO PREMIUM
MARKETING DIVISION, PENGUIN BOOKS USA INC., 375 HUDSON STREET,
NEW YORK, NEW YORK 10014.

For my sister and brother

1

ROSEMARY WYATT stared at the imposing exterior of the house outside the carriage, her hazel eyes filled with dismay. She moved further back into the corner on her side of the traveling coach, not wanting to leave the safety of its protection. As she tied her bonnet strings, her hands shook.

The security of the coach was only temporary. The door to the carriage swung open. "What a relief to arrive at last," Cousin Hortense said, sighing heavily. The elder lady handed the waiting groom her Pekingese and signaled her maid to precede her. "Your father has no idea of the difficulty he has caused me. None at all. I am exhausted, simply exhausted." She sighed again. Rosemary wanted to agree, but the elderly lady did not give her an opportunity. "Straighten your bonnet," she commanded. She inspected her companion carefully, noting with satisfaction that the gray traveling costume hid the girl's ample curves and her bonnet hid Rosemary's too-often-remarked-on hair. Holding carefully to the strap, she pulled herself to her feet and waited for a moment for her knees to stop aching. "Why your father decided to marry with such haste is a mystery to me." Unless the woman were already pregnant, she added to herself. Hortense Wyatt smiled wryly. She had emphasized her cousin's need of an heir for years. "Come on, child. Do not hang back. You do not want to give your future stepmother the idea that you dislike her." The eldery lady leaned on the groom and allowed him to help her from the carriage.

Rosemary followed her cousin up the stairs to the house

her father had rented for the Season. Her girlishly round face
was pale. She took deep breaths and reminded herself that
her father would be close at hand if she needed him.

A footman from the Manor stood beside the butler her
father had hired with the house. The familiar face made her
uneasiness recede a trifle, at least until the butler said, ''Mr.
Wyatt and Mrs. Thorpe are waiting for you in the drawing
room.''

Rosemary handed her bonnet and traveling cloak to the
waiting footman, followed the stately butler, took a few more
deep breaths, and pasted a smile on her trembling lips as
he opened the door.

''Well, Daniel, where is the gel you asked us here to meet?
Let us get this over so I may retire,'' Hortense Wyatt said.

Her cousin, a tall, sturdy man with a handsome face, blond
hair, and blue eyes, glared at her. Then he turned to the lady
next to him and smiled.

''Cousin Hortense, I wish to present my intended, Mrs.
Mary Ann Thorpe. Mary Ann, my cousin, Mrs. Hortense
Wyatt.'' He smiled down at the petite, dark-haired lady at
his side.

A twinkle in her eyes, Mary Ann took the elderly lady's
hand and said, ''Please do not feel that you must stand on
ceremony with me, Mrs. Wyatt. I know how jolting and
upsetting a long carriage ride can be. I tried to tell Daniel
that it would be better to wait for introductions until you were
rested, but he refused to listen.'' She smiled up at the man
she had agreed to marry, and his smile grew wider.

''You will do, gel,'' Cousin Hortense said approvingly.
At least, quite unlike his last wife, the chit was sensible, the
elderly lady thought. She had some concern for others instead
of being completely self-centered, and was different in looks
too. No willowy blond with a wandering eye this time,
Cousin Hortense added to herself as she inspected the petite,
dark-haired woman with the rounded figure. Then she
remembered Rosemary. She glanced around until she spied
the girl standing just inside the door, her hands tightly

clasped, her eyes fixed on her father and his betrothed. "Where is that child? Rosemary, come here. You'd best introduce them, Daniel, and then you can show me my room and leave them alone to get acquainted."

Rosemary took a deep breath, reminding herself how important it was that she present herself well. She walked forward slowly, her eyes lowered. She tried to keep a smile on her lips, but they were trembling so much it was difficult. Daniel Wyatt, familiar with his daughter's expressions, had been watching her carefully since she entered the room. He smiled encouragingly as she glanced at him and then at the lady by his side. "Mary Ann, may I present my daughter, Rosemary Wyatt? Rosemary, Mrs. Thorpe is the lady I have asked to be my wife." The ladies made their polite responses, each trying to evaluate the other.

"Good. That is done. Now, Daniel, show me my rooms. I will instruct the butler to send in the tea tray, Rosemary. Mrs. Thorpe, I know you will understand if I leave you," Cousin Hortense said, letting her voice shake with exhaustion.

With something like dismay, the other two ladies made the polite responses and watched them go. Finally Rosemary remembered her manners and suggested they be seated. The advent of the tea tray eased the situation somewhat. Taking a deep breath, Rosemary looked up from the cup of tea she was pouring. "Cream or lemon?" she asked, her voice so quiet and quivering that the lady sitting next to her had to strain to hear. Talking to strangers had always been difficult for Rosemary.

"Cream." Mrs. Mary Ann Thorpe smiled at her hostess, soon to be her stepdaughter. She was very pleased at the picture the girl made behind the tea tray. Although the girl looked like a child from the schoolroom in her oversize, outmoded clothes, Mary Ann knew that with the right wardrobe Rosemary's childish plumpness, blond hair, hazel eyes, and unassuming manner would ensure her success. And her handsome dowry would not hurt either. "I am quite looking forward to getting to know you. When your father asked me to marry him, I tried to persuade him to postpone the wedding until I had a chance to visit the Manor and meet you. But I am certain you know how impatient he can be.'' Rosemary looked up in astonishment; her father normally planned his actions carefully. He had started making plans for his trip to London at least six months earlier.

Her guest either did not notice Rosemary's strange expression or chose to ignore it. ''Daniel refused to wait longer than three weeks for the wedding. He even tried to persuade me to wed by special license. I told him, however, that I needed the time to have my bride clothes made. Then he told me about you. My dear, I was shocked. I told him very definitely that I had to meet you before we married. If only your father had insisted that you accompany him to town this Season. Men! They have no more sense than babies. Instead of looking for a wife for himself, I told him he should have been looking for a husband for you.'' She laughed merrily, little knowing how her words surprised the girl sitting opposite her.

The cup Rosemary had been handing to Mrs. Thorpe began to shake so badly that some of the tea splashed the younger lady's hand and into the saucer. ''Oh, how clumsy of me,'' she whispered. Quickly she put the cup down and rang her bell on the tray. Although Mrs. Thorpe tried to persuade her that she did not need a fresh cup, Rosemary gave orders to the footman who appeared. ''Take this away and bring another.'' She dropped her eyes to the floor. ''You must think me quite awkward, Mrs. Thorpe.''

''Nonsense. You are a very gracious hostess. Your father, however, has much to answer for, deserting the two of us as he did. You are very kind. I would have refused to meet a stranger on my first day in London. I am afraid I would have retired much earlier than your cousin did. I hope Mrs. Wyatt will suffer no long-lasting effects of the journey,'' she said warmly, a smile lighting her face.

''I am certain Cousin Hortense will be fine once she has

rested.'' Rosemary took the fresh cup from the footman and finished pouring tea. Then she sat back, her eyes on the rug before her. An uneasy silence fell over the room. Rosemary sipped her tea, wishing she were once again in the country.

Finally Mrs. Thorpe cleared her throat. ''Men.'' Rosemary looked up, startled. ''How like a man. Men have no idea of the awkward situations they create. Do you not agree, my dear?''

Rosemary nodded. Even on the best days, which this was not, she could not imagine being more embarrassed. ''Papa has never been comfortable at tea,'' she said quietly, her voice only a little higher than a whisper. ''I am certain he did not think about . . .''

''That, my dear, you may be certain of. That is what men have wives for: to handle the social situations.'' Mrs. Thorpe put her cup on the table beside her. She leaned forward, a smile on her pretty face. ''Were you very surprised when you received his letter?''

Before she had time to think, Rosemary said, ''Yes!'' Then her eyes grew wider, she felt a blush creep up into her cheeks, and tears trembled in the corners of her eyes. ''I mean . . .''

Mrs. Thorpe leaned forward and patted her hand. ''Let us be honest with one another, Rosemary. May I call you Rosemary?'' The younger lady nodded. ''When I discovered that your father had given you no idea of his intentions, I was quite disturbed. From what he said, you have had the ordering of your household for some time, and now everything will change; I will take that away from you. What must you think of the two of us? No, my dear, do not try to make excuses for him. He has made enough for himself. Once you get to know me, though, I am certain we can be friends. Now, what shall you call me? 'Maman?' Rather affected. Perhaps you had better simply call me 'Mary Ann.' '' She sat back and straightened the folds of her fashionable skirts about her. She glanced at the young lady seated opposite her, noting approvingly the silvery blond hair woven into a high knot. Of course, the girl was not as thin or as tall as fashion demanded, but she had a pretty face, and the contrast of her dark brows and eyelashes with her hair would make her striking anywhere. Besides, some men liked women to be more generously endowed, she thought complacently as she gave her skirts a twitch. Daniel Wyatt had more than once praised her own voluptuous charms.

As her future stepmother made her evaluations, Rosemary made a few of her own. Mrs. Thorpe . . . no, she reminded herself sternly, Mary Ann, was younger than she had expected, only about ten years her senior. She was pretty, with her dark hair and eyes. After her father had introduced them, Rosemary had inspected Mary Ann in amazement. The elder lady's muslin gown was *capucine* in color, with a square neckline cut low with blond net that covered but did not conceal her charms. No one that Rosemary knew wore gowns cut so low. Rosemary quickly lowered her eyes and blushed as she realized she was staring again.

Mary Ann chattered away, not seeming to need answers. Rosemary looked at her future stepmother's gown and then down at her own drab gray, a traveling dress chosen for her by Cousin Hortense. She wondered briefly if she would have a chance to buy something as fashionable as the dress her guest wore. She started when Mary Ann said, "Clothes. That must be the first thing we take care of. My bride clothes have already been ordered, but you need something new as well. I wish we had time to order you a complete new wardrobe. I hope you will understand that I am not trying to be critical, but, really, Rosemary, your clothes are sadly out of date. Tomorrow we will visit my modiste. Surely she will have something you can wear for the family dinner tomorrow evening. Your gowns for the ball and the wedding she will make to our designs. Perhaps a clear green or a soft white, not as stark as snow but perhaps the shade of fresh cream. You know the color. And blue, soft clear blue. Yes, I believe those colors will suit you."

"I like blue." Rosemary jumped when she heard her own

voice. "But I should not attend any parties. I am not out."
The thought of meeting new people made her cheeks grow
pale with fear. Her voice quivered as though she were a
woman three times her own age.

Mary Ann looked at her as though she were a calf with
two heads. "Not attend any of the events to celebrate your
father's wedding?" Her surprise made Mary Ann's voice
more shrill than she had intended. "My dear, you do not
have a choice. Can you imagine the scandal it would cause?
Everyone knows you were to arrive today. If you give me
the cut direct by refusing to appear at events in our honor,
can you imagine what the gossips will say?" Mary Ann got
up and crossed to the mirror on the side wall, smoothing away
a frown line carefully. "Besides, your father has said you
often serve as his hostess. What can one more dinner party
matter?"

"You can tell them I am ill," her future stepdaughter
whispered. She clasped her hands tightly in her lap and
thought longingly of the safety of her room. If only her father
would return so that she could escape. All the way to London
she had wondered if her resolve to be brave would last. If
her father returned quickly, maybe she could maintain
control.

"Even if they believed me, there would be talk. Daniel
has explained that you are nervous around strangers and in
crowds. I think I can help you. Rosemary, except at the ball,
your father and I will be close at hand. Even at the ball, I
will try to make certain you are comfortable. If you do not
wish to dance, we can say you turned your ankle."

"You do not understand. I will try. But something
happens. People talk to me, but my heart begins beating so
fast that I cannot hear what they are saying. And I am so
clumsy. I know the steps, really I do, but when I try to dance,
all I can think about is the people around me. Then I stumble.
And then people begin to look at me and whisper. It would
be much better if I did not embarrass you," Rosemary
pleaded. Tears trembled in her eyes.

Mary Ann stared at the young woman she had met for the first time only a short time before. Although she sympathized with her, she did not intend to have her wedding spoiled by any more gossip than was rampant. The announcement of their engagement had already stirred the memories of the *ton*. Stories about her previous husband as well as those featuring Daniel's scandalous wife had put the couple in the center of everyone's attention.

She did not want to delight the gossips by giving them more to discuss. Remembering Daniel's words on the subject when he had agreed to have his daughter come to town, she admitted to herself that he had made up his mind that his daughter would take part in the festivities. It would take more time and privacy than she had to change it at this late date. She frowned for a moment and then moved across the room. Drawing her chair close to Rosemary's, she patted her hand. "My dear . . ."

"You will talk to Papa, make him agree?"

"No." Rosemary gave a moan and hid her face in her hands. Mary Ann wanted to stroke her hair, to give her comfort, but she was afraid that Rosemary would pull away. "Are you uncomfortable in all situations? Or is it only around people you do not know?" Mary Ann asked, her face sympathetic.

Rosemary sat up and brushed the tears from her hazel eyes. She tried to control herself, hating more than ever that cowardly part of her nature that caused her to react to new situations and people with such hesitation. "Strangers mostly." She drew a deep shuddering breath. "But sometimes . . . sometimes even with people I have known all my life. Mary Ann, I do not want to embarrass you or Papa, but I am afraid I will. Then what would people say?"

"Hmmmm. Unfortunately, most of the people invited for dinner tomorrow evening will be my family, strangers to you. You will know your father, of course, and your cousin. She will be recovered by tomorrow?"

"Yes." The word was shaky but not indistinguishable.

"It is too bad that you do not have any more relatives."

"Both of my parents were only children," Rosemary explained apologetically.

"Well, I have more than enough relatives for all of us. Perhaps if I give you a chance to meet a few before tomorrow evening, it would help," she said, willing Rosemary to agree so that she could continue.

Before Mary Ann could explain further, the door opened and Daniel Wyatt entered. "How are the two of you getting along? Don't you think I made a good choice of a new mother for you, Rosemary?" he asked heartily, crossing to stand proprietarily beside his betrothed. Then he saw the tears still staining his daughter's cheeks. "Rosemary, what is wrong, my dear?" He sat in a chair beside her and put his arm around her. "Mary Ann, what happened?"

Rosemary buried her face in his coat and listened as her future stepmother explained. "She is feeling somewhat overwhelmed by the thought of meeting many new people."

"I thought you had overcome that problem," he said, frowning.

Rosemary sat up. "So did I. Papa, I do not have to attend any of the parties, do I? The wedding will be enough?" she asked cajolingly.

"You will attend all of them with a smile on your face," he said firmly. "Then you may choose to live with my cousin in Tunbridge Wells." Rosemary drew her breath in sharply, her face pale and filled with hurt. "I will not allow the sharp-tongued gossips of London to speculate on why my daughter and her future stepmother cannot be in the same room with each other." He stood up and glared at his daughter.

"Daniel!"

"Papa." The two ladies exchanged a rueful glance. Rosemary lowered her eyes and let Mary Ann speak.

Smiling up at her betrothed, Mary Ann got up and put her hand on his arm. "My dear, Rosemary has been nothing but welcoming to me. I am afraid that I was the cause of her distress. You know how formidable the list of my relatives can be.'' A mischievous smile lit her face as she tilted her head toward him; her hand smoothed an imaginary wrinkle on the chest of his coat. "Remember the first time you met my cousin Lady Longworth?'' she asked coquettishly. She laughed softly at the memory.

Rosemary glanced at her father and was startled to see him blushing. "Well, yes,'' he stammered, and ran a finger around the top of his neckcloth. A rather satisfied smile crossed his lips as he remembered their occupation when her cousin had walked into the room unannounced. He took a deep breath and lost himself in Mary Ann's dark brown eyes. For a moment he forgot everything but the buxom enchantress that stood before him. His daughter stared at him astonished. Her father was making a love match; her hardheaded father was in love with Mary Ann. Although she was pleased with her discovery, she felt more alone than she ever had in her life. Would she ever find someone of her own?

"Daniel!'' Mary Ann said sternly, nodding toward Rosemary. He stepped back away from her reluctantly, wishing that the next week were over and they were alone. Mary Ann looked at him and smiled, amazed once more that the tall blond giant had asked her to marry him.

"Papa?'' His daughter's voice captured his attention. He sighed, wishing that for once his life would be simple, uncomplicated. But he had had to deal with Rosemary's insecurities too often to expect that his wish would be granted.

"Yes?''

"I will try. I promise I will do my best.'' For a moment Rosemary's voice broke. Then she hurried on. "Mary Ann has some ideas to help. Papa, you know I do not want to embarrass you, don't you?'' she asked, a note of pleading in her voice.

"Of course he does, don't you, Daniel?'' His betrothed's voice told him that he had better agree.

"Yes, certainly.'' He crossed to his daughter and put out

a hand to her and pulled her to her feet. Putting aside his annoyance, he hugged her. "What is your plan, my dear?" he asked his fiancée.

"Instead of being overwhelmed by strangers, I want her to meet my relatives a few at a time. I am certain Cousin Sarah will cooperate. We can also walk through the ballroom if Rosemary thinks that will help," Mary Ann explained. Rosemary still had a worried look on her face, but she nodded.

Her father smiled at her. "Now that you have met Mary Ann and made some plans, you can escape to your room. I think you will like it. Mary Ann ordered new draperies. I told her you liked blue." He hugged her again and then released her. "I'm going out to dinner, but I will see you at breakfast."

Rosemary smiled briefly and made her curtsy to her future stepmother. "Remember, I will be here early tomorrow so that we can visit my modiste," the elder lady told her with a smile as she offered her cheek for a kiss. Rosemary nodded and slipped from the room. She paused just before she pulled the door closed behind her and looked at Mary Ann again. The lady was a surprise. Rosemary sighed, wondering how this marriage would change her life.

"I told you she would be uncomfortable here," Daniel Wyatt said as he impatiently brushed a lock of hair from his forehead.

"Daniel, how can you expect to plunge her into the midst of this commotion without some upset? Even if she were not so shy, she would have some difficulty. You should have told her about us much sooner, brought her to London as soon as you thought about asking me to marry you."

"I tried to convince her to come to London with me for the Season. As soon as I mentioned it, she turned pale. It was all I could do to get her to promise to think about being presented during the Little Season," he said resignedly. "At least you got her to make an effort now. That is something I have been trying to do for years. But enough of that."

He put an arm around Mary Ann's waist and brought her close to him. "How did you escape without your cousin?" he asked, a wicked gleam in his eyes.

Before she could answer, he was kissing her, his lips sweet and burning against hers. "Daniel, someone will come in," she protested halfheartedly. Her arms crept up around his neck. Then his lips covered hers again. Soon they were nestled in one chair, arms locked tightly around each other. "Daniel," she said, her word merely a sigh as his lips explored her neckline. Her hands played with his curls. As his kisses grew more passionate and his hands continued their exploration, Mary Ann drew back. "Daniel!" The change in her voice told him he had gone as far as she would permit for now.

"Hmmm." He kissed her once again, enjoying the way she melted against him. Then she pulled away and scrambled out of his lap. "You promised not to tempt me like this again," she reminded him, a rather wistful look on her face. His blue eyes were dark with passion, and his neckcloth was partially untied. Mary Ann thought, as she often did, that he was the most handsome man alive. "Please," she whispered.

He stood up, straightened his rumpled clothes, and tossed his hair back out of his eyes. "I never break a promise." A wicked gleam was back in his eyes. "And I promise you that a week from today all this teasing will stop. We may get no further than Hampstead on our wedding journey."

Mary Ann whirled around to hide the excitement in her eyes and the blush in her cheeks. "You just stop this, my love. We must discuss your daughter."

"What about her?"

"How long has she had been . . . ?"

"Afraid?" Daniel let the word drop between them. Then he sighed. "I am not certain. As a small child, Rosemary accompanied my wife everywhere. Her governess complained that Belinda interrupted the child's education too often, but my wife never listened. She enjoyed hearing the comments of our friends when she and Rosemary appeared together. Except for age, they could have been sisters instead of mother and daughter. It would have been better had they been. When Belinda left, Rosemary was heartbroken. I tried; I really did, but nothing I did replaced her mother. And the child looked almost like my adulterous wife.'' His voice was low and harsh.

Mary Ann hurried to him and put her arms around him. ''We do not need to discuss this if it upsets you,'' she said softly, wishing she had never brought up the subject. They both had skirted the subject of their previous marriages, agreeing silently to postpone their discussion until later.

''Do not get the idea that I miss Belinda. Any feeling I had for her disappeared long ago. Except for my pride, I am not certain she had any power to hurt me even at the beginning. We were young, so young. I was only nineteen when Rosemary was born, and twenty-five when Belinda left.'' A flashing smile crossed his face, making her heart beat a little faster. ''And fourteen years later I find you, my love.'' His arms tightened around her. He kissed her deeply.

The door to the room swung open. ''Do not bother to announce me. I am expected,'' a determined voice stated. Hastily the lovers sprang apart. ''Mary Ann, you asked me to call so that I could meet your new daughter.'' An elder lady entered the room majestically, took one look at their guilty faces, and snorted. ''I should have known. Leave you two alone in a room for long and there would be no need for a marriage. And at your ages. No, do not look at me like a woeful puppy, Mary Ann. And you, sir, straighten your cravat.''

''Cousin Sarah.''

''Lady Longworth.''

''Well, where is the gel? Don't tell me she is so hideous you are hiding her from me.'' Lady Longworth laughed heartily at her own joke and sat down on the settee.

"Well," Mary Ann began, giving Daniel a fierce look. "She was exhausted from her journey and has already retired."

"At five in the afternoon? You did not tell me she was an invalid, Mr. Wyatt. We are talking about a young girl, are we not?" The laughter had disappeared from her voice, to be replaced by disapproval.

Mary Ann sat down beside her cousin. "There is one small problem," she began. Daniel snorted.

"Well?" the elder lady asked imperially.

"She is very shy."

"And when she gets nervous, as she does around strangers, she cries or becomes ill or faints," Daniel added. "I tried to explain Rosemary's problem to your cousin, but she would not listen." He took the chair that Rosemary had occupied. "My daughter has promised me that she will try to overcome her fear, but I have no faith in that. At least she seems to like Mary Ann."

"A wise child." Lady Longworth looked from one to the other, not happy about the distressed looks on their faces. After seeing her cousin unhappy for so long, she was determined that nothing would mar this marriage. "What can I do to help?"

A short time later she rose. "Your plan sounds sensible, my dear. Bring her to luncheon tomorrow. I will make all the arrangements. And you, sir, stay away. You will upset the child." Lady Longworth twitched her skirts back into what she considered acceptable order. "It may work. It certainly is better than doing nothing. Of course, if you had not allowed this situation to progress, Mr. Wyatt, there would be no problem. Men!" She swept majestically out of the room. Looking back, she saw her cousin still standing beside her fiancé. "Mary Ann, come along right now. We shall be late dressing for dinner." Blushing as though she were seventeen instead of thirty, Mary Ann smiled at Daniel and hurried after her.

The next day Mary Ann arrived just as Rosemary was finishing breakfast with her father. Ignoring the girl's protests, she swept her into her carriage and away to Bond Street and the modiste. During the three hours of being measured, turned, and evaluated by a modiste, Rosemary had little opportunity to talk. However, when Mary Ann explained about luncheon with her cousin, she protested. "Could we wait for tea? I am so tired," she explained. As usual, her voice was not much louder than a whisper. Her protest was more formality than fear. Except for her fear of strangers and the tedium of standing while her measurements were taken and dresses pinned so that they could be altered quickly, Rosemary had enjoyed the morning. For the first time in a very long time, she felt comfortable in an unfamiliar situation. Somehow shopkeepers and dressmakers had not caused the fear she felt in social situations. She also realized that part of the reason was that Mary Ann, a kind and caring person, ecouraged her to make her own decisions. Usually Cousin Hortense chose both the plates and the fabric.

Mary Ann leaned back against the squabs of the coach and rotated her head wearily. "My dear, if we had more time, of course I would agree. It is cruel to expect you to meet Lady Longworth today, I know. But we simply have no choice. If you plan to carry out the promise you made to your father . . ."

"I do." This time Rosemary's voice was stronger, and there was an edge of steel in her tone. She surprised even herself.

"Remember, my family is giving your father and me a dinner tonight. Viscount Longworth will be the host. Lady Longworth is his mother. She may be a trifle gruff, but she has a wonderful heart. She has always been kind to me, even when . . . Do not let her frighten you. If she asks you questions you do not wish to answer, start fanning yourself. Or . . ." She paused for a moment. "Can you faint? That would be most effective." Mary Ann pulled her pelisse away from her throat, wishing that she were one of the lucky ones who could afford to leave off her corset. The temperature was warm for June.

"What?"

"Your father told her you faint when you grow nervous. I always wished that I had had that talent. To be able to faint on demand would be very helpful at times." Thinking of the scenes her late husband had been famous for creating, Mary Ann decided that the bruises she would have gained when she fainted would have been little to pay for avoiding the disasters.

"I do not faint—at least I have never done so—because I wanted to. You cannot imagine how embarrassing it is to open your eyes and see everyone staring at you. Besides, I have not fainted for a year or so now," Rosemary said indignantly. "Are you certain that is what Papa said? Does he want me to faint?"

"No. That was one of my ideas. Of course, it would not be suitable at one of the parties given for your father and me. I just wondered what my cousin would do if you did," Mary Ann explained, a mischievous twinkle in her eyes.

"You want me to pretend to faint?" Rosemary asked doubtfully, quickly revising her opinion of her new stepmother-to-be. "Mary Ann, do you think it would be appropriate?" Never had anyone suggested that her nervousness might be a talent. The idea intrigued Rosemary for a moment. Then she frowned. "I cannot do that. Think of Papa."

"You are right. It would upset him dreadfully." Mary Ann sighed. "Then you must be prepared for her questions. If you do not wish to answer, simply tell her so. Of course, Clarissa and Stephen will divert her attention for a time. Clarissa is a year younger than you. She has been out for two years. She is causing her mother some heartache. The girl has turned down three eligible suitors in the last few months and, I am certain, several more earlier. I know my marriage to your father has given her mother untold grief.

No one in my family expected me to marry again, you know,'' she said confidentially. A blissful smile made her face sparkle.

Rosemary just sat there, her heart pounding. She was going to a luncheon with Lady Longworth, someone named Clarissa who had already had two Seasons, and Stephen. "Who is Stephen?" she asked quietly, surprising herself with both the question and the interest in her voice. Maybe if everyone in Mary Ann's family were as kind as she was, everything would be fine.

"Another cousin. Cousin Sarah's, Lady Longworth's, second son. He has recently returned from India." The carriage pulled to a stop before a large house that faced the park in the square. "Rosemary, all you have to do is be yourself," Mary Ann said, and patted her hand encouragingly.

The girl took a deep breath and stepped out of the coach, fear trembling in every breath she took. "Be myself," she whispered. She straightened her shoulders and followed Mary Ann up the steps toward the open door.

2

THE VIVID GOLD, white, and Chinese red of the salon where Lady Longworth received them were a perfect background for both Mary Ann and her elder cousin. As the butler ushered them in, Rosemary felt overwhelmed. There were people everywhere, all of them looking at her. Her heart started pounding; she could feel the walls closing in; her face paled alarmingly; she tried to take deep breaths, but all she could do was gasp.

Lady Longworth took one look at her and said quickly, "Catch her, Stephen. She is going to faint!"

When Rosemary came to, she was in the arms of a man who held her against his chest. She could hear his heart beating. Someone pushed a vinaigrette under her nose, and she coughed and sputtered. "Put her down over there, Stephen. Then join your brother," Lady Longworth said.

Mary Ann, her face worried and strained, patted her hand. "Just lie there for a few minutes more, my dear, until your color returns," Mary Ann said softly. Her dark eyes were filled with dismay.

"Oh, Mary Ann, I am so sorry. Please do not tell Papa what happened. He will be so unhappy with me," Rosemary begged, her eyes filling with tears. She held her future stepmother's hand tightly. "Please."

"There is no need to tell anyone anything," Lady Longworth said heartily, giving Mary Ann a stern look. "After the tiring journey you just made and standing while a modiste poked and prodded you this morning, you were exhausted."

She glanced from one to the other, daring them to contradict her. Neither was that foolish. Satisfied that Rosemary was recuperating nicely, she took a seat nearby and signaled for Mary Ann to do likewise. "Now, tell me about yourself," she commanded.

"Cousin Sarah, she needs more time before you begin to question her," Mary Ann protested, smiling reassuringly at the girl on the settee. "Perhaps we could discuss something else for a time."

"Nonsense. She is fine. Besides, luncheon will be served soon. Can't expect me to get to know the gel over the meal."

"I am fine now, Mary Ann," Rosemary said softly. She glanced at Lady Longworth, who was to her right. The elder lady wore the tiniest cap Rosemary had ever seen, just a scrap of lace that enhanced rather than hid the riotuous dark brown curls that had only a hint of gray. Buxom like Mary Ann, Lady Longworth wore a striped gown in gold and white over a gold petticoat. Although she was only average in height, she was a commanding figure. Rosemary was sure she never had any trouble capturing people's attention. When she concentrated her large turquoise eyes on Rosemary, the girl swung her legs over the edge of the settee and sat up straight. "What would you like to know?"

Lady Longworth shot a look of satisfaction at her cousin and smiled. Mary Ann took a deep breath and then let it out slowly as though to calm herself. She smiled reassuringly at Rosemary. "Tell me about your home," the older lady said with a smile.

For Rosemary the request was a happy one. As she described her home, the home farm, their tennants, and the village nearby, she forgot to be frightened. Her face glowed as she talked about helping the vicar with the local festival and overseeing the housekeeping. Mary Ann and Lady Longworth exchanged looks of pleased surprise as the girl forgot her fears and chattered on. They murmured words of encouragement as she explained.

The door to the hall swung open, and Stephen Huntington,

Lady Longworth's second son, stepped in. Rosemary broke off in the middle of a sentence, startled. She glanced at him and then fixed her eyes on the Aubusson carpet as if trying to count its various colors. Lady Longworth glared at him for a moment and then sighed. "Miss Wyatt, may I introduce my son, Stephen Huntington?"

Forced to look up, Rosemary was startled to see him close to her. She blinked and then stared into his deep blue eyes flecked with gold. "Mr. Huntington," she said politely, her voice only a whisper. For some reason she could not look away as she usually did. It had been he who held her, whose heart she had heard. The memory made her heart race and the color come and go in her cheeks.

Completely disregarding the custom of the day, he took her hand in his and raised it to his lips as he would if she were an older woman. "Your servant, Miss Wyatt," he said. Rosemary caught her breath, not certain how to react but enjoying the feel of her hand in his. His mother cleared her throat. Stephen looked over at her and smiled, mischief in his eyes. "Yes, Mother, I know my behavior is most unseemly," he said, a teasing note in his voice. "But I enjoyed it." Rosemary had to agree with him. She smiled up at him shyly. Her hand still in his, he took a seat beside her on the settee. "Why haven't I seen you at any of the balls this Season?" he asked, flirting with her as he did with everyone.

"I have not yet been presented," she said shyly, wondering at her own boldness.

"Then I am very fortunate to have met you before you are introduced to the *ton*," he said, smiling at her. "You will be surrounded by suitors as soon as you make your first appearance." Privately he was amazed. Mary Ann had said Wyatt's daughter was twenty. Accustomed to the flirts just making their bows to the *ton*, he would have said this child was much younger, yet when he had caught her to keep her from falling, she had not felt like a child.

The thought of meeting vast numbers of people made

Rosemary grow pale. She began to breathe rapidly. "No! Oh, no," she said, breathing heavily, her hand covering the pulse beating so hard in her throat. Both Mary Ann and Lady Longworth glared at him.

"You mean I will not have a chance to see you again, to dance with you?" he asked. His exaggerated alarm and the mock horror in his voice told Rosemary he was teasing her. She began to relax again. "I shall have to return to India, Mother," he said dramatically, one hand over his brow. "I shall never recover." Stephen opened his eyes wider to see the effect he was having. The color restored to her face, Rosemary smiled. Her face lost its childishness. Despite his own inner warning that told him she was much too young, that he should tread warily, Stephen felt drawn to her.

"Hush, you silly boy!" his mother said fondly. "And what would I tell your friends when they inquired of me? Miss Wyatt, you must take pity on me. Tell my foolish son that you do not mean to run away immediately."

Rosemary giggled. "Perhaps I should tell my Papa instead," she teased, surprised at her own daring. "Then he would certainly send me home at once." She looked up from under her dark lashes. Although she knew better than to take him seriously, Stephen Huntington's appearance— brown hair streaked with red and gold highlights, his deep blue eyes with golden flecks, the dimple in his cheek when he smiled, and his rugged six-foot body—intrigued her. None of her acquaintances had his joie de vivre, none of them had ever held her close to his chest, and none of them had ever flirted with her the way he was doing, not even when Cousin Hortense had let the size of her dowry become common knowledge.

"Your papa would not send you home before our marriage. I would not let him," Mary Ann said with a laugh. "You would not want people to accuse me of being a wicked stepmother."

"You, Mary Ann?" Stephen laughed. "Can you imagine

her as the villainess in one of those pieces, Mama? No, Cousin, you are simply not tall enough.''

"Stephen!" Mary Ann said, pouting. "You promised never to talk about my height again.''

"And I did not. I simply mentioned your lack of height. Don't you agree, Miss Wyatt?'' He turned to her, his face solemn but a hint of mischief lingering in his eyes.

Rosemary did not know whether to laugh or to respond indignantly. Prudently she decided to do neither, smiling at both Mary Ann and him. While she was trying to decide what to say next, two more people entered the room. Only a short time before, their appearance had distressed her. Now, although her heart raced a bit, Rosemary sat quietly.

"Miss Wyatt, this is a cousin of ours, Miss Clarissa Ravenwood, and my elder son, David Huntington, Viscount Longworth,'' Lady Longworth explained. "And why are you two here?''

"The butler knew better than to interrupt you,'' her elder son explained, a rueful smile lighting his face. He was taller than his brother, with darker hair and his mother's turquoise eyes. "I am happy to meet you, Miss Wyatt. Mary Ann is excited about gaining a daughter.''

The girl who accompanied him was also dark. Her eyes were dark blue like Stephen's. A recognized Beauty, she had not been happy when she was banished from the room. "It is time for luncheon,'' she said unnecessarily. "Are you well enough to join us, Miss Wyatt?''

"Clarissa!'' Lady Longworth glared at the girl, her eyes widening and then narrowing alarmingly.

Rosemary blushed and rose, feeling as clumsy as though she were a baby taking her first steps. She glanced down at her gown, a simple white muslin that the village dressmaker had finished for her only days before, and felt hopelessly out of place. She took a deep, shuddering breath. Stephen, who had risen when his cousin entered the room, took Rosemary's arm in his and patted her hand reassuringly, sending a faint tingling through her. "You will sit beside me, Miss Wyatt. Then I can impress you with all my adventures in India." He smiled at her as if to tell her he was merely joking.

"Perhaps she would rather hear about London parties," Clarissa said, her eyes narrowing dangerously. Then she decided it was in her best interests to be nice to this country cousin, and smiled. "You may take us both in. Then, when she is bored with you, she can hear about my conquests." Clarissa laughed prettily. Rosemary allowed herself to be swept away, uncertain about how to react to the girl.

Despite Rosemary's misgivings, that luncheon was not as difficult as she had imagined. Because it was a family party, no one felt constrained to follow rules for table conversation, preferring instead to talk about the table. Clarissa had kept them all entertained with her clever and sometimes cruel impressions of the fashionable dandies that had flocked around her for two Seasons. The viscount issued a blanket invitation for everyone to help him celebrate his thirtieth birthday in October.

"So old," his brother said with a sigh. "I know what I shall give you: a cane."

"Good. I need it to keep those imps of mine in line. When you come for my birthday, I will introduce you to my children, Miss Wyatt. They will be five on their next birthday."

"Twins?" she asked, intrigued. Her eyes grew even larger as they did when she was interested in something.

"A boy and a girl." His eyes glowed with pride. "I thought about bringing them to town with me since this will be a short visit, but Mother and Nanny persuaded me differently." Only a hint of loneliness tinged his voice. "They are growing up so quickly." He did not mention his wife, and Rosemary, not wishing to pry, kept her questions to herself. Mary Ann later explained that the lady had died of a fever when the twins were only a year old.

"Well, I am glad they are not here. They are into everything, Miss Wyatt,'' Clarissa Ravenwood explained, drawing Rosemary's attention back to her. ''At Christmas they 'helped' my maids unpack for me. She could not find my favorite shawl until we were ready to leave.'' She pouted beautifully.

''You must admit that the dog wrapped in it made an interesting camel in their Christmas play,'' Stephen added, patting her hand.

''And I know whom to blame for using it. The twins would not have thought of it without some outside help,'' Clarissa said.

''Children! Children! Now do you understand why I did not want to bring the little ones? Think what a bad example these two would set for them,'' Lady Longworth said sternly. ''Stephen, apologize for upsetting your cousin.''

He shrugged his shoulders as if he were conceding the match. Then a wicked grin flitted across his face. Only Rosemary, who found it difficult to take her eyes off him, noticed it. He rose from his chair and advanced toward Clarissa, who sat at the end of the table. He knelt beside her, hung his head as though dejected, and asked, ''Forgive me?'' He smiled at Rosemary while he waited for Clarissa's answer. Her heart raced.

The rest of the table dissolved in giggles. ''Very handsomely done, Stephen,'' Mary Ann said when she could control herself.

All eyes were on Clarissa. She waited until Lady Longworth glared at her, enjoying seeing Stephen on his knees beside her. ''You are forgiven,'' she said graciously, and then spoiled the moment by adding, ''but you still owe me a new shawl.''

Stephen fell back as though wounded. Then he nodded and got up. ''Miss Wyatt, you are very lucky to have so few relatives,'' he said confidentially as he took his seat. ''Mine are always getting me in trouble.'' Rosemary giggled. Lady Longworth and Mary Ann exchanged relieved glances.

Although Rosemary's fear returned during the social events

of the next few days, the people she met at luncheon helped her survive. Stephen, especially, was always nearby. That same night, at the dinner party in honor of Mary Ann and her father, he presented himself as her escort. "I'm only an Honorable," he said apologetically as she tried to protest. "Not really important enough for one of the titles. Besides, do you want to explain to my mother that you want to change her seating arrangements?"

Rosemary glanced at Lady Longworth and then looked up at him from under her lowered lashes. Dressed in dramatic black and white with a ruby as large as his thumb in his neckcloth and another twice as large on his hand, he was a gentleman who captured everyone's attention. She did not believe any of the ladies present, young or old, would have protested had Stephen been her dinner partner. But she did not say another word. The thought of sitting beside more than one of the strangers around her, trying to converse with them, made her grab his arm as if it were a vine and she were sinking in quicksand. A stranger on one side was enough. She glanced at him from under her lashes as she had noticed Clarissa doing and smiled. Had she noticed the way certain ladies' eyes narrowed as they watched him smile at her, she might have trembled in fear instead of excitement.

As she sat in the front of the church a few days later, Rosemary gave a sigh of relief, realizing that in only a few hours her excursion into polite society would be over. The experience, though difficult for her, had been interesting. She settled her soft blue sprigged-muslin skirt carefully around her, taking pride in being dressed in the latest fashion. The ladies who lived around her, for whom a visit to Tunbridge Wells was the height of fashion, would enjoy seeing the gowns and bonnets she had bought. Within a week some of the more enterprising would be wearing copies. As she sat there and listened to the music, Rosemary thought about the difference fashionable clothes had made this week. She had to admit Mary Ann was right. Being fashionable and having someone to talk to had made a tremendous difference.

Resolutely she pulled her attention back to the scene before her at the altar. Her father, tall and serious, was holding Mary Ann's hand as though he were afraid she would run away. For just a moment Rosemary looked at him not as her father but as a man. A man not quite forty, he was still handsome, his blond hair gleaming in the June sunlight that streamed through the windows. Although he was not uncommonly tall, he towered over Mary Ann, her head barely reaching his shoulder.

Mary Ann, too, was looking her best. The deep peach of her gown and ribbons on her bonnet made her skin glow and her dark hair and eyes gleam. From the moment she had met Daniel Wyatt at the altar, her eyes had not left his. Rosemary sighed wistfully. Her elderly cousin patted her hand sympathetically, thinking that Rosemary was regretting the marriage.

Attended by only the closest relatives and friends, the wedding was a small one by fashionable London's standards. Across the aisle were Lady Longworth, the viscount, Stephen, and a handful of assorted cousins, most of whom Rosemary had met during the last few days. Stephen noticed her looking at him and smiled, enjoying the difference the last few days had made. Rosemary blushed and then smiled at him, only the corners of her mouth tilting upward just a little.

Although she had made only an appearance at the larger events of the week, Stephen had always been there at her side, ready to help her escape, almost as though he knew how uncomfortable she was. Rosemary believed that she had survived her brief dash into fashionable life simply because he had been so kind. Then she added to herself, "And Mary Ann."

Glancing at the altar once more, she watched her father slide the ring onto Mary Ann's finger, his voice solemn as he repeated his vows. She smiled as she watched Mary Ann listen to her father making his vows.

At times the last week had seemed never-ending. Mary Ann had helped Rosemary cope with a new situation, kept the peace between father and daughter, and completed all the arrangements for the wedding and her move. Rosemary watched as her father smiled down at the lady he had chosen, and caught her breath. Would she ever know the joy the two of them were sharing? Almost involuntarily she glanced at Stephen. He was watching her, a look in his eyes that made her veins tingle with a fire that was unfamiliar. Startled by her own emotions, Rosemary looked away quickly. Her heart was beating like a drum.

At the wedding breakfast a short time later, her excitement was carefully hidden. As the toasts were drunk, Mary Ann reached out with her left hand to pat Rosemary's. The girl was showing the strain of being in a crowd, her lips rather white around the edges. "Are you all right?" Mary Ann asked anxiously.

Rosemary glanced at her father, not wanting to see his happy smile turn into a frown. "I will be fine," she said, wishing she truly believed it. "As soon as you and Papa leave on your wedding journey, Cousin Hortense and I will be on our way also. Do not worry about me. Enjoy your day." She paused for a moment and then rushed on. "I am happy you married my father. I hope that the two of you will be very happy." She blushed with the effort the words had taken.

Daniel, who had heard only the last of the conversation, beamed. "My two girls," he said proudly, too happy today to worry about his daughter. "I told you she would like you, my dear," he told Mary Ann with a smile. He put an arm around each and hugged them. Rosemary looked up in surprise at the public display of affection. Then she stepped back, leaving the two of them alone in the crowd.

"They look very happy," Stephen said quietly. Rosemary jumped, startled. "I am always frightening you. I

apologize.'' The words were serious; his tone was not.
''Perhaps I should start wearing a bell.''

''Like a cat?''

''Yes.'' He took her arm and drew her to a less busy corner
of the room.

''Then I would simply jump when I heard the bell.''
Rosemary smiled at him, wondering at her own daring. ''Do
cats wear bells in India?'' she asked, trying to prolong their
conversation.

''Not any that I saw. Are you pleased with your new stepmother?''

''And what is she to answer to that, may I ask? If she were
to answer no, she would be insulting our cousin. If she
answers yes, she may be doing so only because she is polite,''
Clarissa Ravenwood said, looking her best in the sheerest
white muslin that Rosemary had ever seen. Although
dampening petticoats was no longer in fashion, Clarissa's
dress clung more than it normally would have done. Mischief
peeked out of her blue eyes.

''Mary Ann is wonderful,'' Rosemary said so quickly that
she almost stumbled over the words. ''I am very happy that
she has married my father. He looks happier than I have seen
him in years.'' Her face was earnest, solemn.

''Goose! I was just teasing you. Naturally, you like Mary
Ann. Who would not? Doesn't she look wonderful? I do
wonder, though, why she chose that design for her wedding
dress. When you are as short as Mary Ann, you must be
very careful or you can look dumpy,'' Clarissa said with a
smile that did not take the sting out of her words. After two
Seasons of adulation, she did not enjoy seeing someone
else the center of attention. ''I suppose your father wants
an heir. This time next year we will probably be celebrating
the christening.''

''I think Mary Ann looks delightful,'' Stephen said firmly,
giving Clarissa a warning look. He took Rosemary by the
arm again as though to lead her away.

''And so do I,'' Rosemary added softly, slightly stunned

by the thought of having a brother or sister. Somewhere she found the courage to go on. "And having brothers and sisters would be exciting. I have always regretted being an only child."

"Your father is motioning for you, Rosemary. We will see you later, Clarissa," Stephen said. As they walked away, he said in an undertone, "Good girl." Rosemary looked up at him questioningly. "You handled her just right." She smiled, and he smiled back, his dimple showing. "Now, let us say good-bye to your parents."

When the flurries of good-byes were over, Stephen Huntington and his mother watched the two coaches begin their journey. "Well, that went off very well," Lady Longworth said with a self-congratulatory smirk. "When Mary Ann told me about the girl, I was worried, I tell you. You certainly knew exactly how to make her feel comfortable. It must be from handling all those maharajahs."

"Mama," her second son laughed, shaking his finger at her. "No one handles a maharajah. All I did was talk to the girl to make her feel more at home with us. All you did was frighten the child."

"Hah! She is no child. She is twenty. Should have been presented two or three years ago. Mary Ann will have to take her in hand immediately if she expects to find her a husband," his mother said before she stopped to give her compliments to the butler and the housekeeper. The thought of a husband for Rosemary gave Stephen pause for a moment. He frowned, and then he put it from his mind. He would see her again soon, long before she was presented.

In the carriage she shared with Cousin Hortense, Rosemary could not get the thought of Stephen out of her mind. He had something about him that drew people's attention. She acknowledged that part of his charm might be his stories about India, but that was not all. He had the ability to put people at ease. Because of his attention, these last few days had been bearable. As she thought about them, Rosemary was astonished that she had not been overcome more often by the overwhelming sense of panic she always felt around strangers. Maybe Mary Ann was right and she could learn to control her fear. "Wake me when we stop to change horses," her elderly cousin said, and then went to sleep. Rosemary leaned against the squabs, her eyes fixed on the changing countryside outside, but she too was lost in her dreams.

3

DURING THE MONTH that her father and Mary Ann were gone on their wedding journey, Rosemary slipped back into her regular activities. Occasionally, however, she would stop, her eyes focused inward rather than on the task at hand. More often than not her thoughts drifted to Stephen Huntington, wondering where he was, what he was doing.

Stephen, too, found himself trapped by memories. He would see just a hint of silver-blond curls, and his heart would race until his mind reminded him that Rosemary was not in town.

Cousin Hortense, delighted at the prospect of returning to her home in Tunbridge Wells as soon as the couple returned, spent most of her waking moments making lists and thoroughly exasperating the servants. Only by concentrating on her cousin and enlisting her aid in getting the house ready for Mary Ann was Rosemary able to keep her staff from revolting. With everyone's help, however, she made certain the house was spotless, glistening with beeswax and hard work. The linen especially was in excellent condition, for Rosemary had put her cousin to work mending even the smallest of tears with her tiny stitches.

As the carriage bearing the master and mistress of the house rolled up the drive, Rosemary took one last look at the assembled servants, hoping that their efforts would please her father and Mary Ann. Although her father had never objected to her housekeeping before, he had told her in

London that he expected everything to be perfect for his new bride.

In the carriage Mary Ann settled her bonnet on her head and tied its bow beneath her chin. The last month had been wonderful, but the real test of her marriage would come very shortly as they settled into everyday life. "Is it on straight, Daniel?" she asked anxiously, wishing she had taken advantage of a looking glass at the last inn instead of sharing a glass of wine with her husband.

"You look lovely," he assured her absently, gazing at the fields of grain outside the window and trying to estimate how soon they would be ready to harvest.

"Oh, Daniel, you are not even looking at me."

"My dearest, you always look lovely," he said gallantly as he turned toward her. She was biting her lip, her hands clenched in her lap. He forced her fingers apart and took her hands in his. "Now, what is wrong?"

"What if they do not like me?" she asked, her eyes wide with dread as she remembered the insults she had had to bear in her former husband's household.

"They will." He pulled her close and gave her a hug. "You will see. Rosemary likes you, and that guarantees that the servants will like you too," he assured her.

"They will not resent me for taking over the housekeeping from her?" she asked. It had seemed so simple when they had discussed their plans in London. Now she could think of a thousand objections she wished she had presented.

"How could they if she does not? And I assure you that my daughter will welcome you." His firm tone told Mary Ann that he had heard all the comment on that subject he was willing to tolerate. During the last month she had learned to recognize when he wanted to change the subject. The carriage stopped. A footman opened the door. "See, here she is now," Daniel said, a note of pride in his voice as he noticed the pretty picture his daughter made, the sunlight turning her hair to silver. He helped his bride from the carriage.

"Papa, Mary Ann, welcome home," Rosemary said quietly. "Did you have a good journey?" The ordinary greeting and the pleased smile that went with it did more than her husband's words to alleviate Mary Ann's fears.

"How wonderful everything looks," she said, gazing about her with interest. The housekeeper and butler, who were standing close by, exchanged congratulatory looks. "The gardens are beautiful. Did I tell you that I love roses?" She linked her arms with Daniel and with Rosemary and walked toward the house. "Now, you must introduce me to these important people."

The next few days were extraordinarily smooth ones. Rosemary arranged a tour of the house with the housekeeper and then gave Mary Ann the keys. For her part, Mary Ann consulted with her stepdaughter regularly, trying to include her, not wanting her to feel left out. They discussed changes Mary Ann thought would be beneficial. Finally, for the first time since she had taken up the reins of the household when she was sixteen, Rosemary was free of responsibility.

As soon as Cousin Hortense left for her home, Rosemary took advantage of that freedom. Since her father no longer expected that she be present at breakfast each morning, she enjoyed staying up for hours reading by candlelight and sleeping late in the mornings. And instead of the one hour she usually spent practicing in the music room, she now could work for as long as she wished. The new music she had bought in London fascinated her. And each day she spent time helping to smooth her stepmother's path.

With Mary Ann she visited their tenants. Although Daniel Wyatt did not have a title, his holdings were widespread, totaling several thousand acres. In the past, Rosemary had tried to depend on the local system of gossip to bring her word about who needed her help. She soon discovered, however, that Mary Ann planned to institute more regular visits. Using a map her husband had provided, Mary Ann had Rosemary drive her about the estate and introduce her to the workers.

"I will never learn all their names," Mary Ann complained one afternoon after she and Rosemary had visited several families. "How do you manage?"

"Most of these people I have known all my life. I have to learn only the names of the babies, and even then people are willing to remind me," Rosemary said soothingly. "Do not think you have to learn everything all at once."

Mary Ann pulled the cart to a stop and turned to look at her stepdaughter. "Do you realize how different you are here at home, my dear? You are so relaxed."

Rosemary reddened, her hands clasped tightly in her lap. "I do not understand what you are talking about," she said, hoping she could divert her stepmother's train of thought.

"My dear, do not try to confuse me. Of course you understand. You do not feel out of place here."

"Out of place? Why should I feel that way around people I have known my entire life?" Uneasy as a result of her stepmother's questions, Rosemary shifted nervously. She turned her head away, not wanting Mary Ann to realize how disturbed she was.

"Yes, of course," Mary Ann smiled thoughtfully and changed the subject. "Whom are we visiting next?"

That evening, however, when Mary Ann and Daniel were alone in her bedchamber, the subject came up again. "Are you certain you wish me to present Rosemary next Season?" she asked tentatively as she snuggled up beside him.

He leaned up on one elbow and then bent and kissed her. "Yes." Then he frowned. "Is something wrong?"

"No, but I do think we need to talk." She reached up to smooth back a lock of hair that had fallen across his forehead. Her smile was gentle and faintly pleading.

"Now?"

She nodded. He flopped back on the pillows, a look of disgust on his face. Mary Ann moved closer and put her head on his shoulder. Soon his arms crept around her, drawing her even closer. Mary Ann asked, "Do you really think she will be comfortable in London?"

He pulled away from her, sitting straight up in bed. "She will grow accustomed to it. Look at her here. She visits the tenants and goes into the village. She has even been my hostess when I entertained." He leaned back on the pillows, but he was frowning. "Besides, what kind of life will she have here? Maiden aunt for our children?"

"That was in her home. And I am certain that she knew most of the people you had invited." Her brown eyes held his blue ones captive until he nodded reluctantly. "Have you ever tried to introduce her to society?"

"She goes to parties, and even balls when someone in the shire gives one."

"Parties that are not held here, someplace where everything is new." She reached up to touch his cheek, her fingers trailing across his lips like the breeze tickles the grass.

He took her hand captive, caressing her palm with his lips. Then he sighed. "When she was eighteen, Cousin Hortense took her to Tunbridge Wells for the summer. I had already rented the house in London and planned to present her during the Season the next spring."

"What happened?"

"I never really knew. After several frantic letters from my cousin, I went to see what was wrong. When I got there, Rosemary was locked in her room, refusing to come out. I finally persuaded her to talk to me, but all she would say was that she could not breathe, that she wanted to go home." He frowned. "At first I thought some man had accosted her, but Cousin Hortense assured me that Rosemary had not been out of her sight long enough for that."

"What else did you learn?"

"That Rosemary was the laughingstock of the spa. She would walk into a ball and faint the first time a gentleman approached her. The only events she did not embarrass herself at were musical evenings, and even then she sat in a corner on the far reaches of the room and refused to play. Rosemary, who begged me for a pianoforte as soon as she was tall enough to see a keyboard!" Daniel glanced at his wife, who had once again pillowed her head against his chest, her hand playing with the blond hair that convered his muscles.

''What happened then?''

''I brought her home.''

''And since then?'' Mary Ann looked up at him, a worried expression on her face.

Daniel sighed. ''She has been my hostess. Occasionally she attends parties. But until recently nothing Cousin Hortense or I could do would persuade her to attempt London. Before I left for London, however, she and I talked again. Then she agreed that being presented did have advantages.''

''And now you want me to do it.''

''She likes you,'' he reminded her.

''She loves you. If she would not go for you . . .''

''She has agreed. You will see how she goes along with whatever you plan,'' he assured her.

Their conversation came back to haunt Mary Ann over the next few weeks. Every time she tried to bring up the idea of a London Season, Rosemary simply smiled. Finally Mary Ann decided to let the idea rest for time. She did, however, continue to keep Lady Longworth informed. Her cousin had graciously consented to help with the presentation, and Mary Ann was certain she would have more than one suggestion about how to guarantee that Rosemary's venture into polite society was a success.

Although she would never have admitted it, Rosemary had been wondering about her future. After years of keeping house for her father, she was restless without regular duties. She had enjoyed the first few days of idleness, reading as much as she wanted, practicing for hours. But even her music had been only a hobby, something to occupy her time between visits to the tenants and supervising the household staff. Since Mary Ann had met all the tenants and taken charge of seeing to their problems, Rosemary felt as though she were no longer needed.

Her home, too, had changed. Since the time she had wandered into the library and discovered her father and Mary Ann kissing passionately, Rosemary had hesitated before entering any room except her own. They had not seen her; she had made certain of that by slipping out immediately. But every time she remembered that scene—Mary Ann on her father's lap, her arms around his neck and his hand under her skirt—she blushed. Somehow she had never thought of her father as a passionate man, but she was being forced to rethink her opinions about many things.

What was she going to do with the rest of her life? Mary Ann was an excellent manager. The tenants liked her. Already the women, many of whom had ignored her own suggestions, were turning to Mary Ann for answers to their problems. Although she would never have tried to usurp Mary Ann's authority, Rosemary felt hurt and left out. Was the rest of her life to be spent reading and practicing her music? As she thought of the embrace that she had witnessed between her father and Mary Ann, Rosemary felt a pang of jealousy. Even going to London began to seem the fulfillment of a quest, with Rosemary the bashful knight-errant.

In spite of the affection she felt for Mary Ann, Rosemary knew that her confusion and hurt showed all too well. The more her stepmother tried to involve her in one of the projects to update the house, the more Rosemary felt something familiar slipping away. Even rooms she had cared for the last four years began to seem unfamiliar. After the first few weeks, she found reasons, often so obvious that even her father realized what she was doing, to avoid making the visits to their neighbors, preferring, she claimed, to devote her time to the study of her music. But as the carriage left with her father and Mary Ann, she would stand at the window gazing down the drive, wondering why she felt so alone. Then she would whirl and dash to the piano once more, letting the music absorb her.

As her stepdaughter grew more and more quiet, Mary Ann tried over and over again to include her. Naturally friendly and open, she could not see the hurt in Rosemary's eyes without trying to do something about it. Each day she would seek her out, ask for her help. As soon as the project was finished, Rosemary would disappear. When Mary Ann tried to discuss the problem with Daniel, he would frown and send for Rosemary. The girl would come in quietly, her eyes downcast, and they would talk for a few minutes. Nothing was ever resolved. Even Lady Longworth in her letters suggested that Rosemary's problem was far more complex than they had first believed. "You cannot hope to repair in a few weeks what has taken a lifetime to occur," she said in her letter. "Remember that I am here to help if I can." The letter, arriving shortly after Rosemary's first refusal to accompany them to an evening's entertainment, helped Mary Ann deal with the kind and not-so-kind inquiries by the members of the county society.

As her sense of displacement grew, Rosemary began slipping away early in the morning, finding her way more often than not to the village. Dressed simply, much like other girls she saw around her, Rosemary visited her friends at the inn or ordered new ribbons for a dress. Then she would enter the church, hurrying toward the organ her father had had installed just the last Christmas. He had teased her that the instrument was her Christmas present. Indeed, she had enjoyed it as though it were her very own.

Although it was not very large, it had a wonderful sound, so full that it stirred Rosemary's soul when she played it. Whenever she came to the village, she could always find a boy waiting to pump the bellows, ready to earn the coin she would give him. She enjoyed her practicing, knowing that although her music teacher was the regular organist in the church, sometimes she would be allowed to play for the service. The presence of the organ in the small church had encouraged more faithful attendance recently, even at the evening service.

Her forays into the village caused another problem in her relationship wih Mary Ann. Her stepmother insisted that she take a maid with her whenever she left their own property. Accustomed to coming and going as she pleased, Rosemary protested vigorously. "I have been driving my pony cart to the village since I was old enough to walk by himself. Must I give up my freedom simply because you believe people will gossip?" she asked angrily.

"It would be safer," Mary Ann tried to explain.

For once, however, Daniel Wyatt agreed with his daughter. "She knows everyone, and the village is only a short distance away. Everyone knows that pony cart of hers. Let her have her way in this. She will have to live with restrictions soon enough."

So one day in late summer, Rosemary made her way alone through the village, her blond hair sparkling silver in the brilliant sunlight, dressed in a dress any of the shopkeepers' daughters might have worn. As she passed the bakery, the scent of gingerbread wafted through the door, and she hurried inside. "I knew you could not resist the smell, Miss Wyatt," the baker said, smiling at her as he dusted his hands on his white apron. "How large a piece would you like?" The door opened again, and two strangers came in. "I will be with you in a minute," the baker assured them. He cut a large square and handed it to the waiting young lady. Taking it, she broke off a piece to nibble, and hurried from the shop, enjoying the spicy taste. She smiled and took a deep breath, the fresh morning air and the aroma of the gingerbread mingling in her nostrils. She ate another small piece and continued toward the church. Before she had gone very far, a young boy was running beside her.

Minutes later the two men, each carrying a loaf of bread, walked slowly down the street after her, careful to make it seem they were wandering aimlessly, as people might do when they were strangers waiting for one of their mounts to be shod. The story had convinced the baker, and they did not want to arouse suspicion. They watched as Rosemary entered the church. "Does it match?" one asked the other. The taller man pulled a swatch of hair from his pocket.

"They could 'ave been from the same 'ead," he assured his companion. "Wonder why Uncle wants hair that color."

"You heard him as well as I did. Some old woman ordered a wig, wanted it the same color as her hair when she was a girl. Thought both she and Uncle were imagining things. Never seen hair such a color before."

"Sure is strange. Just wish it 'ad been on someone else, though. Girl looks young."

"All the better. She can grow it again."

"Sure is pretty, all silver and gold in the sunlight. 'Ow we goin' to get it?"

The shorter man looked at his companion in disgust. "Why, just walk up to her and ask her for it," he said, sarcasm dripping from his words. "How do you think? We'll follow her when she leaves the church, until we see our chance. Remember, just hit her hard enough to knock her out. Don't want no death."

"Why is it always me that 'as to 'it 'em?" the taller one complained. His companion glared at him. They both sat down under a tree in the churchyard, eating their bread and watching the church.

As an hour went by, both men began to nod. The taller one dropped off to sleep and began to snore softly. Just when his partner began to grow desperate thinking their quarry had escaped them, the door to the church opened and Rosemary and her young companion appeared. Money changed hands, and the boy ran toward the baker's shop. "Wake up," the watcher hissed in the taller man's ear, and gave him a shake.

"What? What's 'appening?"

"Quiet! Come on. She's leaving." Hiding behind one after another of the tombstones, the men followed as Rosemary made her way to a gate at the far end of the churchyard, a gate almost hidden by trees. Once or twice Rosemary turned around uneasily, but everything looked the same way it usually did. Forcing herself to stay calm and to take deep breaths, she paused and then continued. "Now," the smaller man whispered. His partner swung the sock containing the rock, and Rosemary dropped to the ground. "Look at that, now. You hit her in the hair. What's Uncle going to say if you got blood on the goods?" the smaller man complained.

"If you're doin' your job as you should, the 'air'd already be off and there'd be no danger," his companion said as he watched the other man release the pins from Rosemary's hair and then began sawing it off. "Better be quick about it."

"Lift her so I can get the other side. No, don't put her back down here. It's too close to the footpath. Move her over there." He pointed with his knife, knicking the girl's ear and neck as he gestured toward a tall tombstone.

"Now look who's gettin' blood everywhere. 'Urry! I want to be long away 'fore she's awake." Quickly they finished their job, securing the hair carefully in a long piece of muslin. They made sure that Rosemary was carefully hidden from view. Walking quickly, they made their way back to the blacksmith, paid for the new shoe, and were on their way before Rosemary began to stir.

At the Manor, Mary Ann and Daniel waited until the last possible minute to leave for the picnic luncheon given by Daniel's closest friends, the Margraves. His eyes blue fire, Daniel told his butler, "When my daughter gets home, tell her I want to see her in my office immediately before dinner tonight." He climbed into the carriage and slammed the door. "That young lady is going to change her ways, or I will know the reason why," he said sternly. "Perhaps it is time to put your ideas about a maid into practice."

Mary Ann took one look at his face and filed the sight under "Looks I Never Wish Directed at Me." "Yes, dear," she said soothingly. "But something could have happened. Perhaps we should send someone to look for her."

"How many times has she been late recently? How many invitations has she refused?" He pulled at his cravat, wishing that fashion allowed him to wear a looser neckcloth. He silently worried about his daughter, wishing he could return home.

"She always told us before. This morning she even asked me what dress she should wear. You know she always enjoys herself at the Margraves'," Mary Ann said quietly. "Could we send the groom back to the Manor so that we will know she has returned safely?" she pleaded, turning her large brown eyes on his.

Without acknowledging his own disquiet, he nodded. "If it will make you feel better. But I do not want you worrying until he returns. She has probably forgotten the time." He smiled down at her, wondering why they had not refused this invitation when it first arrived.

When their groom arrived at the picnic spot on the fastest horse in Daniel's stables, both Daniel and Mary Ann exchanged worried glances. The groom threw the reins to a waiting servant and hurried to his master. As he stopped beside Daniel and bent to whisper in his ear, Mary Ann watched her husband's face closely. For a moment it lost all its color. He closed his eyes for a second to hide his tears and then motioned to Mary Ann. They rose and made their excuses hurriedly, uncaring of the babble of voices that rose behind them. "She's at the vicar's," Daniel said in a choked voice.

"Is she all right?" Mary Ann asked in a whisper as she allowed her husband to hand her into the carriage.

Daniel tried to speak, but his throat was so tight that not a sound came out. He cleared his throat nervously and tried again. "Spring 'em!" he ordered, and then sank back on the seat, his hand holding on to the strap so tightly that his knuckles showed white in the bright afternoon sunlight.

"Daniel, tell me! Is she all right?" Mary Ann demanded.

"I don't know," he cried, and angrily brushed tears from his eyes. "The vicar sent a message that we should come at once. He said it was an emergency. Oh, God! How could I drive off to a picnic when my daughter was missing? What kind of father am I? You tried to convince me that I allowed Rosemary too much freedom, and you were right. If only

I had agreed with your ideas earlier. What could have happened to her?''

Mary Ann took his hand in hers and tried to soothe him. "We do not know that would have done any good. Everyone in the village watches over her. Surely nothing serious could be wrong."

"The vicar does not use the word 'emergency' lightly, Mary Ann. I knew as soon as we had pulled away from our door that we should have gone back. But, no, I was afraid of showing my fear. Mary Ann, what shall I do if she is dead?" He leaned his head against her, his eyes closed in despair.

When they reached the vicar's home, the doctor's carriage stood beside the door. Daniel took one look and moaned softly. Then he squared his shoulders and stepped from the carriage.

4

NOT BY A WORD or a look did the vicar reproach them as they walked into the bedroom where Rosemary lay. Only a great sadness filled his eyes. Daniel took one look at the still figure on the bed and turned to the doctor. "Is she dead?" he asked in a voice that was carefully controlled.

Mary Ann had taken one look and covered her mouth with her hand to prevent crying out. She turned her dark brown eyes brimming with tears on the doctor. "She will recover. I gave her something to make her sleep a short time ago," he explained. "She was so frightened that all she could do was cry."

"Come into the parlor," the vicar urged. "My wife will stay with her while we talk." He led them into a simple room where a tea tray waited. "Will you pour, Mrs. Wyatt?"

Praying that she could control her hands long enough to pour the tea, Mary Ann took her place behind the tray. By the time she took the first sip of the strong, sweet beverage, she had herself under control. Daniel had refused tea, and had a tight, angry look on his face.

"What happened?" Daniel asked, his voice shaking with suppressed emotion as he looked from the doctor to the vicar.

"She received a blow to the head and cuts on her ear and neck," the doctor explained. "The cuts probably happened when they were cutting off her hair."

"Her hair? What happened to her hair?" Daniel asked, looking from one to the other. He had noticed only how still his daughter was lying and had turned his attention on the doctor.

"It's all gone." The tears Mary Ann had been holding in could no longer be contained. "She looks like a shorn lamb." She sobbed and searched her reticule for a handkerchief. The vicar offered her his, and she took it gratefully.

"She was not injured in any other way? They did not touch her?" Daniel's tone of voice alerted Mary Ann, and she gulped back a sob so that she could hear the answer, fearing for her husband's sanity if it were as bad as he feared it might be.

"No, apparently all they were after was her hair. According to old Mr. Somers, the innkeeper's wife's father," the doctor explained to Mary Ann, "this used to happen fairly often." She breathed a sigh of relief and saw some of the tension drain from her husband's face. "Of course, they mostly went for girls on the street back then."

"Will she be all right?" Mary Ann asked. "When will she awaken so that we can take her home? How soon will we be able to talk to her?" Her eyes searched the doctor's and then the vicar's faces, hoping for more reassurance than she saw there.

"Do you know who did this?" Daniel's question cut through his wife's. His voice was cold as iron on an icy winter morning. "Does anyone know anything?"

"Some boys taking a shortcut home found her in the churchyard. They came for me, and I brought her here, called the doctor, and sent for you," the vicar said quietly. "There has been little time for anything else."

"We appreciate everything you, your wife, and the doctor have done, Mr. Cunnings," Mary Ann said quietly.

"We need to send for the magistrate immediately," Daniel demanded, his face red and his eyes angry. The vicar and the doctor exchanged thoughtful glances and nodded.

"Daniel." Mary Ann tugged on his sleeve. He looked down at her as if he were not sure who she was. Then he took a deep breath. "Daniel, may I speak with you alone?"

Unused as he was to reading the nuances of a situation, he took one look at her serious face and agreed. "If you will excuse us?" he asked carefully, already walking toward the doorway. As soon as it had closed behind them and he had looked to see that there were no servants listening, he asked impatiently, "Well, what is it?"

"Are you certain you wish to call in the magistrate?" she asked hesitantly, still uncertain whether her new husband expected her to voice her opinions or simply to agree with his. In the two months they had been married, he had seemed interested in her ideas except when they opposed his about his daughter.

"Why?" Daniel ran his hand through his hair. "Get to the point. I need to talk further with the doctor."

"Think of the gossip," she said quietly.

"Gossip. You are worrying about gossip when my daughter has been assaulted? I had not thought your mind so small, Mary Ann! You go check on her while I send someone for the magistrate." He frowned and reentered the room that they had just left, ignoring the explanation she tried to make. The door closed behind him with a loud thud. Mary Ann jumped and walked back toward the bedroom where her stepdaughter lay. She entered the room quietly and stood by the bed, her eyes full of pain both from worry about the girl and from hurt that her husband thought she could be so petty.

"She will be fine, Mrs. Wyatt," the vicar's wife assured her, getting up from the chair she had drawn close to the low bed. "Miss Wyatt is a good, strong young lady."

The two women exchanged worried glances as if acknowledging the problem that lay ahead. "You have been so kind, Mrs. Cummings," Mary Ann said softly. Then she paused as if she were not certain how to proceed. Then she hurried on. "I know I can trust you to be certain the true story is known." As a newcomer to the area, she did not want to offend anyone, yet she was certain the village was already talking and imagining the worst.

"You just sit down here and keep her company. I will see to everything," Mrs. Cummings assured her. "I'll make certain everyone knows the truth." She patted Mary Ann's hand as if to soothe her fears. Knowing the people as they both did, both Mrs. Cummings and Mary Ann realized that although most people would believe the vicar's wife's story, there were always those who preferred to believe the worst. And those people were gossips. "Do you have everything you need?" Mrs. Cummings asked quietly.

Glancing about the room, Mary Ann nodded. She moved the chair closer to the bed so that she could hold Rosemary's hand, and waited. Feeling as exhausted as though she had run from the Manor to town, she closed her eyes for a moment, wishing that when she opened them this would all be a bad dream. Rosemary stirred restlessly, pulling her hand from Mary Ann's. Her stepmother opened her eyes and leaned toward the bed, smoothing the few strands of hair still long enough to fall into the girl's face back away from her eyes. Except for her hair and the small cuts on her neck and ear, Rosemary looked just as she had always done. Mary Ann dampened a cloth and wiped the girl's forehead. The cool water seemed to soothe her, and she drifted back into a more quiet sleep.

When Rosemary awoke sometime later, both Daniel and Mary Ann were at her bedside. She groaned and opened her eyes as though the movement hurt her. Then she saw her father. "Papa," she cried, her eyes filling with tears. She struggled to sit up, but he pushed her back on her pillows.

"I am here, little one," he said quietly, his voice choked with emotion. He reached down and touched her cheek. Sitting on the edge of the low bed, he leaned foward and kissed her forehead.

"Oh, Papa, I am so sorry," she cried, tears running down her face. Mary Ann brushed a few from her own cheeks, wondering how Rosemary had taken such firm possession of her heart in such a short time.

"For what?" her father asked. Rosemary just cried harder.

Daniel looked at his wife as if to ask her what to do, but she was wiping her eyes with the vicar's handkerchief. Shyly the tall blond man reached out for his daughter and pulled her into his arms as he used to do when she was a child. She wrapped her arms about his neck and held on as though she were afraid he would disappear. Finally, when her sobs quieted and the front of his jacket was soaked, he hugged her and then laid her back on the bed. "We have been worried about you," he told Rosemary as he wiped the last tears from her cheeks. "Don't you ever frighten us this way again!"

"Oh, I won't. I promise, Papa." Tears trembled in her eyes again. She moved her head restlessly, as though she could not get comfortable.

"The doctor is waiting to tell us if you are well enough to be moved home," Mary Ann told her, smiling at her to soften her words. "I will tell him you are awake and ready to see him."

"Home," Rosemary whispered. "Yes, please. But I do not want to see the doctor. Just take me home. Please, Papa." She looked up at him, her large hazel eyes pleading. He wanted to pick her up and carry her to safety but knew that would not be wise.

Before he could answer, the door opened and the doctor walked in. "Well, let us see how you are doing, young lady," Dr. Smythe said heartily. "That is some bump you have."

"You will let me go home?" she asked, her voice catching on a sob. "I want to go home."

"Let me see. If you will stand over there, Mr. Wyatt"— Dr. Smythe pointed to the opposite side of the room—"I will examine our patient." He glanced at her eyes, noting that the pupils were still small from the opiate he had given her, but equal. He turned her head gently and carefully inspected the lump behind her ear. "How does your head feel?"

"It hurts," she said plaintively.

"Hmmmm. Probably will for a day or two." He glanced

toward her father. "You will have to be careful in moving
her, but I believe she would be better off at home." He
smiled down at his patient reassuringly. "Expect some
discomfort on the trip, Miss Wyatt." He glanced at Mary
Ann and motioned her to meet him outside the room. She
slipped out quietly and waited for him. After giving his final
instructions to Daniel, he met her. "It will be up to you to
help her with the problem of her hair. She has not let herself
notice it yet. I told Mr. Wyatt to keep her head covered.
Maybe that will keep the servants quiet until you get her
settled in her room. As close as the Manor is to the village,
however, they probably already know what happened. Also,
keep someone with her tonight. She will be in considerable
pain, but I do not want to give her anything else unless it
is an emergency. You have laudanum?"

"Yes." Mary Ann's face was worried. "Shall I give that
to her if she says her head hurts?"

"No, not unless she grows more agitated and you think
she will harm herself. The effects are not always what we
want, not when someone has had a knock on the head. Do
you have any willow bark?" he asked, rubbing his hand
across the back of his neck.

"I do not know. The stillroom is one area that I have not
explored fully."

"Check. If you do, boil some of that and let her drink the
effusion. It will be bitter, but it should help the pain." He
added a few more instructions and then said, "If you have
questions, do not hesitate to send for me."

The carriage ride home was one that Mary Ann would
remember for years. Every time the coachman hit a stone,
Rosemary moaned. Daniel's face grew whiter, and he
wrapped his arms more tightly around his daughter, as though
trying to bear her pain himself. Although Mary Ann had
offered to hold her, Daniel refused, almost as though he
blamed her for what had happened. Sitting opposite the two
of them, Mary Ann wondered how they would survive the
coming days. The dream of living a peaceful life in the

country with a loving husband and daughter seemed farther and farther away.

In the next days Mary Ann knew she had been right. From the evening that they had brought Rosemary home, Daniel slept in his own room—when he slept at all. He was spending most of his time searching for the two strangers, and the rest with his daughter. As soon as Rosemary had been installed in her own bed and was resting comfortably, Daniel had returned to town. He had talked to the two boys who had found his daughter and anyone else who had seen her that day. Both the baker and the blacksmith had mentioned seeing two strangers. The baker even remembered seeing the two men walk in the same direction as Rosemary. But only the blacksmith had seen them leave. Both men agreed the two were the best suspects. But no matter how far Daniel rode looking for more information about the two, he could not find any traces of them. It was as though they had walked through a fairy mist and had disappeared. Nothing would make him stop looking, however. Avenging his daughter was all he could think about.

While Daniel was scouring the countryside, it was Mary Ann who had to answer Rosemary's questions. The day following the injury was a nerve-racking one. First Daniel questioned his daughter about her actions. "Did you see the men who hit you?" he asked, his voice stern. His daughter just looked at him, her face whiter than it had been a few seconds before. "Was it the two strangers who came into the baker's shop when you were there? What did they look like?

"I did not see who hit me," she whispered. The tears rolled down her face. "Why did they do it? What had I done to them?" Daniel looked toward his wife, surprise and dismay written all over his face. "My head hurts, Papa. What made them do it?"

Daniel wiped the tears from her cheeks again and gave her his handkerchief. Mary Ann bustled around smoothing her pillows and wringing out a cloth in cool water to place on her forehead. "How many were there?" Daniel asked as gently as he could. "I want to find them, but unless you can tell me what they looked like . . ." His voice drifted off helplessly.

Slowly, almost painstakingly, Rosemary recounted what had happened. "It was late." She smiled wanly. "You know how I forget the time when I am practicing." He nodded. "I was hurrying. The next thing I knew, I was at the vicar's. Mrs. Cummings was washing my face."

"You just rest. Try to sleep," her father said, his voice gentle and reassuring. "I will be back later." Without a word for his wife, he hurried from the room.

Mary Ann sat down in a chair angled so that she could see her stepdaughter. For a while there was only silence as Rosemary lay there, her eyes closed. From the way her hands fluttered restlessly, Mary Ann knew the girl was not sleeping, but she did not want to intrude on her thoughts. Once or twice she thought one of Rosemary's hands moved toward her head. But it never went further than her throat. Finally the girl opened her eyes and turned her head carefully. "Am I ugly?" she asked, her eyes tightly closed, as though she did not want to see the look in Mary Ann's eyes.

"Ugly? Of course not. Why do you ask?" her stepmother hastened to assure her. She crossed to the high bed and took Rosemary's hand and clasped it between hers.

"No one will look at me. Oh, they glance at me, and then they look hurriedly away. But I have seen the pity in their eyes. What about my bandages? Will I have scars?" She paused and then rushed on. "And my head—why does my head feel so peculiar?" Her voice rose with her panic.

"My dear, the only reason you see pity in people's eyes is that they regret this happened to you. Everyone loves you and wishes you had not been hurt," her stepmother explained, her voice gentle and soothing.

"If everyone loves me, why did it happen?" the patient asked petulantly, as though she were still a child.

"Now I can tell you are getting better," Mary Ann said

with a smile. "Before long you will be up and about as usual."

"Mary Ann, be honest with me. How badly have I been injured? And why did it happen?" Rosemary looked at her stepmother, noting the drawn look on Mary Ann's pretty face.

"I do not know why it happened." The elder lady sighed heavily. "All we can really do is speculate. Your injuries, except for the knot on your head, are slight. We had to put a bandage over the scratch on your neck to keep you from rubbing it raw when you were asleep. You would not leave it alone. The doctor says it will fade quickly. I will let you see for yourself in a moment." Rosemary's maid entered the room then, and Mary Ann waited until she had put down the towels, pulled the copper tub in front of the fireplace, lighted the fire, and then left again before continuing. "The doctor said you could have a bath if you felt strong enough. I thought you might enjoy it," she explained.

"Yes," Rosemary said gratefully. "Is that all?" she asked, hoping that it was but knowing it was not.

"No." Mary Ann took a deep breath and squeezed Rosemary's hand. "They cut off your hair."

"My hair?" Her hands went to her head. Rosemary's eyes grew wider as she felt the short, straggly ends. "My hair?" she asked again, her voice trembling. Tears trembled in her lashes. "They cut off my hair," she said quietly as her tears began streaming down her face. The first thing people looked at was her hair. It was beautiful. She had seen Stephen's eyes when he looked at her. He always looked at her hair.

"It will grow back," Mary Ann tried to reassure her.

"But I never had it cut, not really, only the ends trimmed when it grew ragged. Mama made me promise I would leave my hair long. She said it was my claim to beauty. She told me I would never be as beautiful as she was, but my hair was beautiful. She told me that. It was just like hers." As she was talking, not even realizing what she was saying, Rosemary was running her fingers through her hair as though she were measuring it. "Now it is gone. It changes color when you cut it. Did you know that? Mama told me that. That is why I am never to cut it." Rosemary's voice grew even more childlike. "My hair looks just like Mama's."

"I have cut my hair several times, Rosemary. It always grows in the same color," Mary Ann assured her, blinking back tears as she listened to her stepdaughter babble on.

"Blond hair is different. That's what Mama said." Rosemary stopped. Her face changed, losing the childish expression. "May I have a mirror?" she asked, her voice shaky but definitely that of an adult.

Mary Ann hurried to the dressing table and picked up the only one lying there, an elaborate hand mirror framed in gold. She handed it to Rosemary, who took it and then closed her eyes. She opened them again and raised the mirror. Her eyes widened in horror as she looked at the jagged ends and general unevenness of the hair that remained. "As soon as you wash it, we will have your maid or my dresser trim it," Mary Ann said soothingly. "I am certain it will be quite becoming."

Rosemary simply stared into the mirror again. Then she reached up and pulled a lock of hair straight out from her head. "It is so short," she whispered. "I look like a freak. No wonder everyone looks at me with pity. Mama was right. I am not beautiful. Now Stephen will never notice me again." Her eyes filled with tears once more.

"No one is beautiful with red eyes or a red nose," Mary Ann said briskly. "If beauty is what you desire, you must remember that you should not cry. So few ladies can cry and still look lovely. It is an art that some women are born with, but you were not." She handed her stepdaughter a cloth dampened with lavender water. "Wipe your face with this." While she was straightening Rosemary's bed, Mary Ann filed the statement about Stephen away, certain the girl did not realize what she had said. "Do you feel strong enough for a bath?"

When Daniel returned from his fruitless hunt that afternoon, his daughter was dressed in a frilly nightrobe that she usually refused to wear, and back in bed, her hair neatly trimmed and curled. The short blond curls framing her face made it look less full, less childlike. Although she still mourned the loss of her locks and the unfashionable length of her hair, Rosemary no longer was devastated. Exhausted by her exertions, she dozed peacefully, her headache reduced to a fraction of what it had once been.

Daniel knocked on the door. When no one answered it, he opened it hesitantly, feeling like an intruder. Slipping inside, he walked toward his daughter's bedside and stood there for some time just watching her sleep. Finally he sighed and left. A short time later he stormed into his wife's bedroom, where Mary Ann and her dresser were discussing the repairs to one of her favorite evening gowns. "Why is my . . . ?" he began. Then he noticed the dresser. He frowned.

"Do what you can with it, Harris," Mary Ann said quietly, sending the woman on her way. "What is the problem, Daniel?" she asked, turning to face him, the mirror of her dressing table reflecting the tumbled mass of curls that had slipped out of the knot that usually kept them off her neck.

"Why is Rosemary alone? I told you to keep someone with her at all times. Are my wishes constantly disregarded? Is this the way my household behaves when I am not around?" he ranted. Mary Ann bit her tongue, reminding herself that he was under tremendous stress. "Well, what have you to say for yourself?" he demanded as he ended his tirade.

His wife took a deep breath and fixed a serious look on her face. "Rosemary begged me to allow her some time alone. She was exhausted after her bath."

"Bath? I did not give my approval for her to take a bath," he said angrily, pacing around the room furiously.

Mary Ann resisted the impulse to dash to the rescue of a pair of Meissen figurines that trembled every time he walked by the small table where they sat. "Yesterday the doctor told me she would probably rest easier after she had

had a chance to bathe. We were very careful. I know she did not have a chance to grow chilled. Both her maid and my dresser were there constantly, as I was.'' She smiled up at him, noting as she always did the way his blue eyes seemed so dark against his fair skin. ''What did you discover?'' she asked softly. She moved to the chaise longue and patted the place next to her suggestively.

Daniel ignored her, taking a chair across from her. ''I learned no more than I already knew. It is as though those men were evil spirits. One minute they were injuring my child; the next they had disappeared.'' His anger drained from him as he sighed. He put his head in his hands as though he were too weary to hold it up any longer.

''Do not let anyone else hear you say that!'' Mary Ann said sharply. She crossed to the door to the hallway, opened it, and checked the hallway. Next she checked the door into his bedroom.

''What? Mary Ann, what are you doing?'' he asked, his face puzzled. ''Has something happened I know nothing about?''

''No. Just do not mention evil spirits again!''

''You cannot believe in such things!''

''Of course I do not! But the servants might. You know how easily rumors start. If one of them heard what you said, it would be all over the Manor in minutes and in the village shortly thereafter. Watch what you say,'' she said seriously.

''You know I did not mean it,'' he said in disgust, seeing her reaction as just another example of how women over-reacted to a situation. ''Everyone agrees that those two strangers that were in the village yesterday were probably the ones. I wish I could find them.'' He pounded his fist into his other palm. ''I would not wait for the magistrate. How dare they strike down a defenseless girl?'' His face was dark with anger. He rose again and resumed his pacing. ''Well, they will not get away so easily. Someone must have seen something.'' He walked toward the door to the hallway.

"And if you do not plan to stay with my daughter, I will," he said angrily.

"But you have not had any sleep. How will you be able to look for those men tomorrow if you do not sleep tonight?"

"I do not want my daughter left alone. Not for a moment!"

"You go to bed. I will sit with her," Mary Ann said firmly. She sighed, wishing she could do more to relieve his anger and guilt. "Go to bed, love." She patted his cheek and shoved him toward his own bedroom door. Without thinking of the sleepless hours his wife had already spent, he nodded. As soon as the door had closed behind him, Mary Ann sighed wearily. She looked at the bed behind her. Then she picked up her embroidery and walked from the room.

5

ROSEMARY'S PHYSICAL injuries healed quickly. By the end
of the week she had returned to most of her normal household
activities. Only a thin red line remained on her neck, and
her headache had disappeared. Daniel, however, was still
scouring the countryside, with as little luck as he had had
that first day. His temper, usually so even, was as ragged
as his looks. When he came in so late Saturday evening that
only a footman and his valet were waiting up for him, he
slammed into his bedroom, waking Mary Ann, who had tried
to stay awake to talk with him. Pulling her robe about her,
she stumbled toward his door. Yawning, she waited until
she heard the door to the hall close. Then she walked in,
climbing into Daniel's bed before he had a chance to tell her
no. "Did you find them today?" she asked, hiding a yawn
behind her hand.

"No," he said angrily. Unconsciously he reached out and
pulled her close, needing some kind of reassurance. "And
that . . . that magistrate told me he had more important things
to do. He wants me to stop looking for the men!" Daniel rose
because his brother has a title, he thinks he can tell me what
to do. He wants me to stop looking for the men! Daniel rose
on his elbow, looking down at Mary Ann's sleepy face, his
anger cutting deep lines into his face. The hours that he had
spent in the saddle during the last few days had turned his
skin a deep tan.

"Are you going to listen to him?" Mary Ann asked softly,
reaching up as she usually did to smooth back a lock of hair

that had fallen on his forehead. He had streaks in his blond hair that had not been there only days ago. He lay back and closed his eyes. When he did not answer her after a few moments, she asked, "Daniel, what are you going to do?"

"I don't know," he finally said, the words coming out as though they had been forced. "My only daughter is attacked and there is nothing I can do." His tone was hopeless.

"What about a reward? Surely if you offer enough money, someone will come forward," she suggested, wanting to restore his confidence.

"I have already done that. Most of the information has been unreliable or the men do not fit the description once I find them." He sighed. "Lately I have been wondering if the story about two strangers is just that, if someone else hit her."

"You think someone in the village would hurt your daughter?" Mary Ann's voice revealed her astonishment.

"No, not really. I simply do not know what to do anymore. I cannot sit around doing nothing, but I have nowhere else to look."

"Tomorrow we will go to church. Everyone needs to see that Rosemary's injuries were not as serious as they have been rumored to be, and then on Monday you will go back to your regular activities managing this estate," Mary Ann said as calmly and as rationally as she could. "I can keep your household running, but I know nothing about the estate. When someone has new information for you, he will know where to find you."

He sighed again. "You are right. Thank God I found you. I do not know how I would have survived this without you." He kissed her good night and drifted off to sleep. Mary Ann lay there in the darkness, her heart too full to sleep right away. Her fears that he blamed her for what had happened to his daughter seemed so foolish now. She nestled against him, listening to the steady beat of his heart.

The next morning was golden, not a sign of rain or mist.

Both Mary Ann and her stepdaughter were dressed in the latest style. Mary Ann wore an apple-green spencer over an oyster-white muslin gown sprigged in a matching green, with both the skirt and spencer decorated with matching ribbon. Rosemary wore a pink sprigged muslin. To hide her missing hair, she wore curls around her face and a bonnet worn over a lacy cap. As they waited for Daniel to join them, Rosemary walked nervously about the room. When Daniel walked in a few moments later dressed in a dark blue coat, crisp white cravat, linen figured waistcoat, and buff trousers, anyone who saw them would have been forgiven for thinking them the perfect English happy family.

Their happiness did not last very long. From the moment she saw the churchyard with all its tombstones, Rosemary went white. She bit her lip but got out of the carriage, taking her father's arm and holding on as though she were afraid to let go. Even the soft pink bow on her bonnet and the pink ribbons around her neckline did not add any color to her face. Mary Ann glanced at her sharply and then hurried her inside to their own pew. During the service, Rosemary sat quietly, making the responses as though she were asleep. Even the music did not reach her. Although her lips were moving during the responses and the hymns, neither Mary Ann nor Daniel could hear her voice.

After the service the real ordeal began. As they made their way out of the church, Mary Ann and Daniel greeted their friends and acquaintances. After they left a group, a buzz would break the hush that had fallen when the Wyatts arrived. Most men had a handshake for Daniel. The women, their eyes bright with curiosity, ignored Rosemary and asked Mary Ann impertinent questions. Their eyes darted from stepmother to daughter as if ferreting out the details. A few pulled their children away from Mary Ann and Rosemary as though the ladies had the plague, ignoring any remarks addressed to them. Instead of a congenial group of neighbors enjoying their usual chat after services, the congregation broke into groups in which people would chatter for a moment excitedly and than as casually as possible turn to stare at the Wyatts, especially Rosemary. Except for a few like the baker and blacksmith, even the townspeople stared at Rosemary, gossiped behind their hands, and then hurried home, their faces concerned. Only the Margraves and the vicar showed real concern, inquiring about Rosemary's health and well-being. The others simply gossiped.

To Mary Ann's horror, Rosemary grew even more pale and began to shake. She did not collapse, however, until they were safe in their own carriage. Then she dissolved in tears. "I won't to back there! I won't, I won't!" she said, sobbing.

Daniel, helpless to ease her pain, put his arms around her. He looked over her head at his wife, his expression grim, as though reminding her that it was her idea to attend church that morning. Fortunately, the journey to their home was a short one. As they began the trip up their drive, Mary Ann handed her stepdaughter a handkerchief. "Wipe your eyes, dearest," she suggested. "You do not want the servants to see you in tears." Obediently Rosemary sat up and began wiping her face. Daniel raised an eyebrow as if to suggest that nothing could keep the information from the gossip mill. Mary Ann frowned at him.

As soon as they reached the Manor, Rosemary averted her face and ran up the stairs to her room. Daniel and Mary Ann followed her as casually as they could. "Tell Cook to put back our meal for a half-hour," Mary Ann told the butler. Then she too hurried up the staris. She paused outside her stepdaughter's door. Then it opened, and Rosemary's maid walked out, her face puzzled. "Is Miss Wyatt all right?" Mary Ann asked.

"Oh, Mrs. Wyatt, I don't think so. She is crying as if something terrible has happened. I am afraid she will be sick if she goes on. And she told me to go away." Obviously it was the last that was the most disturbing to the maid, who had been with Rosemary since she was sixteen. "She ought not be alone like that, but what was I to do?"

"You did just as you ought. I believe you should tell Cook

that Miss Wyatt will have luncheon in her room today. Tell her that she might need some coaxing to eat," Mary Ann said soothinly. Somewhat calmed, the maid nodded and walked down the back stairway to the kitchen. Mary Ann opened her stepdaughter's door and stepped inside. "Are you all right, Rosemary?" she asked, and then wanted to call back her foolish question.

"Go away," Rosemary said, her face muffled by her pillow.

There was a knock at the door. Before Mary Ann could answer it, the door swung open and Daniel put his head in. "Is she all right?" he asked, carefully keeping his eyes on his wife. Ever since Rosemary had grown up, he had hesitated before entering her room, not wanting to embarrass her or himself.

His wife shook her head. "Come in," she whispered. Together they walked over to the bed where Rosemary lay, still facedown. "Rosemary, you cannot lie there crying like that. You will make yourself ill," Mary Ann said, her voice low and soothing.

"Please, baby, talk to us," her father added, running his hand through her short curls. Neither by word nor action would the girl acknowledge them. Finally, convinced that their presence was doing more harm than good, Mary Ann pulled Daniel out of the room.

"Her maid is bringing her luncheon on a tray," she told him. "Perhaps it will be better to let her rest until then. We can talk to her later." They walked to their own rooms, exhausted by the events of the morning and the storms of the heart they had yet to conquer. When the door to their suite had closed behind them, Mary Ann pulled off her bonnet and put it carefully on a small table. "Daniel, I did not imagine what happened in church this morning. Are people around here really that cruel?" She turned to face him, anger written in the lines of her face.

He put his arms around her, glorying once again in the way she responded to him so eagerly. She melted against him. He closed his eyes. "No, no more than anyone else. Part of it is my fault."

"Yours? How?" she demanded, pulling back just a trifle so that she could look up at him, her deep brown eyes puzzled.

"You know your background. Rosemary's mother did not have the best reputation. When she was a girl, she had been forced into the typical mold and married off as soon as possible. As soon as Rosemary was born, she began to have affairs. I was determined that my daughter would be reared differently. Therefore, I gave her a far different education, brought her up with more freedom so that she could have a chance to discover who she was before she married. Cousin Hortense warned me that I was ruining her. Now I have." His tone was level, but his eyes revealed his anguish.

"Do not blame yourself for this. You did not cause those men to hurt your daughter."

"No, but I certainly did little to protect her. You warned me. 'Send a maid with her,' you said, didn't you? But would I listen?" He began to pace around the room as though he could work off his anger by himself.

"Daniel, no matter what we feel or think, we cannot go back and change what happened." His wife's soft voice was neither loud nor harsh, but it stopped him. He turned to look at her, a question in his eyes. "What we need to do now is decide how to handle the situation. Both you and I have been the center of gossip before, and we can survive this. But Rosemary does not deserve it. What we must decide now is how to protect her," she said firmly. She glanced at the clock on the mantelpiece and sighed. "Our meal will be ready. Maybe after we have eaten, we will be able to think more clearly."

Although the idea was a good one, nothing they did or said that day helped them cope. Rosemary refused to eat, to talk to them, to come out of her room. The servants behaved as though there had been a death in the house, moving into the rooms silently, their eyes carefully averted.

The situation grew steadily worse over the next week. Rosemary stayed in her room, subsisting on pots of tea. Both Daniel and Mary Ann tried to talk to her; nothing moved her. After one of their sessions with Rosemary, Daniel would rush to the stables and spend the rest of the day inspecting his properties. His wife was not as lucky. She had to contend with the servants, who had somehow decided that she was to blame for what had happened to their master's daughter. And society had turned its back. Although she would not have left the house with Rosemary in the state the girl was in, Mary Ann did not even have the pleasure of turning down invitations. They had ceased to arrive. Only the Margraves, the vicar and his wife, and the doctor dared brave public opinion by visiting the Manor. Using the strength she had learned in her first marriage, Mary Ann did not allow her emotions to show in public, revealing them only to her husband and in her letters to Lady Longworth.

In her room Rosemary brooded. She looked out into the beautiful countryside and saw only a frightening unknown, full of people who thought she had done something wrong. She had never believed that she could feel so uncomfortable in the church she loved. The feeling of all those people surrounding her, staring at her, had surprised her. She knew those people, shopped in the village, visited with them. How could she be afraid of someone she had known all her life? As the week progressed, her fears grew. She jumped whenever the door to her room opened. Even her maid had stopped scratching for permission to enter because Rosemary always refused to answer. As a result, Rosemary would look up and suddenly there would be someone in the room with her. She never spoke, hoping that if she ignored the person, he or she would not be there when she turned around again. But whoever it was always stayed and tried to force her to talk, refusing to leave her alone.

Her father was the worst. He would come into her room in the morning, his face hopeful. "Rosemary, come down to breakfast with me," he asked every morning. When she did not answer and turned her face back to the window, he would leave, his face clouded and unhappy. Alone, Rosemary stared out into a bleak future. How could she explain the way she felt, how afraid she was? What was going to happen to her?

Mary Ann was more practical. She called the doctor. He made Rosemary open her mouth, listened to her breathe, took her wrist between his fingers, and frowned. "I can find nothing wrong with her, Mrs. Wyatt," he said after he had inspected Rosemary carefully. "The scratch is disappearing; the knot on her head is gone. I can find nothing else wrong with her." He frowned. "There is a doctor in London, a man who is known for his treatment of the disturbed. Perhaps . . ." He hesitated, for he was unsure how his suggestion would be received. Both Mary Ann and Rosemary turned to face him. Rosemary's eyes were wide with horror. "Perhaps you need to take her to see him."

"No!" Rosemary screamed. "No! I will not allow him near me!"

"And I would not even suggest it. Thank you, Doctor. I appreciate the time you have given us," Mary Ann said coolly as she walked him to the door. "The footman will see you out." She closed the door to Rosemary's room behind him and turned to face her stepdaughter. "So you have not forgotten how to talk."

"I am not disturbed. I am not! I do not need to go to London to see that doctor. I will be fine. I will come down to dinner this evening. You and Papa will see. I am fine," Rosemary cried. She kept her eyes on Mary Ann as if she expected her stepmother to bundle her up and ship her off immediately.

"Your actions this week have disturbed your father and me," Mary Ann said gently. "We have been worried about you."

"I am better. I will come down to dinner this evening," Rosemary promised, the thought of being taken to London to see a doctor who would believe she had lost her mind filling her with dismay. The stories she had heard of Bedlam rose to terrify her.

"Good." Mary Ann took her stepdaughter's hand. "Rosemary, neither your father nor I want you to visit this doctor. All we want is to help you. Obviously going back to the place where your injuries occurred was wrong. I should have thought about how you would feel, how frightened it would make you," her stepmother apologized. She clasped both of Rosemary's hands within her own. "Can you forgive me?" She led her over to the window, where there was a padded window seat wide enough for the two of them.

"Forgive you? You did nothing, Mary Ann," Rosemary said quietly. She brushed tears from her eyes angrily. "That church has been part of my life since I was born. Now I never want to go near it again."

"My dear, you must not blame the place for what happened. What happened to you could have happened anywhere."

"It is not the place," her stepdaughter said in a whisper. Mary Ann looked at her, surprised. "Oh, I was frightened when we drove up and I remembered coming to, my head hurting." She paused and took a deep breath. Then she looked down at the dull brown muslin she had chosen that morning, a dress that Cousin Hortense felt suitable for gardening. She pleated her skirt nervously.

Hearing the door open quietly, so quietly that Rosemary, who was deep inside herself, did not hear it, Mary Ann put her finger to her lips and then motioned Daniel to come closer. His boots were muddy, and it was obvious that he had come straight from the fields. His wife wondered idly who had sent for him. She waited for him to take a seat and then asked, "If it was not the place, what was it? What has kept you in your room all week?"

"I never want to see them again!" Rosemary cried, shutting her eyes and shuddering.

"Who?"

"All those people who stared at me. Stared and turned

their backs on me." She shivered again. Mary Ann put her arm around the girl, marveling at how much weight she had lost that week. "It was worse than the ball at Tunbridge Wells. There at least I knew I was afraid because most of the people were strangers. I know most people at church, but they frightened me more than any strangers could. Why did they stare so? What is wrong with me?"

"Nothing is wrong with you, little one. Nothing!" Daniel said angrily, crossing to where they sat. Rosemary looked up, startled at first, and then ran into his arms. He tightened them around her. "Except you are too thin," he added, trying to lighten the mood. "We will have to tell Cook to prepare all your favorites."

"I am not hungry, Papa." She tried to smile at him, but managed only a rather watery tilt to her lips. She took a step or two back from his arms but kept hold of his hand. She looked from her stepmother to her father. "Why did they do it? Why did they stare at me so, turn away from me?" Her hazel eyes were filled with pain.

Her father wrapped one of her short curls around his finger, trying to find the right words. He looked helplessly at his wife. She smiled wanly at him and said, "Some people are always ready to believe the worst, Rosemary. And others feel guilty. They were so close by and could do nothing when you were hurt, can still do nothing. It makes them uncomfortable. You are a reminder that something could happen to one of them, to members of their families." She brushed a tear from her stepdaughter's cheek and gave her a hug, hoping she would not have to say more.

Her hopes were quickly shattered. "What do you mean, they thought the worst?" Rosemary asked.

This time Mary Ann left the answer to her husband because she was not sure just how much her stepdaughter knew. Daniel cleared his throat nervously. He looked at Mary Ann with pleading in his eyes; she simply shook her head. "Do you remember when your menses started?" he asked. Mary

Ann raised her eyebrows slightly, startled at his accurate terminology. Her mother had left it to her governess to explain, and, prude that she was, the elderly lady had called it "the woman's curse." For months Mary Ann had been certain she had some dread disease. Then she had been sent away to school, where some of the bolder, more informed young ladies had given her more reliable facts.

"You did not understand what Cousin Hortense had told you so you came looking for me." Rosemary blushed and nodded. "Do you remember everything I told you?" She nodded again. He paused and closed his eyes, trying to find the best words. He opened them again, fixing them on Mary Ann.

This time she could not resist their entreaty. "What your papa is trying to say is that some people have started the rumor that the men who hit you on the head also took advantage of you," she said gently.

"They didn't, did they?" Rosemary stared at both of them with wide, scared eyes.

"No," Mary Ann hastened to assure her. "But sometimes truth does not matter to people." She winced inwardly as she saw that Rosemary understood what she was trying to say.

"Then it will not matter to them what I do, will it?" the girl asked hopelessly. "My reputation is already destroyed."

"It may not matter to them, little one, but it matters to Mary Ann and me," her father told her firmly.

"And it should matter to you," Mary Ann added. The three of them looked at one another for a few moments.

Rosemary pulled back from them and walked over to the window to stare out at the bright blue-and-gold day. "What am I to do?" she asked, her voice breaking. She whirled around to face them again. "What am I to do?"

It was the opening Mary Ann had been waiting for. "My cousin, Lady Longworth, has made a suggestion. I wrote to her soon after you were injured. She spends the months of July through September in Bath. She has a home on the

Royal Crescent near the Upper Assembly Rooms. She thinks you should come stay with her.''

Her stepdaughter laughed bitterly. "I can see myself now. If I am reacting so badly to people I have known all my life, I will probably faint if a stranger looks at me. Then people here *and* in Bath will have a chance to talk about me.''

"If you do not want to go, you do not have to," her father assured her. He took her hand and led her back to the window where she and Mary Ann had been sitting when he first entered. "We will think of something else.''

"I will not go to Cousin Hortense. She has probably heard all about it from one of her cronies and has already made up her mind that everything is my fault. I can never do anything right as far as she is concerned." Daniel and Mary Ann exchanged rueful looks. Rosemary's thoughts followed the same lines as theirs had. The girl sighed and looked at them as if she could read her future on their faces. She closed her eyes and asked, "I cannot stay here, can I?''

"Of course you can.''

"Do you want to?''

Mary Ann's question made her stop and think. "What do I want to do?'' Rosemary laughed easily. "Can I go back to the way things were three weeks ago?'' she asked, already knowing the answer.

"Would you want to?'' Her stepmother's question surprised her. She raised her head and stared at Mary Ann. "You were already unhappy, Rosemary,'' the elder lady reminded her. Daniel looked from one to the other, confused.

Rosemary thought about the way she had felt since Mary Ann arrived. The changes had really begun when she received her father's letter announcing his coming marriage. London and, she had to admit, her attraction to Stephen had made her look at her world differently, had made her restless. "You are right,'' she said quietly. All the childishness seemed to disappear from her in that moment. "But I do not know what I want to do now. May I think about this, please?''

Her face, childish no longer, was serious as she thought of leaving her home to live among strangers.

"Take as much time as you like," her father assured her. "Just do not forget to come down to dinner. You are too thin." Both Rosemary and Mary Ann made a face at him. They looked at each other, smiles of understanding lighting both their eyes.

Although Rosemary did not leave the grounds of the Manor, over the next few days she walked around the gardens, practiced the piano, and thought. Before dinner one day, she asked, "If I go to Bath, will the two of you go with me?" Her father frowned. "Oh, not forever. Just until I grow a little more comfortable there?" Her voice trembled slightly.

Her father and stepmother exchanged glances. "Of course we will," her stepmother reassured her.

"We will stay as long as you need us," her father said heartily, pleased that she was willing to take this step.

"Or until harvest begins," his daughter teased him. Then she grew serious again. "I am not certain I will be able to do this, but I refuse to stay here simply so some people can stare at me and talk about me. At least if they talk about me when I am gone, I will never know it." She paused; her face blanched. "You do not think the gossip will spread to Bath, do you?"

"With the connections of most of the people around here?" Mary Ann asked, raising her chin haughtily. Rosemary and Daniel laughed. Serious once more, Mary Ann asked, "How soon do you wish to leave?"

6

ALTHOUGH THEY DID NOT leave as quickly as Rosemary wanted, they arrived in Bath in what Mary Ann considered record time, within two weeks. As the carriage pulled up in front of Lady Longworth's house on the Royal Crescent, Rosemary glanced around her. "Everything is so pretty. It is almost as though your cousin lives in the country. Who else lives in these homes?" She was trying very hard to be enthusiastic about her visit to Lady Longworth.

"At one time the Duke of York had a home nearby, but I am not certain if he visits Bath any longer," Mary Ann told her, pleased that Rosemary was showing some interest in her surroundings. Since they had made the decision to bring her to Bath, Rosemary had been very quiet. She had not remained in her room staring out the window and refusing to eat. Neither had she seemed to care about anything. Cook was in despair because she only picked at her food. As a result of her uninterest in eating, everything except for the dresses her maid had hurriedly altered hung on the girl.

"Does your cousin know the duke?" Rosemary asked in a tiny voice. Her eyes were wide and frightened.

"I am certain she has seen him, but Lord Longworth, my cousin's husband, not her son, often disagreed with the king and did not hesitate to tell him what he thought. As a result, his son, the duke, avoided my uncle."

"Your cousin has met the king?" This time Rosemary's eyes were wide with surprise.

"You might too, if you allow Mary Ann to present you

next Season," her father added, delighted that his daughter
was finally showing some interest in society. His wife
glanced at him. His daughter's face paled alarmingly. He
looked from one to the other and fell silent again for a
moment. Then he said hurriedly, "Of course, whether you
go to London or not is your choice. You will have to decide
that for yourself." For a few moments there was only silence,
causing Daniel to regret his words.

Then, as though he had not spoken, Mary Ann answered
Rosemary. "The king does not come to Bath. And as late
in the summer as it is, the town may be thin of company.
Many people are leaving to entertain at their country homes."
She smiled at the groom who opened the carriage door,
followed her husband from the carriage, and stood waiting
for her stepdaughter. "Remember, if Lady Longworth asks
too many questions, you can always faint. It worked very
well last time," Mary Ann said in a whisper. Rosemary
giggled nervously.

Her father, startled, turned to look at her, ignoring his
hostess. Then he realized what he was doing and hurried up
the stairs to make his bow. "Pretty is as pretty does, Mr.
Wyatt," Lady Longworth reminded him as he tendered his
apology. "I think I shall have to keep you at my side in order
to teach you some manners," she said coquettishly, tapping
the side of his face with her fan. He looked helplessly at Mary
Ann. His wife, a wide smile on her face, simply kissed her
cousin's cheek and whispered a few words that made both
the elder women laugh. "Now, come see my surprise," Lady
Longworth demanded. "You can inspect your rooms
presently."

Rosemary, who was not certain how much Lady Longworth had been told, glanced at her hostess. She saw nothing
but welcome on the lady's face. She followed her parents
into the morning room, willing herself to accept the welcome
she saw. After two nights on the road, she longed for a bath
and a quiet corner, a place where she could escape. But even
though she had dreaded it, this journey had not been as

difficult as the ones in the past. The strangers—maids and ostlers mostly—that she encountered did not overwhelm her as they sometimes did. Maybe Bath would be equally free of threatening situations. She sighed and prepared to smile.

Her polite smile became a real one as she saw who was waiting within the room. "Stephen . . . Mr. Huntington," she corrected herself, and blushed.

He bowed but kept his eyes on her, delighted with the changes he saw in her. Instead of the little girl whom he had amused in London, he now faced a lovely young lady. With all her childish plumpness gone and her curls framing her face, Rosemary was the ideal blond beauty. "Miss Wyatt," he acknowledged. He crossed the room to make his bow to her. She glanced at her stepmother uncertain how to respond.

"Since you are now my daughter, I think you can call him Stephen," Mary Ann said kindly. "What do you think, Cousin Sarah?"

The eldler woman looked from her son to the pretty blond, her eyebrows raised in speculation. "As family, it would be ridiculous to stand on formality." Longworth walked in and made his bow. "You already know my elder son." Rosemary made her curtsy. "And here are my grandchildren. Julia, James, present yourselves to Mr. and Mrs. Wyatt and their daughter, Rosemary." Two dark-haired, blue-green-eyed miniatures of their father walked slowly forward, their eyes searching everywhere, their faces puzzled. Already aware of correct social behavior, Julia made her curtsy and walked over to her father. James made his bow, walked over to his grandmother, and tugged at her skirt. After rearranging her dress, she bent down so he could whisper in her ear. "Where is the little girl?" he asked in a whisper as loud as most people's ordinary voices.

Her face flaming with embarrassment, his sister marched over to him, her tiny mouth set in a firm line. She stopped right in front of him and leaned in close so that her face was almost touching his. "You be quiet," she demanded. "Grandmama said we could have tea down here if we were nice.'' She frowned, her hands resting on her hips. ''And you had better be nice.''

''Julia, what did I do?'' her brother asked, his bewilderment evident on his face. ''Papa, did I do something wrong? Are we still going to have tea with you?'' He walked over to his father and leaned against him, his face showing his confusion.

''Yes, you will have tea with us,'' his father reassured him. ''Julia, when your brother needs to be corrected, I will do it,'' he told his daughter firmly, resisting the impulse to gather her in his arms when her face clouded with threatened tears.

Daniel and Mary Ann carefully hid their smiles as they watched the twins glare at each other. Lady Longworth and Stephen exchanged looks that said they had seen this scene enacted many times. Rosemary, however, shifted nervously. She remembered all too well how embarrassing it was to make a social blunder and have everyone watching her. She walked over to James and smiled at him. ''When I was Julia's age, I would have loved a brother just like you,'' she said. She flashed a look at her father and Mary Ann, a look far more mischievous than anyone expected. Mary Ann blushed. Julia opened her mouth as if to ask a question. Then the little one thought better of it. She crossed to the settee and sat down, arranging the white figured muslin about her as though she were being presented to the queen. ''Then I would have had someone to have adventures with. Come over here with me and tell me how you spend your days.'' Rosemary smiled. James, realizing he had found a friend, put his hand in hers and followed her to his sister. Looking at the little girl, whose eyes were fixed on the toes of her shoes, Rosemary added, ''I would have liked a sister too.''

James took a seat beside Rosemary. ''You didn't have any brothers or sisters?'' Julia scooted a little closer, as if she wanted to hear better. Rosemary simply shook her head. ''Well, most of the time I am glad Julia is around,'' he said, as if it pained him to admit the truth. His sister flushed and wiggled just a little before she remembered her manners. "Because she is, I do not have to have lessons alone. Julia and I have lessons every morning. I like geography best. Someday I am going to India like my Uncle Stephen did," he told her proudly.

"And what about you, Julia? What do you plan to do?" Rosemary asked, trying to include the little girl in their discussion.

"I am going to be an Incomparable," she said firmly, sticking her tiny nose in the air.

"Julia," her father said sternly, his face red.

"And you thought I would get in trouble," James said under his breath, but still loud enough to be heard clearly. He shot her a look of triumph.

"You will come here to me immediately," her grandmother said firmly, and motioned Julia to her side. When the child was standing in front of her, her head hanging, Lady Longworth told her quietly, "Ladies who try to puff up their own importance often find that no one wants to have them around. I believe you have something to say to everyone." Her grandmother stared at her, not giving an inch before the pleading in those clear blue-green gyes.

Julia looked at her father. He frowned at her. She hung her head and said in a rush, "I am sorry."

With effort the adults kept their faces straight. "Children, go find Thomas Two and tell him we are ready for tea," their grandmother suggested. "Thomas Two is my butler," she explained to Rosemary. "His older brother is Longworth's butler. The twins had a problem with names until we numbered them."

"The twins have grown so much since I saw them last," Mary Ann said. "I do not remember that they were so willing to talk to strangers."

"That is something that has developed recently. I blame their Uncle Stephen; whenever he is at home, he visits them in the nursery and encourages them to discuss everything they have been doing," Longworth explained.

"And you and Mama never go near them? Do not believe him, Mary Ann. Both of them are just as bad. Anytime I wish to find my brother, I go looking for the twins. Besides, I have missed five years of their lives. I need to catch up," Stephen said, his eyes laughing. He glanced at Rosemary as if to ask her to agree with him. Her heart raced.

Although Rosemary had chosen Bath simply as the better of two bad situations, she found herself enjoying the city. The children helped. They had their own routines, but part of each day they spent with the adults. Two mornings a week Julia visited the Pump Room with her grandmother, while James rode with his father and his uncle.

On the first day Rosemary visited the Pump Room while Lady Longworth drank the waters, both Julia and Mary Ann accompanied them. Before the crush of new faces could overwhelm Rosemary, Julia had her by the hand. "We must fetch Grandmama's glass. The pumper knows me. I do not know how Grandmama can drink the waters. They smell." She said the last in a very low tone and then looked around to see if anyone else had heard her. She sighed. Rosemary bit her lip to keep from laughing. Julia was so serious that she would not hurt her feelings for any reason. As they walked through the room, Julia pointed out people she knew, making her curtsy to the ones that called her by name. "You must always be polite," she instructed Rosemary as though she were the elder. "When you are presented, some of these ladies will invite you to their homes. It is always wise to plan ahead." Rosemary lost her smile at the thought of being presented. "Of course, if they have ugly daughters, they will not want you around. You are prettier than Cousin Clarissa, and she is a recognized Beauty," Julia told her friend as though her word was law. Ignoring the little girl's compliments as childish prattlings, Rosemary thought, not for the first time, that Julia sounded just like Lady Longworth. She glanced around her, pleased that her gown was as modish as any other.

Then Julia's words sank in. "I am not pretty," she told the little girl. "But you are."

"Yes, you are. I heard Uncle Stephen telling my father. He said you were vastly removed."

Rosemary stared at her, not knowing whether to reprove her for repeating other people's conversations or to ask her to explain. Discretion won, and she said nothing. Julia's words, however, kept her so occupied that she did not notice the attention she was receiving. As a result, she was able to greet the people surrounding her stepmother and Lady Longworth with composure.

The days without Julia were more difficult. Then she was expected to fetch Lady Longworth's glass and walk beside her as the lady made her progress through the room, stopping to greet an acquaintance here, a friend there. Because their stay in the Pump Room was always brief and no one expected her to respond other than to smile, nod, or curtsy, Rosemary survived. After the first day without Julia or Mary Ann, when she was certain she would embarrass her hostess, she tried to explain her fears to the lady. Lady Longworth simply said, "If you grow faint, there will be a dozen doctors here instantly. You could not hope for any better care than that." She smiled at her and patted her cheek, noting that they would need to visit a modiste soon. The child's clothes simply hung on her. "We will go today," she said, and walked on, leaving Rosemary to wonder what she meant.

Rosemary had thought her visit to the modiste in London had been exhausting, but to Lady Longworth, choosing the correct attire was a serious business. For a week they visited one shop after another: gowns in one, shoes in another; in yet another, gloves. Then they had to purchase bonnets and fans.

Lady Longworth had watched as the modiste took Rosemary's measurements. She narrowed her eyes and walked around the girl, studying her carefully. She picked up a bolt of white muslin and held it under Rosemary's chin.

"Not that one," she said thoughtfully. Then she picked up a bolt of figured muslin that was more the color of thick cream. Holding it under the girl's chin, she turned to Mary Ann and asked, "This is the right color, don't you agree?"

Feeling like a calf on display at the trading fair, Rosemary stood there while they considered the best colors for her wardrobe. At first she simply did not care. However, when the modiste permitted her to move, she began to glance through the fashion plates in order to have something to do. Every once in a while a gown would attract her, and she would wonder what Stephen would think of her in it. During the last week she had found him often by her side. Although he was supposedly in Bath to inspect an estate he wished to buy, he had spent most of his time visiting with her and his niece and nephew. "I want this gown in a muslin figured in blue," she finally said, holding up the fashion plate.

Lady Longworth raised her eyebrows, looked at Mary Ann, and waited. "She chose her dresses when she was in London," Mary Ann admitted. "And they were very becoming."

"That traveling gown was not one of them, was it?" Lady Longworth demanded. She would have preferred to make all the decisions. "Puce does not become you, Rosemary, not enough pink." She smoothed the skirt of her ensemble, made from her own design and featuring a long sleeveless pelisse with a pointed hem in turquoise over an oyster-white long-sleeved muslin gown figured in the same color as the pelisse.

"Cousin Hortense picked that dress out. In London I ordered only a few gowns, mostly ones I needed for that week," Rosemary explained quickly. She respected Lady Longworth's opinion on fashion and did not want to give her a false impression.

"Well, let us see what you have chosen." Carefully the three of them inspected the fashion plates. "Just the thing. Very simple, very elegant," the elder lady said with a smile. Rosemary glowed. "Now, let us look at fabric." After that,

Lady Longworth simply made a few suggestions but let Rosemary make her own decisions.

When they arrived home from shopping each day of the week, all Rosemary wanted to do was collapse on her bed. Instead, on three afternoons she had to receive guests with Lady Longworth and Mary Ann. The first time, she was so nervous that she would do something wrong, her hands were shaking so badly that she could hardly carry the cups of tea to their guests. Once that task was finished and she had taken her seat, she was surprised how comfortable she felt, almost as comfortable as she had been when she had served as her father's hostess. Of course, she had met all of the people before at the Pump Room. Just then Stephen and his brother came in. Rosemary looked up at the younger man and smiled. Stephen caught his breath and then smiled back. He reminded himself, not for the first time, that he had to proceed slowly. He looked at her again, his eyes on her lips. She felt the warmth and blushed.

As the week wound to a close, Daniel and Mary Ann called their daughter into the morning room. When she came in, Daniel was pacing nervously while Mary Ann sat quietly, her hands folded in her lap. "What is wrong?" Rosemary asked hesitantly, wondering if the gossip had followed them to Bath.

"Nothing," her father said quickly. She merely looked at him, her eyes wide with astonishment. "I had a letter from my bailiff. He is concerned about the state of the fields. He wants me to have a look at them." He stopped, dreading her reaction. How would she survive without some member of her family nearby for security? he wondered.

His daughter gulped and lost some of her color. "Is Mary Ann going to stay here?" she asked, her voice only a whisper. As soon as the words were out of her mouth, she wished she could recall them.

Her stepmother and father exchanged anguished looks. "I will if you really need me," Mary Ann said quietly. Daniel crossed to stand behind her, his hands resting lightly on her shoulders and one finger lightly caressing her neck. She closed her eyes and rested her cheek against his hand. The thought of being separated for more than a few days was almost more than she could bear. But if Rosemary needed her . . .

Thinking about staying in Bath alone made Rosemary tremble. She closed her eyes for a moment so that she could control her thoughts and fears. When she opened them, she smiled. "I need you, but Papa needs you more," she said courageously. "With harvest coming soon, you will need to be on hand to supervise the party for the tenants. Besides,I will see you in a month. You will be at Long Meadows to celebrate Lord Longworth's birthday?" In spite of all her resolution to be brave, her voice trembled slightly on the last question.

Her father hurried to her side and took her in his arms. "That is a promise, little one. Remember, if you need us, you have only to send us word. We will come immediately." Mary Ann nodded her agreement. He stepped back a moment and looked down at her. "You do know you can go home with us if you wish." He looked deep into her eyes, as if he could read her very soul.

"Thank you, Papa." Rosemary kissed him on the cheek. "I will stay here," she said bravely, trying to smile. Her father hugged her again. One tear trickled down her cheek. She hastily wiped it away. No matter what her father said, Rosemary knew that returning to the Manor was the last thing she would do. Bath, with all its new faces and strange places, was far less frightening than facing all her "friends" again.

The day her father's and Mary Ann's coach pulled away from the house on Royal Crescent, Rosemary felt all her panic returning. She walked back into the house, her smile fading and her color disappearing. Lady Longworth took one look at her and sent a footman for the children. When they arrived, she asked, "Shall we have a picnic for morning tea?" The children clapped their hands and agreed.

Just as they were making their arrangements, Stephen and his brother walked into the room. "Were you going to leave us behind, Mama?" her younger son asked. He assumed a hurt expression, his eyes twinkling merrily.

"We thought you would be off on your own business. You do not want to trail around after an old woman, a young lady, and two mischievous children." His mother smiled at him to soften her words.

Lord Longworth said with a smile, "Mama is right. I already have another engagement. But I will see you two this evening and have supper with you." He smiled at his children, who sighed at his temporary loss, and then directed all their attention on their uncle.

"Will you come, Uncle Stephen?" James asked. "You and I could ride behind the carriage. You would like that, wouldn't you?" His smile was a picture of innocence. His shirt that only a short time before had been crisp and spotless was crumpled. It had begun to work its way out of his trousers, one tail hanging down under his jacket.

"No, you can't," his sister protested, her eyes filling with tears. "You went riding with Papa and Uncle Stephen yesterday. Papa promised it would be my turn next." She crossed to where her father stood and leaned up against him, her face upturned. Her crisp white muslin frock was as neat as when she had put it on.

"James, your sister is right. Unless we hired horses for everyone, it would not be fair. And your grandmother does not like to ride," he reminded his son. He motioned the boy to come closer. Then he turned him around and tucked his shirt back into his trousers. James blushed, but his father finished the task and patted him.

Rosemary opened her eyes wider, startled by the ease with which Longworth straightened his son's clothes. Her father, much as he loved her, would have called her nurse to redress her. "Do you think you would be willing to be my escort, James?" she asked. The quiet drama of family life unfolding before her made her fear recede, but a strange longing gripped her heart. He nodded, turning his head to see if his father approved. A smile was his reward.

"Stephen, will you escort Julia and me?" his mother asked, trying to smooth her granddaughter's feelings. Julia did so hate to be left out of anything.

"I would be delighted," he said, smiling merrily. He glanced at Rosemary, pleased to see her smiling at him. His mind raced with plans to ensure that she would sit beside him in the carriage. "Where shall we go on this picnic?" The children's voices bubbled forth like spring water. Each had a suggestion.

"Mama, Rosemary, I will leave the three of them in your capable hands," Longworth said, his eyes twinkling.

"I resent that," his brother said sternly. "I thought I was going along to protect them."

"They just want you to think that," his brother said as he walked out the door. Laughter echoed through the room as he walked down the hall.

Surrounded by the twins, Lady Longworth, and Stephen, Rosemary did not have time to think about being alone in Bath until she was in bed that evening. Then she wept a few tears until she dropped off to sleep.

7

ALTHOUGH SHOPPING for new clothes took far longer than Rosemary would once have thought possible, neither that nor the children took all of her time. But to her surprise, she missed her father and stepmother far less than she had imagined. Lady Longworth made certain her charge had little time alone during the day to worry.

To Stephen's dismay, his mother began to plan small social gatherings to keep her guest busy. Had she kept her guest list to her usual friends, ladies of her own age, he would not have been as unhappy. However, she included younger ladies, once with daughters and sons about Rosemary's age. Although he did not protest openly, his face revealed his displeasure. Grimly he canceled his own plans so that he could be present to give Rosemary his support.

At first the at-homes were difficult for Rosemary. There were so many people to remember, each one ready to talk to her, to discuss the latest tidbits of gossip. After her father and Mary Ann had been gone for a week or so, Rosemary was certain that no one came to Bath who did not call on Lady Longworth to keep her up to date with the latest gossip. After her own experience, Rosemary did not enjoy hearing someone's flaws examined publicly.

She would pass around the tea, praying she did not destroy someone's favorite gown by spilling it. Stephen would help her. More than once their hands touched as they reached for the same saucer. A shock tingled up her hand as though she had touched a wool carpet on a very cold day. He smiled at her. She lowered her eyes hastily. Then she would take her seat, trying to ignore the conversations around her. As often as she dared, she glanced across the room where Stephen sat. Caught up in exploring her feelings for him, she did not worry about the compliments the gentlemen gave her, comments that would have had her blushing only hours before.

Gentlemen who had recently searched for reasons to avoid afternoon calls insisted that their mothers or aunts call on Lady Longworth. Those who were so unfortunate as not to have been introduced began appearing at the Pump Room early each morning until they found someone to make their introductions.

"Will you be attending the ball this evening at the Upper Assembly Room, Miss Wyatt?" one gentleman asked the first afternoon he called. Like his friends, he had heard of her and arranged an introduction. She was looking her best in an afternoon gown of a clear lemon yellow. Its square neckline and sleeves *à la mameluke* were trimmed with ribbons of Devonshire brown. The combination had caused a controversy when Rosemary first proposed it; Lady Longworth and the modiste had declared the brown too dull and the yellow unsuitable for a blond, but Rosemary had persisted. From the attention of the gentlemen that afternoon, her eye for color, always good, had been correct.

Before Rosemary's color faded away completely at the thought of attending a ball with so many strangers, Lady Longworth said, "Not this evening. Perhaps next Monday." Stephen, who had been watching the scene from across the room, took a step or two toward her. His mother was faster than he. She sat beside her guest and smiled at the young man who had asked the question. "You must not let our stay-at-home attitude confuse you, sir. Everyone is always welcome during the afternoons I am at home." He blushed so brightly that even the young ladies smiled.

Deftly turning questions from curious ladies aside, Stephen gave Rosemary time to recover her poise. Then he casually got his mother to move so that he could take her place beside Rosemary. She smiled up at him thankfully.

Stephen's presence as well as that of the viscount and his children helped Rosemary face the strangers that Lady Longworth introduced by ones and twos at each at-home. When Longworth and the twins left for Long Meadow, Stephen became her lodestone, her philosopher's stone, who transformed her fear into laughter. Her greatest worry was that he too would disappear.

One afternoon when all their visitors had left, she gathered her courage and asked him, "When are you leaving Bath, Stephen?"

"Are you tired of me already?" he asked, a smile on his face to show that he was only teasing. He stood there as though her answer did not mean anything to him. His throat tightened unbearably as he waited for her reply.

Her face lost color. "No, of course not. How could I be?" she asked, her words stumbling over one another. He began to breathe normally again. "You have been so kind to me, allowing me to share your home, your family. Helping me adjust."

Wanting something more than gratitude, Stephen kept his smile with an effort. "It is the least I could do." Rosemary looked up at him, her hazel eyes wide and puzzled, wondering why his words made her feel so empty. "Besides, being in Bath has given me the chance to look for an estate in this area," he reminded her. And keep an eye on you, he admitted to himself. The at-homes were no easier on him than they were on her as he watched gentlemen several years younger than he rush to her side.

Lady Longworth shifted in her chair, looking from one to the other, not at all displeased by what she observed. "Have you found an estate you would consider purchasing? When did you find it? You have rarely been gone for more than a few hours."

"Yes. I saw it yesterday while you and Rosemary went to your dressmaker's. There are some problems, though. My man of business looked at it this morning and thinks the heirs are asking more than it is worth. The property has been neglected for some time and will need a sizable investment before it will begin making a profit.'' Her son sat down beside her on the settee and stretched out his long legs.

"Are you going to pursue it?'' his mother asked. "Maybe you should keep on looking. There may be something closer to Long Meadow.'' A frown creased her forehead. Although an estate close to Bath would ensure that she would see her second son at least during the summer, she would rather have her sons living near each other and near the dower house she called home.

"There are not that many suitable estates for sale, Mama. At least not in the counties where I would like to live. I looked in Norfolk, but Thomas Coke of Holkham has standing orders with his agents to purchase whatever become available. Naturally, people there give him first refusal.''

"Is that fair?'' Rosemary asked, frowning. "Papa says his holdings are already enormous. What does he want with more land?''

"What do any of the large landowners want with more? I am certain your father increases his holdings whenever he can. Land represents power and wealth.'' Stephen relaxed his tense shoulders and let his voice soften. "The house on the estate I am interested in buying is in poor condition. After we meet with the agent for the heirs and give him our counteroffer, will you and Rosemary look over it and give me some suggestions on how to begin to make improvements?''

"You are determined, then?'' his mother asked, a tiny frown creasing her brow. "You do not need to buy an estate, Stephen. You know your brother has offered to put one of his at your disposal.''

"It would not be the same. Even if he allowed me to do exactly as I wished, I would always know that the land belonged to him.'' Rosemary looked up, startled. She remembered how she had felt when Mary Ann had taken over the housekeeping duties at the Manor. Even though her step-mother had tried to give Rosemary a voice in the day-to-day running of the household, the girl had always felt as though she were outside looking in. "I want land that is mine, that will be my children's after me. If not this estate, then some other." His voice was as serious as his face. He looked at Rosemary, pleased to see her nodding her approval.

"Then we will do what we can to help you," his mother said firmly. A satisfied smile lighted her face. Whether he realized it or not, her younger son was thinking of the future. She glanced at her guest and noticed with satisfaction the way the girl watched Stephen from under her long eyelashes when she thought he was not looking at her. "Do you agree, Rosemary?"

"Certainly, Cousin Sarah." The words were demure, but the look in the girl's eyes was anything but. Stephen was thinking about children. "Will we be able to visit it before we leave for Long Meadow?"

"If everything goes well, I will escort you there at the beginning of next week. We are meeting with the representative of the heirs in the next day or so to see if they will accept a lower price," Stephen said, a serious look in his eyes. "The heirs, nieces of the former owner, are living in Canada and the West Indies and do not want to be absentee landlords."

"Living so far away from their properties could cause problems," Rosemary said, echoing statements she had heard her father make on more than one occasion. "If the bailiff is not honest, both the landlord and tenants can suffer."

"Well, the bailiff on my estate will find me looking over his shoulder," Stephen said firmly.

"Just like your father and brother," Lady Longworth said, her pride evident in the tone of her voice.

Over the next few days the ladies saw little of Stephen as he met with agents and his man of business. Even though she was busier socially than she had ever been in her life, Rosemary felt alone, even more alone than when her father and stepmother had left. As if she realized what Rosemary was feeling, Lady Longworth expanded their social activities. In the mornings they shopped; in the afternoons she insisted that Rosemary accompany her on visits or accept invitations for picnics or carriage rides. Although she was uncomfortable around so many new people, the girl managed to cope with the changes in her companions and her way of life. At the ball held in the Upper Assembly Rooms, no one who saw her at the beginning of the evening would have realized how nervous she was. She even surprised herself. For a short time, she began to think once more of going to London for her presentation.

During the first two country dances, she followed her partners' lead, wishing only that Stephen were there to lead her out instead of the gentlemen whose names were on her program. After the second dance, she glanced around the floor, searching for Lady Longworth. Realizing her chaperone was nowhere in view, Rosemary allowed her partner to escort her to the side of the floor. As soon as they realized she and her partner were alone, several other gentlemen made their way to her side, surrounding her. A familiar blackness crept over Rosemary as she realized she was surrounded. Then she slumped and would have hit the floor if one of the gentlemen had not caught her.

"Put her down here. Then leave. Give her room to breathe," were the first words that Rosemary heard as she began to come around. She opened her eyes, expecting to see on her hostess's face the annoyed expression her cousin had always worn. Instead Lady Longworth looked worried. "Do not worry, my dear. You are fine. A gentleman caught you before you could hurt yourself. Just lie there a moment and get your breath again," the elder lady said in a soothing voice. Rosemary closed her eyes, not wanting to see the usual staring faces surrounding her. "If I had not gotten so involved in my gossip, this would never have happened. I know she must not overdo," Lady Longworth explained to one of her friends. "I did so want her to enjoy herself. She has missed so much this summer."

Fully recovered, Rosemary admired the way her chaperone enlisted everyone's sympathy. She opened her eyes once more and glanced around, certain that the ring of people that had surrounded her in the past would be there again. The tightness in her throat eased as soon as she realized that instead of being in the ballroom surrounded by staring eyes, she was in an antechamber with only her hostess and two of the elder ladies.

"Are you all right, my dear?" one of them asked, holding her vinaigrette under Rosemary's nose.

The girl took a deep breath and coughed. Swinging her legs off the settee, she sat up and nodded. "I hope I did not ruin the evening for anyone, Cousin, Sarah," she whispered, blushing deeply in embarrassment.

"Nonsense. This was even more exciting than having you faint dead away in my drawing room. Did I tell you," she asked her friends, "about the first time I met Rosemary?"

"Yes!" they both exclaimed, having already been entertained by the story more than once.

"Cousin Sarah," Rosemary protested, and turned even redder. "May we go home now?"

"After a few minutes. I think it would be wise to put in an appearance in the ballroom, just so people can see you are truly recovered. Do you agree, my ladies?" Lady Longworth looked at her friends, who nodded vigorously.

"Do I have to?" Although that was not what she intended, Rosemary sounded like a petulant child.

"Unless you wish to drink three full glasses at the Pump Room tomorrow morning." Lady Longworth smiled, but her voice told Rosemary that she would carry out the implied threat unless the girl did as she was told. A few minutes later, the four of them reappeared in the ballroom, Rosemary blushing brightly. "She grew too warm," Lady Longworth explained as everyone flocked around them once again.

Rosemary plastered a smile on her face and tried to think of green meadows filled with flowers rather than the mass of people around her. Noticing how pale her charge was growing once again, Lady Longworth made their excuses.

During the short carriage ride to the Royal Crescent, she asked, "How long have you been afraid of being surrounded?"

"Surrounded?"

"Rosemary, do not try to fob me off. The first time it happened in my drawing room in London I blamed it on your nervousness at meeting new people. But you knew most of those people tonight. And by no means of the imagination could the people at the Assembly Rooms tonight be called a crush, and there were only six of us that day in London. And it never happens when it is a musical evening and you are sitting in the back." Rosemary stuttered and stammered as they pulled up to their door. When she tried to make her escape after they had entered the house, however, Lady Longworth detained her. "I think we should discuss this now."

"But I still feel rather weak," Rosemary protested. She was not certain why, but she knew that she did not want to talk about the causes of her embarrassing behavior. Cousin Hortense, her father, and Mary Ann in her turn had asked her questions after each episode. No one had ever been satisfied with her answers.

"Just a few minutes, my dear. Then you may go up. Perhaps you should have breakfast in bed tomorrow morning," her hostess said solicitously. The look on her face was the same as the one Rosemary had seen the day Lady Longworth had decided that Rosemary would accompany her to the Pump Room for the first time. "Let us sit in the morning room. I just want to ask you a few questions." The elder lady sat on the settee and gestured for Rosemary to take her seat beside her. The flickering candlelight gave the familiar room eerie shadows.

Settling the skirts of her new dress, Rosemary looked with

dismay at the small rent in the blond net that covered the cream silk. The tear gave her something to focus on, a chance to escape the uneasiness she felt whenever anyone questioned her.

"How old were you when this began happening?"

"What do you mean?"

"Rosemary, when was the first time you remember feeling the sense of panic that you felt tonight?" Lady Longworth's tone was patient but firm.

"After the dance. When my escort brought me back from the dance floor," she said in a whisper, hoping to concentrate her hostess's attention only on that evening.

"You did not feel it while you were dancing?" Even though she knew the girl was still avoiding the real question, Lady Longworth willingly followed her lead. The girl's answer intrigued her.

"No, no, I did not!" Rosemary stood up, her face revealing her surprise. "When I was dancing, I remember talking to my escort, listening to the music, and counting my steps. It was not like the last time I tried to attend a ball. Oh, not like the one for Papa and Mary Ann either. At both of those, I was frightened before I ever arrived there. Even at the last one I attended at home with Papa, I could not even get out on the floor." She smiled at Lady Longworth. "Tonight I danced two dances. I did not stumble or forget my steps. I talked to my escorts. I really talked to them."

Lady Longworth let Rosemary babble on, absorbing every word the girl said. When Rosemary fell quiet once more, a delighted smile on her face, the older lady said quietly, "You go on up to bed now. We can talk about this more in the morning." She watched her guest leave, and sat there quietly for a while until the candles began to sputter. Then, a thoughtful look on her face, she made her way up to her own bedchamber.

The next morning, as Lady Longworth sat propped up in bed drinking her chocolate, her son poked his head into the room. "Your dresser assured me you were awake and ready to receive visitors," he said, taking a seat at the foot of the high bed. He refused the offer of a cup of chocolate. "Thomas Two told me when I arrived home last evening that you and Rosemary had gone to the ball at the Upper Assembly Room. You should have sent me a message so that I could accompany you."

"And tear you away from your beloved estate? I assume since you have been there the last three days that everything is going well?" his mother asked, smiling at him.

"Very well. The agent accepted our offer so readily we wondered how low he was willing to go. Still, the price was reasonable. Mama, you must go out there with me soon. There is so much to be done." She nodded, still smiling. "But I am still upset that you did not send someone for me so that I could escort you last night. Rosemary must have been terrified. I should have been there to protect her."

"Not at first." Her son frowned at her, confused by his own emotions. He was pleased for Rosemary but felt as though she had taken a step away from him. "Stephen, what do you think I have been doing these last few weeks? Rosemary knew almost everyone there. With so many people already having left for their estates, I was certain she would have no trouble. And she needs to learn to rely upon herself, not me or you."

"What happened?"

"She danced the first two country dances."

"The first two only? What happened then?"

"She fainted." Stephen stared at his mother, startled by the abruptness of her statement. "Oh, someone caught her. My dresser said she has already received a bouquet from him this morning. He must have been up with the dawn." Her voice was quiet and level, almost as though she were thinking aloud. She tapped her fingernail against the thin china cup she held in her hand. "She was quite excited when she realized that she had actually danced."

Stephen gritted his teeth, thinking of the young men who had flocked to their home each afternoon, wondering who had won the right to lead her to the floor. Then he controlled himself. "What are you planning, my dear?" he asked, a solemn look on his face. The thought of Rosemary dancing with someone else had sent a frisson of alarm up his spine. The look on his mother's face made him wonder if he needed to take her into his confidence. "Should I warn Rosemary to beware of your machinations?"

"No. I mean her no harm, my dear." She smiled at him again, pleased at the way he was reacting. "And Rosemary has already learned to hide."

"What do you mean?"

"Rosemary did not develop this fear of crowds simply to gain attention. If she did, she is not acting like any attention seeker I ever knew." A mischievous gleam lit her eyes. "I have known a few young ladies who would have tried this if they thought they could get away with it. Your cousin Clarissa, for one," she said, the merest hint of a laugh in her voice. Then she grew serious again. "Daniel is determined that Rosemary be presented during the Little Season. If she is to be comfortable, we must get to the root of the problem. According to her father, she was a very outgoing child before her mother left them. We must then discover what caused her to change."

"Do you think it had something to do with her mother?"

"Possibly. I wish I knew what Rosemary was thinking."

"Well, if anyone can find out, I have faith that you can. Perhaps you can entice the famous Dr. Mesmer—is he still in London?—or one of his students to investigate her case," he said only half-seriously.

His mother looked at him thoughtfully, an interested look on her face. "The French said he was a charlatan."

"Do the English always believe what the French say?" her son asked. "You told me he had given some amazing demonstrations. In India I learned not to be so skeptical of the powers of others. They have *fakirs* there who can sleep on beds of nails and never have a scratch on their skins."

"But that is not the same thing. Besides, Mary Ann told

me that Rosemary had hysterics when their doctor suggested that they call in another doctor. I would not want to cause any problems. We are making progress—slowly, it is true. Let me have a few more weeks. If I know nothing more by then, I will agree and secure Daniel's and Mary Ann's permission to investigate that avenue.''

He frowned. "Mama, I was just teasing. Surely you would not consider subjecting Rosemary to such a man?''

"I will do whatever I need to do to help her overcome her problem,'' she said firmly. Then her voice lost its serious tone. "Tell me more about this estate. When can I see it?''

8

THE FLUSH of excitement Rosemary had felt the evening before disappeared in the bright light of morning. Once more she had fallen short of what was expected of her. Would Cousin Sarah send for her father and Mary Ann? she wondered, remembering Cousin Hortense's reaction when she had fainted at the ball at Tunbridge Wells. Slowly she dressed. Almost without thinking, she rejected the soft blue muslin gown her maid had laid out for her, reaching instead for one of the drab gray dresses left over from the days when her Cousin Hortense had supervised her wardrobe. Only when she put it on and saw how it hung about her did Rosemary change her mind, accepting her maid's choice.

"Shall I run a ribbon through your curls, Miss Wyatt?" her maid asked. "Mr. Huntington's man always passes along his master's comments when you wear your hair that way," she explained, her face turning red.

"Mr. Huntington has returned?" Rosemary asked, her eyes wide with pleasure.

"Late last night. Lady Longworth's dresser said that he was having chocolate with his mother this morning. Do you want ribbons in your hair?"

"Yes." Rosemary sat quietly until her hair met her maid's approval. Inside, the despair she felt earlier gave way to a flutter of excitement. Even if she did not always see Stephen during the day, just the knowledge that she might made that day a little brighter.

By the time she ventured from her bedroom, Stephen had

already left. Rosemary glanced at the bouquets she had received, pulled the cards, and wandered listlessly about the house, her mind once again fixed on the evening before. Finally she returned to her room to write her thank-you notes, feeling that somehow she had let her hostess down. Her depression lasted until she and Lady Longworth met for a light luncheon.

"Have you any pressing engagements for this afternoon?" the elder lady asked, her face calm and pleasant.

"Why, ah, I do not think so," Rosemary stammered, wondering what her hostess had planned and fearing the worst.

"Good. Stephen has asked us to inspect his property this afternoon. He has promised us tea."

"The sale has gone through, then?" Rosemary asked, her eyes lighting up with interest.

"Yes. Will you accompany me? Stephen said to warn you to wear something you do not mind getting dirty. The place has been neglected for years."

"I am looking forward to seeing the estate. Is it far from town?"

"An hour or so. I told him we would leave as soon as luncheon is over. It is such a relief to me to know that he has found a home. I have worried constantly that he would decide to return to India if he could not find some place of his own. My dear, during the years he was so far away, I never had a moment of complete peace because I worried about him so much."

Neither of the ladies made a hearty meal. Rushing through the removes, they hurried, forcing down a few bites of their favorite dishes so that they were soon ready to leave.

Although he knew that the estate he had purchased lacked many amenities the ladies were used to, Stephen seemed to stand taller as he showed them around the gardens. They had been long neglected but held the remnants of beauty. Spying two roses close to the wall, Stephen cut them, trimmed the thorns, and presented them to his guests. "For the loveliest ladies I know.'' His mother laughed and walked further up the once-neat path. Rosemary stopped, her eyes growing wide. She looked up at him. Her eyes locked with his. Her lips parted. Stephen took a step toward her, his eyes serious. Her heart began to race. He bent his head toward hers, his eyes on her lips. She shivered excitedly.

"You will need an army of gardeners, Stephen," his mother said, breaking the spell. Rosemary lowered her eyes, her heart still pounding. She looked up at him through her eyelashes. The look in his eyes made her heart beat even faster.

With regret he turned to his mother. "I have already thought of that, my dear." He glanced back at Rosemary, his longing all too evident to his doting mother. "They have orders to begin on Monday. What do you ladies suggest I do with this tangled web?"

"If you have already hired gardeners, I am certain you must have a plan," his mother said firmly, knowing that he was not one to start a project without considerable study.

"Only a general one, Mama. I only know I want roses. Lots and lots of roses." He was staring at Rosemary as he said it.

"White ones and pale pinks?" she asked, her face alive with excitement.

"Any color you suggest," he assured her. "Maybe you and Mama could sketch a diagram of what you think would look good and where to put it." His mother glanced at him and then at Rosemary, wondering if the girl knew where this might lead.

"I suppose we could. Would that be all right, Cousin Sarah?" Rosemary asked, her smile lighting her face like a sunrise. A small hope that she had been trying to ignore burst into bloom.

"Certainly," her hostess assured her. She glanced at her son, noting his bemusement, and then looked back at Rosemary, who now had her eyes fixed firmly on the path in front of her. The girl's cheeks blazed with color. "Are the gardens all you plan to show us today?'' she asked, keeping her own counsel although vowing to write to Mary Ann and Daniel immediately.

''No,'' Stephen said hurriedly. ''Just remember, the house has been badly neglected. It will need a new roof before anything else is done. I have hired many people from the estate who were willing to come in and clean, but they have had a monumental task. Do not expect too much.'' He took a deep breath and led them up to the front door. It swung open, and he caught a glimpse of dull wood and dirty walls. He took a deep breath, wondering if he had made a mistake.

''Do not just stand there blocking the way. Let us go in,'' his mother said firmly, pushing him to one side. Rosemary followed her hesitantly. Both ladies were pleasantly surprised. Although the wood paneling of the entry was dull and lifeless, they could tell it was of excellent quality. The staircase that rose from the marble floor was graceful, the balustrade elegant. ''Very nice.'' Rosemary nodded. ''Shall we look at the rooms down here first, or begin with the kitchens?'' Lady Longworth asked, determined to see it all.

''Not the kitchens,'' Stephen pleaded. ''You can come back and see them later. I told the bailiff I hired to tell the cleaning crew not to worry too much about them first.'' Rosemary and Lady Longworth exchanged glances of resignation.

''You tell him,'' his mother whispered. ''He may listen to you.'' She nodded at Rosemary.

The girl glanced at her as though she did not want to get involved. Before the silence could grow uncomfortable, Stephen asked, ''Tell me? Tell me what?''

''You should have begun with the kitchens,'' Rosemary said patiently. ''A good kitchen and a good cook can do much to keep the staff happy. And you will never find a good cook if you do not have a good kitchen. How did you plan to feed all the people you have hired?''

''Feed them?'' Stephen looked from one to the other. ''I am supposed to feed them?''

"Where is this bailiff of yours? He should have explained this to you," his mother said firmly.

Stephen looked somewhat embarrassed. "He did ask to see me yesterday. I could not find him before I left for Bath," he explained. He glanced at Rosemary to see if she were upset with him. She smiled reassuringly at him. "I suppose we should begin with the kitchens?" he asked rather sheepishly.

"Lead the way, son," his mother said resolutely. "Watch your step, Rosemary."

On the ride back to Bath that evening, the ladies consulted their notes, agreeing that the house was charming. The rooms were comfortable. However, even with as many people as Stephen planned to hire, it would take several months before it was completely habitable. The few pieces of furniture that were worth salvaging needed to be recovered; the entire house had to be painted; new wall coverings, rugs, draperies, china, silver, and glassware would have to be ordered. "Can you take notes in this jolting carriage, Rosemary?" her hostess asked. "If so, we need to draw up a plan not just for the garden but for the whole house. Add toweling and sheeting to our list."

Engrossed in ordering linens and furniture and everything else needed to restore the house to its former glory, Lady Longworth and Rosemary worked steadily through the rest of September. Two or three days a week they ordered the carriage and went to the estate. Each time she went and saw one after another of her suggestions put into place, Rosemary felt a thrill, a sense of homecoming. She worked with the gardeners to ensure the grounds would be the vision of loveliness she and her hostess had intended, talked with the women who were overseeing the cleaning, consulted with the housekeeper and butler, one of Thomas Two's younger brothers, about putting other plans into place—all without her usual sense of fear. Although Rosemary thought little about her unusual behavior, Lady Longworth noted with pleasure the progress she was making in dealing with strangers and new situations. If Rosemary had been asked for her opinion, she would have said that she was too busy to be nervous.

As busy as they both were, each of the ladies wrote to Daniel and Mary Ann Wyatt each week. The first letter that arrived from his daughter had Daniel ready to order his carriage and head back to Bath. Only when Mary Ann read him her letter from Lady Longworth did he relax slightly. "I still do not believe that she should force my daughter to meet all these strange men. What is she thinking of?" he asked, a faint hint of worry adding a rough note to his voice.

His wife looked up at him, a tiny smile creasing her mouth. She said nothing for a while, letting him worry, and then asked wryly, "And how do you expect her to present Rosemary during the Little Season if she does not accustom her to company now?" She tilted her head just a trifle and twinkled her eyes at him. "We did take Rosemary to Bath in order that she would grow more comfortable with strangers."

"No, we did not! We took here there because she was not comfortable here." He frowned and began pacing around the morning room that Mary Ann had just finished redecorating in her favorite peach and cream shades. "And look how everyone is treating us now. Butter wouldn't melt in their mouths. That old woman who had the audacity to snub my daughter sent us an invitation to her Harvest Ball. What did she hope to accomplish? Well, let me tell you it will be some time before I cross her threshold again or she crosses mine. Too bad, her husband is an interesting person when you get him away from her. She is rearing her daughters to be just like her. Thinks she's better than everyone else around her since her niece married a baron."

Mary Ann rose gracefully and moved to cut him off in his circuit around the room. He stopped as she walked in front of him and put her hands up on his shoulders. "I have already refused her invitation, my dear," she assured him. "What else did Rosemary say?"

Daniel smiled down at her. During the journey home, more

than once he had been ready to turn around, to retrieve his daughter. Only the knowledge their home might not be the best place for her stopped him. He loved Rosemary and wanted the best for her, but as her only parent, knowing what was best had been difficult. He knew others in his same situation who had simply found a female relative to take charge, hired a governess, and put the child in their hands. He had never been able to do that.

From the day that his wife had left, Rosemary had wandered around with the saddest look on her face. She had clung to him as though she expected him to disappear too. And there had been the nightmares. Only when he held her did his daughter's sobs stop. After a while Rosemary's company had become a habit: breakfast together, tea in the afternoon as they discussed her lessons, and a good-night kiss. Of course, as she had grown older, he had stopped visiting her room to kiss her good night, fearing to invade her privacy, choosing instead to kiss her before she went upstairs after the evening meal. Cousin Hortense had protested that he was spoiling the girl, but Daniel had never truly believed that. He had protected her, maybe more than he should have, he admitted to himself, but he had never spoiled her. Rosemary had never asked for much. He had failed her when he ignored her fears, thinking she would grow out of them. Now he felt guilty for deserting her, no matter that Lady Longworth believed she would progress faster without him. He smiled. "Rosemary says I will be horrified when I recieve the bills. Apparently Lady Longworth believes shopping is good for all problems."

Some days later they both received new letters from Bath. Hesitantly Mary Ann opened hers, not certain she wanted the real world to intrude into her idyll. "Daniel, Cousin Sarah says Rosemary went on a picnic with some of her new acquaintances. Does she mention it?" she asked, glad that the news had been good.

"I think so. She sent me a long list of the places Stephen has taken her. I will have to write to your cousin and congratulate her on her success. My little girl's finally taking her place in society." Mary Ann noted the proprietary smile on his face. "Wouldn't that old harridan who gave her the cut direct have apoplexy if she knew? Her platter-faced daughters are wallflowers."

"Do not gloat, Daniel. Cousin Sarah says Rosemary is still very nervous, especially if Stephen is not around. Apparently that has not frightened any of the young men off. Cousin Sarah says Rosemary receives one or more bouquets a day. You know, that is really quite remarkable. Bath must be quite empty of company by now." She continued reading her letter, frowning slightly.

Her husband looked up from his daughter's letter. "What is wrong? What did your cousin say?"

"Not anything really. She simply mentioned that Rosemary fainted at a ball at the Upper Rooms. Apparently after the second dance, gentlemen surrounded her, requesting that she dance with one of them."

Her husband's face grew dark. "And what was your cousin doing at the time? Who told her to take my daughter to a ball?"

"I believe you did, my dear," Mary Ann reminded him gently.

"Oh," he said, his face registering his dismay.

"There is good news. Rosemary danced the first two country dances without a problem. And this was on an evening when Stephen was not there to lend them an escort."

"An improvement, I must admit. Your cousin has done wonders. I wish we had tried this earlier. But what is that about Stephen? Rosemary's letter is full of his name."

"Cousin Sarah is not certain. It may simply be an infatuation. He has been extraordinarily kind to her."

"All your relatives have been. I am not certain what we could have done without Lady Longworth's help."

"You would have thought of something," Mary Ann assured him. "Would you mind if this is more than an infatuation?"

"Between Rosemary and Stephen?" he asked, his face serious.

"Yes." She looked at him, trying to read his thoughts.

"I do not know. My first reaction is to say yes. It is hard for me to think of my daughter as a wife. Yet girls younger than she are married. I would not want her to spend her life alone. Before I decide, I would want to see them together, to have a talk with him and with her."

"Stephen's very wealthy."

"And Rosemary's portion is a large one. Besides what I will give her, she has a large inheritance from her mother. But money, as necessary as it is, is not the most important thing in a marriage." He walked across the room and pulled her from her chair, putting his arms around her. "I want her to have someone who loves her for herself."

Mary Ann laid her head on his shoulder. She closed her eyes. "I hope she finds him, my dear," she said so softly that Daniel almost missed it. "I hope she finds him."

Miles away, Stephen watched Rosemary walking toward him and wondered if he should write to her father. Then he shook his head, reminding himself that he would see Daniel Wyatt soon. He was in no hurry. Now that his mother and Rosemary spent almost every day with him, he no longer felt threatened.

Stephen laughed ruefully, marveling how helpless he felt around the sweet blond beauty who walked toward him. He, who had faced man-eating tigers, was as gentle as a lamb around her.

Rosemary saw him waiting for her and hurried forward. "You must come see, Stephen," she said excitedly. She held out her hand to him. None of the gentlemen she had met recently made her feel like he did.

The temptation was more than he could resist. He took her hand and pulled her slowly towards him, giving her an opportunity to pull away. Her eyes grew wide. She took a step toward him, then another and another until she was in his arms. He lowered his head and kissed her. Hearing a noise on the path behind him, he let her go and stepped back.

Rosemary, her eyes sparkling and her lips red with his kiss, reached out a hand toward him. He shook his head. Then his butler appeared from around the bend in the path. "Lady Longworth requests your presence in the salon as soon as possible, Miss Wyatt. She asked me to remind you of the musical this evening."

"Thank you, Thomas," Stephen said quietly. "Please tell her we will join her immediately." When they were alone once more, he smiled at Rosemary. "Later," he promised. He took her arm and guided her to where his mother waited.

9

By THE TIME Daniel and Mary Ann arrived at Long Meadow, Rosemary and Lady Longworth had been in residence for more than a week. They had, however, postponed their departure from Bath as long as possible. Only a desperate plea for help from her elder son had pried Lady Longworth away from many projects she had taken in hand at her second son's estate. In fact, had Stephen not added his insistence, the ladies might have stayed in Bath indefinitely. "When the visit to Long Meadow is over, you can return to help me finish everything. My man of affairs assures me that all the major work will be finished by then. Maybe you and Rosemary would be willing to stay with me for a time." Stephen looked at Rosemary to see her reaction, but her bonnet covered so much of her face that he could not be sure he had seen her smile.

"Do say we might, Cousin Sarah," Rosemary said slowly.

"If your parents do not object," the elder lady said thoughtfully. She smiled at her son. "I expect to see you shortly, sir," she reminded him. He nodded, his eyes never leaving what he could see of Rosemary's face.

The week before the other guests arrived at Long Meadow was a delightful one for Rosemary. Unlike Lady Longworth, she had no specific duties to perform. And the viscount had an excellent music room. He had added a pianoforte to his collection as soon as he returned from Bath. When the twins learned of Rosemary's arrival, they begged her for additional lessons. "The music teacher Papa hired makes us practice our scales," James complained.

"He never lets us have any fun," his sister added. "I wish you could stay here and teach us music." She opened her eyes wide and let her bottom lip poke out.

Rosemary had to bite back a laugh at the pitiful face the child was making. Had she not known what a little manipulator Julia could be, she might have been taken in. "If I were to undertake your instruction, I would be worse than any other instructor alive," she told them, her eyes narrowing dangerously. "You would not only have to practice your scales for two hours a day but also spend at least another hour of fingering practice after that."

"Three hours? Monsieur LeClerque makes us practice only a half-hour a day." James looked at Rosemary again, his eyes wide and troubled. "I think you are having fun with us."

"Of course she is," Julia said in a scolding tone. "Nobody practices three hours a day. Now, Rosemary, come with us. We want you to teach us to play a song for Papa's birthday. I already embroidered him a handkerchief, and James made him something too, but we wanted something special, something we could do on his birthday. Do you have something that would be easy for us to learn? I have been practicing every day." She pulled on Rosemary's hand until the older girl bent down. "James has not," she whispered in her ear.

Although Rosemary had expected to grow tired of the lessons, the twins were determined. Each morning and afternoon they joined her in the music room and practiced. James, who played the bass because it had fewer notes, plodded along. Julia learned the notes the first day. The only real problem that presented itself appeared when Rosemary had the children play the parts of the song at the same time. James plodded slowly along while Julia raced ahead. For a while it was musical chaos.

Just when Rosemary was ready to throw her hands up in despair, the door to the room opened. "Is this a music lesson?" Stephen asked, covering his ears with his hands.

"Uncle Stephen." James hopped off the piano bench and ran toward his uncle at full speed. Just before he slammed into Stephen, his uncle picked him up and tossed him in the air.

Julia turned around on the piano bench and smiled at her uncle. Then she glared at her brother. "That is a sour look for such a sweet girl to have on her face. Does it mean that I will not get a kiss from my favorite niece?" her uncle asked. He smiled at Rosemary, causing her pulse to race as she wished he was offering the kiss to her.

"Of course not, Uncle Stephen. But James is doing everything wrong. We will never get the song right if he stops to play with you."

Her brother stomped over to the piano bench and planted himself in front of her. "You cannot blame this on me. I played the notes right. Tell her, Rosemary. I did not miss a note, but she did." He stuck out his tongue at his sister and turned to stalk away.

"Do not be so hasty, James," his uncle told him, looking over his head at the young lady dressed in a blue muslin that made her hazel eyes blue by reflection. He smiled at Rosemary, a slow smile that warmed her very heart. "Tell me more about this project."

"We are trying to learn a song to play for Papa's birthday," his niece told him. She looked at her brother, her face full of indignation. "But James does not play it right!"

"Yes, I do. You are the one who is wrong."

"No, I'm not."

"Yes, you are."

"Am not!"

"Children, I have heard enough," Rosemary said. She took both of them by the hand and led them over to two chairs. "Sit here. You both know your notes well. Now you need to learn to put the parts together. Let me show you."

Stephen walked over to the piano as she took her seat. "Maybe if I played James's part and you played Julia's, they would understand better," he suggested. She nodded and slid down the piano bench so that he could take his place beside her. His shoulder brushed hers, and his muscled thigh felt warm through her dress. "I may have suggested more than I can achieve. It has been a while since I have played," he whispered in her ear, noting with delight the way her short curls teased her earlobe.

She smiled at him, glad to have him close to her once more, and then said out loud, addressing the twins, "We will go through the song slowly at first so that you can hear both parts." She smiled at Stephen. "Then we will play it again at the tempo written." Stephen raised his eyebrow and grinned.

By the time they played it for the second time, both Julia and James were at the piano. "Uncle Stephen, will you help me while Rosemary helps Julia?" James asked.

"But I wanted Uncle Stephen." Julia pouted.

"Shame on you. I know Nurse has taught you better manners. Rosemary has given you her time, and now you shun her. Cupboard love if I ever heard of it," their uncle scolded, his face serious but his eyes dancing.

"We did not mean it, Rosemary," the twins said seriously, their eyes fixed on her face.

"If you do not help us, we will never be ready." Julia stuck out her lower lip and let it quiver. "You play much better than Uncle Stephen."

Her uncle fell back, clutching his heart. "A thrust to the heart. I am wounded."

"Where? Let me see!" James shouted.

"Stop this foolishness this minute," Rosemary scolded. She did not try to hide her laughter. "We have only three days before your father's birthday. Let us concentrate on our song." She looked about the room until she found the object she was looking for. "Stephen, bring the metronome over to the pianoforte." As soon as she had set the rhythm she wanted, she told the children, "Listen for a moment." For a minute the only sound was the rhythmical ticking of the instrument. "Now, play the song again, trying to match the rhythm. Do not worry if you do not get it right at first. We will work on it.'' She glared at Stephen, warning him not to agitate them further.

The foursome were finishing their practice for the day when Daniel and Mary Ann Wyatt arrived. Hearing the bustle outside, the twins hurried out into the hallway. When she heard her father's voice, Rosemary quickly followed, the skirts of her pink afternoon dress held up out of her way.

''Here is my wayward daughter now,'' her father said as he held out his arms to welcome her. Rosemary flew into them, then, remembering her manners, blushed and took a few steps back. ''So elegant, do you not agree, Mary Ann? Obviously this time away from us has refreshed you,'' her father said proudly. Rosemary smiled up at him and then kissed her stepmother on the cheek.

''She has certainly been a help around here the last few days,'' Viscount Longworth said, joining them with a smile. ''My twins have enrolled her help on a project of theirs. I am surprised she is not exhausted.'' The twins, who had wrapped themselves around his legs, looked up at him reproachfully. He dropped a hand on each of their heads and laughed. ''You remember my brother, Stephen Huntington, and my children.''

''Cousin Stephen, Rosemary's letters have been full of what you have been doing to your estate.'' Mary Ann held up her cheek for her cousins' kisses. ''I am happy that you have found something you like.''

''Come. Come. I am certain you are exhausted from your journey,'' Lady Longworth said. ''Do you wish to go up to your room to refresh yourself? We do not expect the others until tomorrow, so we will be able to have a comfortable coze before supper this evening.''

Mary Ann glanced up at her husband, and he nodded. His face wore a look that his daughter had never seen before. ''You come up with us, Rosemary. I have so many questions to ask you,'' her stepmother suggested.

''If their chattering bores you, sir, my brother and I will

be in the library," Longworth told Daniel. "Any servant can direct you. If not, we will see you later this evening."

As soon as they were settled in their rooms, Daniel and Mary Ann ordered tea for the three of them. "Tell me about everything," her stepmother urged.

"You cannot imagine the number of dresses that Lady Longworth believes a lady should have, Mary Ann. If we had gone shopping every day, I believe she would have found something to buy each time. I am sorry, Papa, but the bills will be frightful," Rosemary said apologetically. She had always dreaded giving her father the household account to peruse, but he rarely complained.

"I am certain you will not beggar me," he assured her. "If you do, I will spend your money," he teased. "But I have heard enough about clothes for today. How have you enjoyed your stay in Bath?"

Her face rather solemn, Rosemary paused thoughtfully. "Lady Longworth has kept me busy. She has refused to let me worry or brood. Even when I fainted at the Upper Assembly Rooms—"

"What?" her father said, his face worried.

"Hush," his wife said quickly, motioning Rosemary to continue.

"Even then, she acted as though I had done nothing to be ashamed of. Before long, she had everyone believing it, even me."

"Good," Mary Ann said with a smile. "But you did not spend all your time fainting at balls. Tell me about the rest."

"The last few weeks we have been helping Stephen refurnish his estate. He let me pick out the colors for the master suite and the morning room. Even Lady Longworth assured me that they were the perfect choices." Mary Ann and Daniel exchanged glances. Daniel made a note to get to know Stephen much better during this visit. Although he was pleased to see the changes in his daughter, he was not certain she was ready for marriage. That evening as they ate their meal, he watched the younger man carefully.

Guests began arriving the next morning almost before they finished breakfast. In the confusion of helping Lady Long-worth assign rooms and getting the visiting children trans-fered to the nursery, Rosemary had little time to be afraid. Her father watched in amazement when she did not pale or grow faint even when surrounded by strangers. During their talk the previous evening, he had been impressed by how grown-up she seemed. He felt the smallest twinge of regret as he watched her look up, catch Stephen's eye, and exchange a glance.

Mary Ann read his expression correctly. "She is quite a young lady," she murmured consolingly. "What do you plan to do about that relationship?"

"What relationship? Until he approaches me or she decides to say something, I suppose I will have to pretend I am blind."

"Do you wish me to ask Cousin Sarah about it?"

"No, leave it for me. You have enough to take care of." He smiled down at her protectively. "May I interest you in a slow walk about the gardens?"

Clarissa had been one of the first to arrive that morning. She had not been happy to see Rosemary already in residence or the looks the blond and Stephen had been exchanging. Lingering in the hallway near Rosemary, she said cattily, "I would think Mary Ann would have more pride than to look at him that way. Lud, Rosemary, I do not understand how you can stand it. Your father and Mary Ann are acting like a pair of fools. I just know everyone is talking about them." Clarissa twitched the skirts of her red kerseymere dress into place, wishing she had chosen something cooler like the aqua muslin Rosemary was wearing. Her mother had tried to convince her she would be too warm, but, as usual, she had not listened. She looked at herself in the mirror, noting the way the red of the gown made her skin seem even whiter. "What are you wearing to the ball?" She smiled, knowing that the ball would be one place where Rosemary would not show off to advantage.

Her gloating came to naught, however. From the moment she entered the drawing room and saw Rosemary dressed in a cream lace overdress with a rose-pink underslip standing beside Stephen, resplendent in midnight blue and stark white with sapphires on his hand and in his cravat, she was miserable. When the two of them insisted that everyone follow them to the music room for a special predinner surprise, her stomach twisted itself into knots as she watched them encourage the twins to play their song. Her displeasure increased during dinner, so much so that her mother called her to her side during the lull before the ball and reminded her that a lady does not reveal her emotions. She flushed and turned away angrily.

Had she known that Rosemary had not lost her fear but only learned to hide it better, perhaps she would have been happier. As one after another young man solicited her hand for a dance, Rosemary reminded herself sternly that she did not want to do anything to spoil the evening for her father and Mary Ann. Shortly before they were to go down for the evening, they had called her to their rooms to give her the news. She was going to be a sister. She had laughed and hugged them both, delighted with the news. They had wanted to tell her the evening before, but the dressing bell had sounded before they had the chance.

"I plan to tell Cousin Sarah tomorrow," Mary Ann explained. "We wanted you to know first." She glanced at her stepdaughter to make certain the girl's reaction was not just a brave front. The smile that spread across Rosemary's face reassured her.

The news sustained Rosemary throughout the evening. She managed to dance one or two dances with mere acquaintances as well as two dances each with the viscount and Stephen and one with her father. Clarissa, with whom Stephen danced only once, even though she held the supper dance open as long as she dared, gritted her teeth and flirted madly. Her eyes narrowed dangerously as she watched Stephen lead Rosemary into the supper room.

Stephen had left nothing to chance. As soon as he arrived at Long Meadow, he had insisted that the supper dance was his. All evening while he danced with others, he watched Rosemary. Whenever he noticed her smile grow white around the edges, he would hurry to her side and whisk her to the safety of his mother's or Mary Ann's side. His care plus her excitement about the coming baby made the ball bearable. Although she felt faint several times, Stephen was always there, and she never succumbed.

The next morning she slept later than usual, awakened only when her door flew open and Julia rushed in. "Come see!" The little girl stopped when she realized Rosemary was still in bed. Her face fell. "I am sorry. I did not mean to wake you," she said as she walked back toward the door.

"Come back here," Rosemary said quietly. Julia walked back to the bed, her feet dragging. "Now, hop up here and tell me what I am going to see."

"You'll come? I told James you would. The big cat in the barn has new kittens. I wanted you to see them before my cousins find them." In the last few days Julia had not enjoyed her home. There were too many nurses, governesses, and tutors about for her comfort. And too many children.

"Go ring the bell for my maid. I suppose we must hurry?"

"Yes!" Julia jumped off the bed, her skirts flying, her dignity forgotten in her excitement.

A short time later they were on their way to the stables, Julia running ahead and then back to Rosemary. Clarissa, who had been told in no uncertain terms by her mother that they would leave no later than eleven that morning, watched them cross the yard. Although she had danced every dance the evening before, she had had to share the attention she craved, and she did not like the feeling. Even the twins had deserted her. Her eyes narrowed. She turned and hurried into the hall.

In the barn James waited impatiently. "What took you so long?" he demanded.

"She was still in bed," his sister told him, her amazement evident in the tone of her voice.

"Be quiet. If she hears us, she will move them," he said importantly. "Follow me." They climbed the ladder that led to the loft full of fresh-mown hay. "Do not try to touch them. She might bite you," he told his sister and Rosemary quietly. "See! There are five of them."

"They are so little. And look, their eyes are shut. I wonder if Papa will let us have one for the nursery," Julia said. She reached out a hand to touch one but drew it back quickly when Rosemary frowned and the mother cat growled.

"You will have plenty of time to find out. They will not be ready to leave their mother for quite some time. I am certain the other children will want to see them too. Why don't you run and get them?" Rosemary suggested. "I will stay here and make certain the mother does not move them before you get back."

Reluctantly, with many backward glances, the children slid down the ladder. Then they rushed from the barn. Before they had been gone for more than a moment, Rosemary heard the ladder they had used drop to the floor. "Hello, is anyone there?"

"Yes," Clarissa said smugly. Rosemary glanced over the edge of the loft and then stepped back hurriedly as she grew dizzy.

"Could you put the ladder back in place? It must be around there somewhere," Rosemary asked. "The children must have dislodged it."

"I do not see it anywhere. Perhaps I should hurry to the house and get some help," the other young lady suggested, her smile satisfied.

"Do hurry. The children will be here in a few minutes to see the kittens."

"I will," Clarissa reassured Rosemary. She rushed back to the house, where her mother waited impatiently. "I needed

to take a walk before I had to ride for hours in that carriage,"
she explained. She turned to a footman. "Tell the nursery
attendants that the head groom said he did not want the
children in the stables until later this afternoon." He nodded
and hurried on his way. Clarissa watched him, a smile of
satisfaction plastered on her face.

As time passed, Rosemary grew nervous and then resigned
to her imprisonment. She finally lay back and closed her
eyes. When she awoke sometime later, the cat and her kittens
were nowhere to be seen. But she could hear the rattle of
harness in the stable below. "Hello, is anyone there?" she
called as she had done earlier.

"Rosemary, is that you?" Stephen moved back across the
stables so that he could see into the loft. "What are you doing
up there?"

"James and Julia brought me to see some kittens. Then
they rushed off to bring the other children to see them. They
must have dislodged the ladder as they left, and I could not
get down," she explained. "Clarissa promised to send help."

"Clarissa? She left for home hours ago." His face grew
stern. "Wait a minute until I get this ladder in place. Then
I will be up."

"There *is* a ladder. That's peculiar."

Not as peculiar as Clarissa being involved, he thought to
himself. He clambered up the ladder and looked around.
"Where are these kittens you came up to see?"

"I went to sleep, and I suppose the mother took them away."

"How long have you been up here?" he demanded, taking
in her sleep-flushed face and disarranged hair.

"I don't know, but I'm hungry. Julia gave me time only
for a cup of chocolate before she rushed me out here." She
turned to him, her face worried. "Do you think something
has happened to the twins? I know they were planning to
return immediately. Are they all right?"

"Perfectly fine." He swung off the ladder and into the
loft, sliding toward her. His boot, which had not cleared the
ladder, knocked it loose, sending it crashing to the floor

below. "I hope their nurse releases them from the school-room soon," he said ruefully, looking at the ladder below. "Some rescuer I am."

"But you tried," she said firmly, trying to reassure him. She put her hand on his arm much as she touched James or her father. The reaction was not the same. Her fingers tingled and her heart raced. She took her hand away hastily, backing up slightly.

He followed and sat down beside her in the fresh hay. "Someone is certain to come soon," he said, his eyes fixed on her face. Her hair was a cloud of silvery curls that caught the dim light and sparkled. He reached up and brushed away the hay that had caught there. Then he froze, his eyes never leaving hers. Slowly, as though trying not to frighten her, he cupped her face with his hand. He bent toward her, his eyes still on hers.

When their lips met, her eyes closed. Her heart pounded. Her arms, almost as though they belonged to someone else, reached out and curled around his neck, holding him close to her. They sank back against the hay, their kisses deepening. Finally he pulled away reluctantly. Then he sat up, enjoying the picture she made, her hair tousled and her dress rumpled.

She blushed under his burning gaze, but she did not look away. He put out a hand and pulled her up to his side, resisting his desire to wrap his arms around her and to give her more than kisses. "I have been wanting to do that again since last time," he told her, his low voice sending ripples of excitement through her.

"You have?" Her smile grew wider. As he had done for her earlier, she reached up and brushed the hay from his hair.

"Every day. And last night at the ball I wanted to smash the faces of the men you danced with when you were not with me. I was even jealous of your father and my brother." He laughed ruefully, keeping an eye on her for her reaction.

Her eyes opened wide, as they did when she was startled.

Her heart pounded with excitement. "Jealous? You were jealous of me?" She wanted to reach out and touch his face, but was still too shy.

He smiled ruefully. "I am almost embarrassed to admit it," he said as he reached out and took one of her hands in his. They both took a deep breath as warmth spread to the rest of their bodies.

"Do not be. I did not like it when you danced with Clarissa and the other young ladies," she said so quietly that he had to strain to hear her voice. She blushed again and looked at their clasped hands. His tightened around hers.

They sat there for a few minutes, neither willing to interrupt the anticipation, the tension in the air, the heart-pounding excitement. Just when Rosemary's nerves were stretched to their limit, Stephen cleared his throat. She jumped. His grip on her hand grew tighter, as though he were afraid she would pull away. He tried to speak and his voice cracked much as it had done when it was changing. He cleared his throat again, noting to himself that his knees were shaking more now than they had done when he had met the maharajah for the first time. Rosemary simply sat there enjoying his hand on hers, willing the moment to go on forever.

For the third time he cleared his throat. She looked up at him, her eyes wide and full of trust. He knew that what he was going to do was against the bounds of propriety, but he had left those far behind when he had kissed her. "Rosemary, may I approach your father?" he asked. His words tumbled over one another so that she was not really certain that she had heard what he said.

"I am certain my father will be happy to see you," she murmured. Her fear of strangers and refusal to attend large social events had left her largely unprepared for his declaration. She had dreamed. The hours she had spent working on the house on his estate had been filled with dreams of sharing the house with him, of their children. The kiss they had shared set her dreams blazing. Now she was not certain that what she was hearing was not part of her dreams.

Stephen sat there, his eyes fixed on her downcast face, trying to read her emotions. He reached over with his other hand and tilted her face up to him. "Rosemary, will you accept my offer if your father agrees to my suit?" he asked solemnly. He held his breath, waiting for her reply.

Her eyes opened even wider, appearing much too large for her face. Her mouth shaped a silent O. Then she flung herself forward into his arms. "Yes," she said almost in a whisper at first. "Yes!" she shouted.

Laughing, he fell backward, pulling her down with him until her lips were right above his. Then he kissed her, letting his lips tell her of his love. Neither of them heard the commotion below them or the ladder being raised into place. James pushed his way up the ladder before the adults. "Are the kittens still here?" he asked. Then his eyes grew wide. In his less-than-quiet voice, he asked, "Why're you kissing Rosemary, Uncle Stephen?"

Startled, the two of them sat up, staring at the viscount and Rosemary's father, who had followed him up to the loft. "Yes, Stephen, do tell us what you are doing with my daughter?" her father demanded, the light of battle in his eyes.

10

THE CONTRAST between those moments in the hayloft and the rest of the day was almost more than Rosemary could bear. Once again she was the center of everyone's attention and one of the ones at whom questions were directed. Her happiness faded quickly. The fact that most of the faces were kind or the questions were gentle did not matter. All that mattered was that Stephen was beside her, giving her strength to face the disapproval that was evident in the faces around her and in their questions.

Even that was taken from her finally. "May I use your library, my lord?" her father asked Longworth formally. The viscount nodded. "If you would accompany me, Mr. Huntington?" Although he framed the remark as a question, one look in Daniel Wyatt's face told Stephen that he had no choice. He had known this time was coming from the moment he heard his nephew's voice. He smiled at Rosemary and squeezed her hand. Then he walked from the room, his back straight in the dark blue coat he had changed into as soon as they had returned to the house. One by one the other gentlemen left the room.

As soon as the door had closed behind them, Lady Longworth sighed. "For such a quiet child, you can cause the biggest problems, Rosemary." If Rosemary had been listening carefully, she would have recognized the glee in the elder lady's voice.

"What problem? I do not understand why it is wrong to

be in a hayloft with Stephen when I can walk through the garden alone with him any evening.'' The memory of their questions still echoed in Rosemary's ears. Her conviction of her innocence gave her strength now that the men were gone.

''The difference is the seclusion. And even that might have been overlooked, since everyone here is family, except for the fact that you looked so thoroughly kissed and delightfully rumpled,'' her stepmother explained. ''One look at the two of you covered with hay, and everyone knew exactly what you had been doing.'' Rosemary blushed, the red of her cheeks in competition with the soft pink of her kerseymere dress. Only the fact that she had been shivering with cold had released her from her father's thundering scold. Even then he had insisted that Mary Ann accompany her to her room so that she could don a gown more suitable for the changing October weather and comb the hay from her hair. ''My dear, had it been just the two of our families alone here . . .''

''I would never have been alone in the hayloft. Clarissa lied to me. She said the ladder had disappeared and she would send help.'' Rosemary's face was full of confusion. ''What did I do to her? Why would she do such a thing to me?''

Lady Longworth sat beside Rosemary and patted her hand. ''We will probably never know. What I do know is that her mother will receive a very strongly worded letter about the young lady's manners. They will receive no more invitations from my family.'' Sparks of anger glittered in her turquoise eyes. Both of the other ladies were glad that emotion was directed at someone besides them. Then Lady Longworth said softly, her voice gently chiding, ''No matter who created the possibility of the situation, my dear, it is you and Stephen who must bear the blame. Had you called for help or he dropped down from the loft, or even if you had not gotten so . . . so involved! My dear, you have not been presented, have not had a single offer of marriage.''

''Yes, I have,'' Rosemary said quietly, a thrill of joy

shooting through her as she remembered how shy Stephen had been when he asked if she were willing for him to offer for her.

Both of the older ladies stared at her in shock. "Your father knows nothing of it," her stepmother said firmly. Rosemary smiled a secret smile.

"Who is he? He will not interfere? He will not come forward?" Lady Longworth asked, wondering if she had nursed a viper in her home.

"He already has. At least I think he will have by now," she added. She stuttered just a bit, wondering for the briefest moment if Stephen had really meant what he had said. Then the memories of his words, his arms, his lips, flooded her once again. Her smile made the two elder ladies catch their breath.

"Who is he?" Mary Ann demanded, frowning at her stepdaughter. Until today everything had been so wonderful. True, Rosemary still was not completely comfortable around many people, but she was better. And she had been so happy when they had told her of the baby, so excited. Whom could she have become involved with?

Before Mary Ann could get out that question, her cousin asked, "Who is he? Mary Ann, I swear to you that she did not make the match when she was with me."

"Yes, I did. In fact, you and Mary Ann were the ones who introduced him to me," Rosemary said. A mischievous sparkle lit her otherwise solemn face.

"Well, no matter who he is, he will have no chance now. With all the gossips in the house today, your reputation is in shreds, and you and Stephen will have to be married right away," Mary Ann told her firmly. She remembered her husband's wish for his daughter and her own unhappy marriage and regretted that there was not another option.

Lady Longworth glared at her guests. "I do not know whom you are talking about, young lady. I supervised you carefully and know very well that you made no assignations. You were never alone with any gentleman except for . . ."

She paused. The expression on her face changed from indignation to amused delight. "You little minx," she said happily, giving Rosemary a quick hug.

"What is going on?" Mary Ann demanded.

"Rosemary?"

"Stephen asked me if he might approach Papa, Mary Ann. He planned to see him this afternoon anyway, but . . ."

"The situation was his undoing, hmmm. I shall have to tease my son about his lack of control," Lady Longworth said smugly. "Just like his father. Never liked to wait for anything. He was even in a rush to be born."

"Stephen? Stephen wants to marry you?" Mary Ann could hardly get the words out. Relief rushed through her. "And you obviously were ready to say yes." Rosemary nodded. Her face was pink with happiness. "How wonderful." She hugged Rosemary gratefully. "This changes everything." Mary Ann looked at her cousin. "How can we eliminate some of the talk? We do not want them to begin marriage as the latest topic of gossip for the *ton*." Rosemary blanched in fear. Her hands began to shake again.

"Leave everything to me, everything but your husband, that is," her cousin said, smiling. "Talk to him soon. Make certain he will not put any obstacles in our path or say anything to contradict our stories."

"You do not know Papa well if you think you can change his mind once it has been made up," his daughter said fearfully, looking from one to the other with wide eyes, certain her dream of happiness would slip from her grasp.

"My dear, as you will learn before very long, a loving wife has more resources at her command than a daughter. And with Mary Ann's recent announcement, I am certain he will deny her nothing." This time it was Mary Ann who blushed.

"I will do my best," she promised, a gleam of excitement in her eyes. "Do you wish to be married from the church at home, Rosemary?" she asked hesitantly. She thought she knew the answer but believed she should give her step-daughter at least a chance to respond.

All color left Rosemary's face as she thought of the church she had attended most of her life. She shook her head slowly. At one time her dreams had been filled with just such a hope. As soon as she finished reading a romance, she would picture herself entering the church on her father's arm, the hero waiting for her at the altar, a sense of excitement filling her. "No, I do not want to go back there!" Her face grew more thoughtful. "You do not think the vicar will feel slighted? I would not want to do anything to hurt his feelings."

"If we arrange things carefully, I am certain he will understand," Mary Ann reassured her.

"Just a small intimate ceremony here at Long Meadow, I think, or would you prefer Bath?" Rosemary's future mother-in-law asked. She should have realized just how serious her son was as he showered Rosemary with his attention and invited her suggestions about the estate. She had had her hopes but was afraid he would retreat if she asked him too many questions.

"Bath? Why would she want to be married in Bath?" Mary Ann asked impatiently.

"She does have acquaintances there."

"I thought this was to be small, intimate, merely family," Mary Ann said. Her face wore a frown. "We will have to invite your Cousin Hortense," she said thoughtfully, looking at Rosemary.

The girl frowned too. "Must we? She will go on so, especially if she finds out what has happened. And she will. And then everyone will know."

"But if you do not invite her, she may talk even more," Lady Longworth explained. "Better to give her something positive to say than leave her wondering."

"But she will not say anything positive. She never does," Rosemary protested, determined that they would see her side.

"She will have to be invited," Mary Ann said firmly. "Of course, she may choose not to come."

"That will never happen," Rosemary said gloomily. Then her face grew brighter. "She does not like to travel even on the best of roads," she reminded them. "If we have the wedding here, she would have to hire a carriage and travel on roads that are not the best in the country. And it may rain." She sighed happily, already thinking of the letter she would write to her cousin.

"Then the marriage is to be here?" Lady Longworth asked with a satisfied look on her face.

"If Stephen will agree," her future daughter-in-law said quietly.

"He will. Now, let us think of a date."

"Daniel will insist that it take place immediately," Mary Ann said firmly. Rosemary nodded.

"Nonsense. If we are to quiet the talk before it has a chance to spread, we cannot act so hastily. Besides, Stephen's estate will not be ready, and it is too early to go to London." Lady Longworth tapped her fingers against the arm of the chair as if calculating. "Mary Ann, you will have to talk with him. Convince him to see reason."

"Well, we will have to order her bride clothes. And she will need something special to be married in."

Rosemary, who had been dreaming of walking down the aisle toward Stephen, had missed the last few exchanges. But when Mary Ann mentioned a gown for the wedding, she spoke up, "I already know what I want to wear."

"Well, for heaven's sake, do not tell your father."

"Which gown are you talking about?" Lady Longworth asked, her brow furrowed as she tried to remember the extensive wardrobe they had ordered for the girl.

"The white one. You must remember. At first you thought the cloth had yellowed until Madame showed you the fabric near the window."

"Why that one? What about the white with the deep blue

pelisse?'' Lady Longworth asked, remembering at last the dress to which Rosemary was referring.

"This one has a matching pelisse trimmed in blond lace. The dress has a little ruff that hugs my neck. It is lovely, with just the faintest pattern in the material. And there is a matching bonnet," Rosemary told her stepmother, a vacant look on her face as she thought of herself in the gown walking toward Stephen.

"Gowns later," Mary Ann said practically. "Now we must decide on a date before your father and Stephen return. How long should we wait, Cousin Sarah?"

"A month, I think. Rosemary and I can return to Bath. Perhaps you should come with us if you feel able to travel," the elder lady said thoughtfully. "We will need to order new linen. Too bad we will not have enough time to monogram it."

"There are all those sheets and pillowcases I sewed when I was growing up," Rosemary reminded them. "They are packed in lavender at the Manor. At least Cousin Hortense said she packed them away."

"I will write to the housekeeper tomorrow. She is certain to know what was done with them," Mary Ann said. "As to Bath, well, shall we wait to decide about that?" She exchanged a meaningful glance with her cousin. "Now, whom should we invite for the ceremony? Everyone who is here now, for certain. I do hope they will refrain from gossip."

"Nonsense, my dear." Both of the other women turned to look at Lady Longworth, stunned expressions on their faces. "Let us encourage them to talk. We will simply have to direct them as we want them to go. Emphasize that this is a love match."

"Well, it is," Rosemary said defensively.

"Of course, my dear." Her future mother-in-law patted her cheek and smiled. "Now, let me send for paper and pen—and a tea tray. All of this emotion has quite exhausted me."

"And me," her cousin replied. "Are you certain our relatives can be manipulated that way?"

"They are observant. They must have seen Stephen and Rosemary at the ball. I saw all that gossiping behind the fans. And most of them are willing to be kind. You could see that this afternoon. After all, they are family. Any gossip could be detrimental to their plans as well as ours."

"At least the worst gossip of them all had already left."

"Who is that?" Rosemary asked curiously. Suddenly she had realized that these people she was talking about were going to be her relatives too, people she would associate with for the rest of her life. The viscount's birthday had been a revelation for someone who had so few relatives. True, most of the family had attended her father's and Mary Ann's wedding, but at the time Rosemary had assumed that was a special occasion. From the talk during the visit, she realized that they met several times a year, rotating from one country home to another. Only the October gathering was always at Long Meadow. That meant she would be expected to be the hostess for this group someday. She turned white and began to shake again.

"Rosemary, what is wrong?" Mary Ann hurried to her side, her vinaigrette in her hand. "Here, smell this." Her stepdaughter took one whiff and stepped back. "If your father were to walk in and see you in a faint, he will think the worst. I would never be able to convince him of anything. Quickly, now. Think calm and soothing thoughts." She grimaced. "I never thought I would ever say that. My mother said that to me before my first wedding."

"I think, Mary Ann, that you should sit and rest. You must take care of yourself and the baby. Leave everything to me," her cousin said soothingly. "See. Rosemary has lovely color in her cheeks again. Ah, here comes the tea." She smiled up at her butler. "Put it here. Thank you, Thomas. This looks very refreshing. Make certain the gentlemen have something also. Something filling perhaps. I have a feeling they will need food to counteract all that brandy I am certain they are swilling." She turned to Rosemary. "Men have the most annoying habit of indulging in drink just when you wish them clearheaded. Have you found this to be true also, Mary Ann?"

"More often than I would like to admit. Oh, Daniel does not overindulge. In fact, he often forgoes his port after dinner and joins me for tea." As soon as the butler and footman left the room, Mary Ann changed the subject abruptly. "I wonder what the gentlemen are talking about? They have been in the library for a long time."

"You do not think Papa would hurt Stephen, do you?" Rosemary asked hesitantly, her eyes wide and frightened.

"More likely my son would hurt your father. Oh, do not look so worried, child. I am certain nothing happened. I admit I would not like to have been in my son's shoes when the library door closed behind him, but he managed to get himself into the situation"—she glanced over at Rosemary, her face rather stern—"and I am certain he can talk his way out of it."

"If they would just tell us what they have decided," Mary Ann said with almost a yawn. "I think I will go absolutely mad if they do not come out soon."

"Rosemary, pour your stepmother a cup of tea. Bring me some too," Lady Longworth demanded. "Then sit down and write what we tell you to." Once again she began tapping her fingers against the arm of her chair. "No more than thirty guests, I would say. Fortunately, most of our overnight guests left uncharacteristically early this morning. When it becomes known that I have one fewer eligible son, several of those mothers will gnash their teeth." She smiled in private glee, thinking of the disappointment on more than one face. "Whom else beside Rosemary's Cousin Hortense should we invite?"

"The Margraves. I would like to have them at my wedding. They are neighbors of ours. I played with their children until they grew up and went to town. I still correspond with their daughter. She married during her first Season. Now she has a darling little boy.''

"Not relatives. Of course, since you have so few connections, it would be good for you to have someone of your own there. Shall we invite your friend as well as her parents?''

"She no longer travels. Her husband was injured in a hunting accident last year, and she rarely leaves his side.''

"That attention does her credit, I am sure . . ." Lady Longworth began. Then the door opened. Daniel Wyatt and Stephen Huntington entered the room. Although neither man looked very easy with the other, much of the tension was gone.

Rosemary darted to Stephen's side. "Are you all right?'' she asked quietly, searching his face for the marks she was certain her father would have left there.

"What did you think I was going to do with him, Rosemary?'' her father asked impatiently. "I am not a brute.''

Stephen smiled down at her and reached for her hand. "I am fine.'' He glanced at her father, who nodded. "Will you come to the library with me?'' His eyes held a hint of excitement. He smiled again, and her face lit with happiness. She looked at the other people in the room and then nodded.

As soon as the door had closed behind them, Lady Longworth asked, "Well, what have you decided?''

Daniel Wyatt looked at her and laughed ironically. "Even if the situation had been different, that son of yours would not have listened if I had said no.''

"But you did not, did you?'' his wife asked, her face anxious.

"If I had, would I have let them leave the room like that? In a few minutes, when they have had a chance to talk, I want you to go to the library,'' he said, looking at Mary Ann in a way that reminded her of their stolen kisses when they were engaged.

"I will go," Lady Longworth said, just a hint of a smile on her face. "You two need to be alone." She narrowed her eyes and smiled at her cousin. "I am certain you have much to discuss." Danial looked at her, confused by her lack of questions.

"Thank you, Cousin Sarah," Mary Ann said quietly. "I am weary, and I not feel quite well." In fact, her face did have a green tint to it. Unlike other pregnant ladies, Mary Ann experienced morning sickness only in the afternoons.

"Get her up to her room immediately!" the elder lady ordered, her face worried. "Call her maid; have her bring up some dry husks. No, you get her upstairs, Daniel. I will send her maid up straightaway."

His heart racing, Daniel Wyatt picked up his wife and carried her from the room, ignoring her protests. "You weigh no more than a large bag of grain," he reminded her. "Besides . . ." He bent his head close to hers and whispered in her ear. She giggled and made no further attempts to dissuade him.

When Stephen and Rosemary entered the library and closed the door behind them, he reached out and pulled her into his arms. She went willingly although rather shyly. "Look at me," he said quietly. She glanced up. His eyes were blazing with love and passion. He bent his head, his lips coming closer. Her heart began to pound. Unconsciously, her tongue moistened her lips.

"Stephen," she whispered as his lips covered hers. At first the kiss was soft and gentle, a promise. Then it deepened as his passion flared. Her lips parted, giving him the freedom he desired. He took it eagerly, introducing her to new excitement, new desires. She moved forward, trying to get closer to him, her hands caressing his shoulders. Only her fear had made her feel so strongly before. Now that was forgotten as she learned desire.

His arms pulled her closer to him, her soft breasts crushed against his chest. As her chest heaved when she tried to take a breath, he thrilled with the movement. One hand made its way to the side of a breast; the other clasped her bottom, pulling her hard against him. He could feel the reaction she was causing and knew he should pull away. But he could not. Her lips were too sweet, her hands too exciting. One of her hands slipped inside his jacket, inside his waistcoat, lying just above his heart. He stopped his own exploration for a moment to encourage hers. "Yes, sweet," he whispered as her fingers slipped inside his shirt. His fingers had found the ties on the side of her gown. She felt them there and froze. Stephen immediately pulled his hand back, cursing himself for rushing his fences. He smiled at her again, and she relaxed. She lifted her lips invitingly. He accepted her invitation. Neither heard the knock at the door.

"Well, I see you have managed to entertain yourselves quite well," Lady Longworth said, her voice dry.

"Mama!"

"Cousin Sarah!" Rosemary stepped back from Stephen and tried to straighten her disarray. Stephen brushed her curls back from her forehead and wished he could take just one more kiss. Rosemary looked up into those blue eyes flecked with gold and read his desire. She moved a step or two closer, forgetting Lady Longworth completely.

"Hmmmm." Both Stephen and Rosemary turned around, their faces warm. "Have a seat. No, not next to each other. I want you thinking, not just reacting to each other. Daniel told us he accepted your suit." She snorted. "I wish you had waited to make your declaration until you were someplace beside a hayloft. If you had no consideration for your own consequence, you could have given some to mine and to your brother's." She glared at him for a moment. Then she closed her eyes briefly, took one or two deep breaths, and continued. "You will be married in a month. I assume you had not gotten around to telling him, Rosemary." She looked at the girl, who hung her head.

"Mama, I do apologize for embarrassing you, but it was not intentional," her son said, trying to determine whether she was truly angry or merely annoyed.

"I know. We have no more time for apologies. Stephen, you will need to return to your estate. See that everything is proceeding as planned. Rosemary and I will return to Bath, so you do not have to look as though I am banishing you. She will be only an hour away." Stephen looked at his mother and then at his intended and smiled. Rosemary's heart began to beat faster. "And I will bring her out to see you occasionally. Have you had time to think any further than that?"

"Yes. I do not want to rush the work on the estate. After our wedding journey"—he smiled at Rosemary again, and she blushed—"we will go directly to London. I must be there at the end of next month. Having Rosemary at my side will make the dull social rounds more exciting. And I am certain Mama will appreciate your help in planning our ball and other entertainments. Then we will see what these old gossips have to say."

Although she had been willing to consider being presented, Rosemary had assumed that her marriage would make that unnecessary. Her eyes widened in shock. Her face paled. The memory of what had happened in her own church returned to haunt her. What if Lady Longworth could not stop the gossip? She could imagine the stares, the cuts direct, the hum of gossip each time she appeared. And the strangers. She would be surrounded by strangers. Memories of the men who had crowded around her, pleading for a dance, made her gasp for breath. It might be worse in London. She had survived her last trip to the capital, but then she had had the support of her father and Mary Ann. With a baby on the way, Mary Ann would not be there. And Stephen could not stay at her side always. She gasped, her heart beating heavily. "No, Stephen! No!" she whispered as she lost consciousness.

11

"ROSEMARY, ROSEMARY!" Stephen's frantic voice and his hands on her shoulders shaking her were the girl's reintroduction to the world she had escaped for such a brief time.

"Give way, Stephen. Let me put this under her nose," his mother commanded, shoving herself in front of him. For a moment Rosemary was confused; then memory rolled over her like a wave crashes against a rock. She moaned and tried to pull away. "Sit up. Open your eyes." Lady Longworth took a deep breath and hardened her usually soft heart. "This will never do."

"Mama, just let me talk to her," her son pleaded, noting the light of battle in his mother's usually flawless turquoise eyes. "Let her have a few moments to recover. Then we can talk."

"Talk is what we must do, and do it now, Stephen," his mother said firmly. "Rosemary, sit up." Startled by the sharp tone where she usually found a sympathetic one, the girl swung her feet off the settee and did as she was ordered. "That is better," Lady Longworth said, giving a mental sigh of relief. "Now, what do you mean, no? Are you refusing my son?"

Rosemary ignored her, addressing Stephen instead. "If you want a wife to help you entertain in London, you must find someone else," she said very softly, her eyes filled with regret.

"I do not want anyone else. I want you," he told her.

"Do you want him branded as a despoiler of young ladies?" his mother asked fiercely.

"No, of course not," Rosemary said, horrified.

"Mama, leave her alone," Stephen said as he sat beside Rosemary and wrapped an arm around her waist. She laid her head against his shoulder, glad for his support.

"If you do not plan to marry the man, I would suggest that you avoid embracing him," his mother said dryly.

Rosemary blushed and tried to pull away, but Stephen would not let her go. He turned her face toward him and asked, "Why did you say you would not marry me?" His voice and his face reflected his confusion and hurt.

Lifting her hand to brush away a lock of hair that had fallen on her forehead, Rosemary blinked rapidly to hold back her tears. "You see what happens. In the last four months I have been involved in two scandals. What if that happens in town?" Once more she tried to free her hands from his in order to pull away from him. Once more he held her close.

"If you were married and fainted as you did just now," lady Longworth said practically, "everyone would assume you were *enceinte* and think nothing more of it. Married women are always increasing."

"Cousin Sarah!" This time Rosemary managed to yank her hands from Stephen's and cover her red cheeks.

"Well, just look at Mary Ann. She was positively green this afternoon, and no one thought anything of it."

"You and I were the only ones there," her future daughter-in-law reminded her. Her response delighted the older lady, who began to see more spirit than she had given the girl credit for. "Besides, it will soon be apparent that the rumor is not true."

"How do you know? By the time you have been married for a month or so, it may very well be. And the Little Season is so short you do not have anything to worry about."

"Mama, do not embarrass Rosemary or me any further," Stephen said in tones so much like his father's that his mother's heart jumped for joy. "We will work it out."

"And just how do you intend to do that if she faints every time London is mentioned? It is not as though you will be going there by yourself. This business of yours will require all our presence. I am even thinking of suggesting that the children accompany us," Lady Longworth said thoughtfully. "Rosemary, your father and Mary Ann could make part of our party also."

"Mary Ann? You want her to go to town in her condition?"

"Of course. Did you think she should sit at home, letting herself be wrapped in cotton wool? Nonsense. She needs to be kept busy. She will worry enough without having extra time on her hands." She paused. "If there are enough of us there to keep you company, do you think you could manage? You did very well in Bath. And look how successful this visit has been." Lady Longworth's voice had lost its sharp edge and was faintly pleading.

"I am so afraid, afraid I will not be everything you want me to be," Rosemary said softly, facing Stephen. "All my life I have wanted to make Papa proud of me. Always I have failed. What if I failed you too? I would not be able to bear it!" She raised her tear-filled eyes to his. She bit her bottom lip to keep it from quivering.

"The only way you could fail me is if you refuse to marry me," he said earnestly. "Rosemary, I love you. I want you with me for the rest of my life, not just for a short time in London. If going to town for the Little Season distresses you this much, then I can cancel my plans." He smiled at her, willing her to agree, to reassure him. However, the thought of discarding the plans he had already made worried him.

"No, you cannot," his mother said angrily. "Too much work has gone into this for you to back out now. I suppose we could postpone the wedding until after Christmas, although people are certain to talk. Rosemary can return to the Manor with her parents to wait for you. I am certain Clarissa will be happy to be your partner whenever one is needed. Maybe the gossip will not hurt our plans." Leaning back in her chair, Lady Longworth noted with satisfaction how Rosemary's eyes snapped wide open at the mention of Clarissa's name. She had not grown wise in the ways of the *ton* without learning how to manipulate people very well. She waited. She was not disappointed.

"You keep talking about a plan, about business. Why do you have to be in town then, Stephen?" Rosemary asked. The thought of watching him drive off to the capital, where there were bound to be bevies of beautiful girls waiting to snare him, was very unsettling. Her hand reached out for his, clasping it tightly.

"As soon as I purchased my estate, a friend of my father's, someone who knows the king quite well, presented my petition to him. Apparently the king is amenable to giving second sons titles."

"If the family has enough land and money," his mother added, her face revealing her pride. "And if the man is wealthy in his own right."

Stephen frowned at her and then continued. "My father always wanted me to have a title of my own; it was one of his greatest disappointments that he was not able to do this for me. Just when he thought he had everything set in motion, he and the king quarreled. When he lay dying, he made me promise to pursue the idea," Stephen explained. "If it were left to me, I would be happy to go on as I always have done. But I could not break my word to him. You do see that, do you not, Rosemary?"

Rosemary nodded, her face thoughtful. "But why do you have to be in London if your petition has already been presented?"

"It has been presented, not accepted. Stephen must be there to wait on the king himself. We must entertain," Lady Longworth explained. She smiled at Rosemary, wishing the girl had more town bronze so that she would understand the nuances of the situation. Usually very astute in handling people, Lady Longworth was focusing on her son's problem only, determined to smooth his way.

"The king? You are going to entertain the king?" Rosemary felt her chest begin to tighten as it had just before she lost control.

"No." Lady Longworth and Stephen exchanged glances. The older lady sighed. Patiently, at though explaining to a child, she added, "We must entertain those families who have influence with him, make certain they will speak for Stephen if the king makes inquiries about him." How could the girl be so naive? she wondered.

"Oh." Rosemary sighed. She looked from one to the other as if trying to make up her mind about something. "Would it not be better to wait until the Season to proceed?"

"And would you go with me then?" he asked hopefully.

Before she had a chance to voice her refusal, Lady Longworth said firmly, "We cannot wait. You know how precarious the king's health is. What if something happens to him? Besides, if you do not appear now that the petition has been presented, you will be insulting both the king and your father's friend." She frowned. "Once Stephen has his title, he will want to take his place in the House of Lords, like his father and brother. The skills he learned in India will be very useful there."

"That means you will be spending part of every year in London?" Rosemary asked quietly, too quietly.

"I had planned to," her love told her, his face serious and his blue eyes dark with uncertainty. "Rosemary, I know you will be able to do this. Look at how well you succeeded in Bath."

She pulled away from him and stood up, her hands clasped tightly before her. She walked over to one of the shelves of books, staring unseeing at the titles. Then she turned back to face them. "You know more than I do, Stephen. If I could only believe that this were possible. What kind of wife would I be if Stephen had to be worrying about me all the time instead of concentrating on other things? My dear, as much as I want to marry you"—she took a deep breath and then said hurriedly—"I cannot be your wife."

The door to the library opened just as she began her last words. Mary Ann and Daniel, who had begun to worry when Rosemary did not appear, stood frozen in the doorway, their faces reflecting their shock. "I thought you told me she had agreed to marry you." Daniel Wyatt said angrily, crossing to stand in front of the younger man. He reached down and lifted Stephen from his seat. "If you have been lying to me—"

"Papa!" Rosemary screamed, running to Stephen's side. "Daniel!"

"Mr. Wyatt, put my son down. If you wish to reprimand anyone, you might begin with your daughter. She is a fickle little thing, first agreeing to marry my son and then changing her mind." Lady Longworth looked at Rosemary, disapproval in every line of her face. The sympathy she had shown the girl had disappeared when her son's happiness was in peril.

"She did what?" Daniel swung his daughter around to face him. She dropped her eyes before his, shaken by the anger she read in his. "Daughter, I do not think you understand the situation." His voice was cold, and each word was a polished sound, precise and clear. "You will marry Mr. Huntington. You have no choice. You gave that up this morning when you decided to act the hoyden with him in the hayloft. Do I make myself clear?" She did not answer, and kept her eyes fixed on the carpet. He gave her a little shake. "Do you understand?" She nodded. He breathed a sigh of relief. If she had refused, he was not certain that he would have had the strength of will to force her through the ceremony. "Good." He noted the pallor of her cheeks and the way she had to bite her lips to keep them from trembling. "I think you have had enough excitement for now. Perhaps you should retire and rest until it is time to dress for dinner." Quickly she made her escape. Then Daniel Wyatt turned to his wife's cousins. "What happened?" Drawing Mary Ann to his side, he sat down on the settee that Stephen and Rosemary had vacated just a short time before.

Quickly Lady Longworth gave them the details of what had happened. Stephen sat quietly, his face serious, obviously deep in thought. Finally he broke into their conversation as though he had not heard a word they said. "Mama, as much as it will upset you, I am going to write and cancel my petition."

His future father-in-law got up, his shoulders straight. "I cannot permit you to do that," he said firmly. "My daughter must not interfere with your carrying out your father's wishes. My honor would be destroyed if that happened."

"You do not control my actions," Stephen said angrily, remembering how rough Wyatt had been with his daughter.

"Stop it, both of you!" Mary Ann said. Her voice reflected the strain she was under. "Nothing good will come of making angry remarks or hasty decisions. You think about what you want to do, Stephen, but do nothing until you have spoken with Rosemary. I am going up to her now. Make my excuses to the others this evening. Say that I am exhausted"—she took a deep breath and realized that her exhaustion was a reality—"and Rosemary is keeping me company. We will have our supper on trays." Lady Longworth got up to accompany her. "No, I am certain you have other things to do, Cousin Sarah. Let me talk with her by myself. She is a reasonable person. Had we introduced the idea gradually, this problem would have seemed much less overwhelming." She looked up at her husband. "Will you come up with me?"

"Certainly." Daniel put his arm around his wife and led her from the room, the pallor of her face causing him to worry again.

An uneasy silence fell when the door closed behind them. Realizing that she had not handled the situation well, Lady Longworth waited nervously for her son to break the silence. He did not, but simply sat there as though lost in his own world. Finally she could bear it no longer. "Are you never going to talk to me again?" she asked plaintively. "Stephen?" When he did not answer her, she began to grow angry. "Stephen!" He still did not answer. "As I recall, you and Rosemary were the ones who precipitated this problem. I admit that within the last hour I have exacerbated the situation, but I refuse to allow you to blame me for everything. Do you understand me, son?''

"Did you say something, Mama?" he asked, pulling himself from the recesses of his mind. As usual when he was trying to solve a problem, he had shut off his awareness of the world around him. It was a useful technique that he had learned from a wise man in India.

"I was trying to talk to you, Stephen," she said impatiently. She crossed to stand near her elder son's desk, once her husband's, and ran her hand thoughtfully over the smooth, rich inlaid wood along its edge. She took a deep breath or two to try to marshal her thoughts, to improvise a solution.

Before she made up her mind what to say, Stephen said quietly, "Mary Ann had the right idea."

"What?"

"Too much has gone on today for any of us to think clearly. Maybe tomorrow Rosemary will listen to me, let me explain." He got up and walked across the room, his blue eyes somber and serious. "But you must realize, Mama, that I plan to marry Rosemary no matter what. If I have to give up Father's idea, I will. She is the one I want to spend the rest of my life with." He willed her to understand, his eyes locked to her turqouise ones.

For almost five minutes they just stood there looking at each other. Then Lady Longworth smiled sadly. "All I want is for you to be happy," she said as she reached up to cup his face with a hand.

He covered her hand with his. "Then you had better get busy so you can find a way to change Rosemary's mind," he said impishly. He kissed her hand. "My future is in your hands."

"Stephen!" she exclaimed, all her lethargy leaving her.

"Make my excuses for dinner, Mama. I am going for a ride."

Both she and Mary Ann used their evenings well. Lady Longworth smiled as she swept into the drawing room, looking her very best in an elegant gown of deep purple silk. As the conversation stilled around her, she smiled sweetly. "You were talking about Stephen and Rosemary, I assume," she said as if the situation were unusual. "And I did so want the announcement tomorrow to be a surprise." She sighed, almost as dramatically as one of the leading actresses would have done.

"Announcement? What announcement?" Everyone crowded around her, clamoring for more information.

"I really should not say." She smiled and held up her hand as if to ward off their questions.

"Mama, do not keep them in suspense," her elder son said mischievously. "Tell them."

"But neither Stephen nor Rosemary is here," she protested, "and the announcement is not really mine to make." She allowed Longworth to lead her to a chair. "Besides, I am certain everyone must have guessed since learning what happened this morning."

"Guessed?"

"Do you know what she is talking about?"

"It must have something to do with that hayloft episode," one of the gentleman said. "Should have known it was all a hum."

"What do you mean," one of the Huntingtons' cousins asked.

Just then Daniel Wyatt walked in, and conversation stopped once more. He walked over to Lady Longworth and her son. "Mary Ann asked me to give you her regrets this evening. Not feeling very well. Rosemary's staying with her. All the excitement this morning was not good for a lady in her condition." He made the last statement in a low voice, but everyone around them heard him clearly. He glanced around the room, noting the eyes fixed on him. "Did everyone already guess?" he asked just as the note from Lady Longworth had asked him to do.

"No. These slowtops claim they know nothing." She smiled up at Daniel and at her elder son, David. "After Stephen's actions at the ball last night, I thought everyone would know." She leaned close to Mrs. Darylrimple, one of her husband's cousins, and said quietly, "Clarissa certainly must have known something. She and her mother left before noon today."

"Ohhh." The older lady smiled. "I thought Clarissa had her sights fixed on the wrong person," she said maliciously. Her youngest daughter and Clarissa had come out the same Season. Although her daughter had had some small success and had married at the end of June of that year, Clarissa had always let the girl know, often very bluntly, that she was not the Beauty of the family. "That young lady had better lower her expectations or she will be left on the shelf," she said, smiling broadly. "I wonder if her mother realizes what is going on. She often misses so much." She smiled happily, thinking about the letter she would write before she retired that evening.

"So true," Lady Longworth agreed.

"Are they going to wait until after she is presented to be married?"

While they were talking, the others in the room had moved closer, straining their ears to hear what was going on. With the word "married," a ripple of nods and comments flowed around the room. "Naturally, I knew."

"Anyone would have guessed. You saw them last night."

"Cousin Sarah's just trying to make the best of a bad situation," said a tall man with a face already marred by his dissolution.

"Nonsense. I saw the way he looked at her when he helped her up on her horse the other day."

"And the way she followed him with her eyes at the ball," the speaker sighed as she fanned herself vigorously. "So romantic. Will the wedding be in London, Mr. Wyatt?"

"Wedding? What wedding?" he asked with a smile and a wink.

"You cannot keep a secret in this family," Longworth said heartily. He too had been given his instructions earlier that evening. "Better give up, Daniel."

The butler announced dinner before anyone else could insist on information. As the guests talked around the table, the upcoming marriage was on most people's minds. Although none of those most closely involved would give definite comments, by the end of the evening almost everyone felt as though he or she had been the first to know about the coming marriage.

While Lady Longworth was putting out the fires of gossip in the drawing room and dining room, Mary Ann was soothing her stepdaughter. The task was not an easy one. When she had reached her room that afternoon, Rosemary had cried herself to sleep. Abut thirty minutes later, her maid woke her. "You were screaming, Miss Wyatt," she said. "You probably were too warm in that dress. Let me help you take it off." Rosemary moved sluggishly, trying to ban the feeling of terror that haunted her. She had been dreaming of London, London when she was a child. Every time she had the dream, that was all she remembered whenever she awoke. No matter how hard she tried, everything else escaped her. Undressed at last, she went back to bed.

When she awoke several hours later, she saw Mary Ann lying on the chaise. She closed her eyes, hoping her stepmother had not realized that she was awake. Mary Ann simply lay there waiting for Rosemary to acknowledge her presence. When she could no longer bear to lie still, Rosemary turned over. Then she sat up, still silent. Mary Ann simply waited.

"Why are you not at dinner?" her stepdaughter finally asked.

"I was not particularly hungry."

Pulling on her dressing gown, Rosemary walked to the dressing table, picked up a brush, and began to run it through her hair. Nervously she glanced in the mirror. Mary Ann was still lying peacefully on the chaise, her eyes closed.

Rosemary dropped the brush and turned around. "You might as well scold me now," she said. Her face and the way she held her shoulders reflected both her anger and her guilt.

"I do not plan to scold you." Mary Ann sat up. Nothing in her face or her body revealed how nervous she was. "You are twenty years old, almost twenty-one. Very soon even your father will have no authority over you. You will be able to do as you wish," she said quietly. "Daniel said that your mother's fortune comes to you on your twenty-first birthday."

"I know," Rosemary said impatiently, nervously fingering the silk ribbons that tied under her bosom. She took a deep breath, wishing Mary Ann would say what she had to say and leave. All she wanted was to be alone. Even as she thought those words, she had to admit they were not true. She wanted Stephen.

Once again Mary Ann let silence fall. She closed her eyes and took a few deep breaths, wishing that she were far away from the trouble and turmoil of the present. If she had known the problems she would have to face when she married Daniel, she thought. She sighed and smiled ruefully. She would have married him anyway. Remembering his care for her that afternoon, she relaxed, letting her cares slide away.

Rosemary was not that easily forgotten. "Mary Ann," she asked, "why are you here now?"

"I thought you could use a friend." Mary Ann swung her legs over the edge and sat up. She walked across the room, noting as she did that Lady Longworth had given the girl one of the best guest chambers. She stopped beside her stepdaughter. "Have you thought about what you are going to do until you come of age?"

"Come of age? Mary Ann, what are you talking about?" Rosemary swung around angrily, confused, afraid.

"You have said you do not wish to marry Stephen." Rosemary's heart ached at the thought. "When we returned to the Manor, you said you never wanted to go there again.

When Lady Longworth leaves for London, where do you plan to go? I assure you that your father will resist any attempt of yours to set up your own household. You will need to wait until you have your fortune under your own control to do that.''

"My own household? What are you talking about? I do not plan to live alone. Think about what people would say.''

"Then you are going to live with your Cousin Hortense?''

"No!'' Usually meek and timid, Rosemary slammed her hands against the dressing table, wincing as they stung with the force of the blow.

Her stepmother sighed, closing her eyes for just a moment. She straightened an imaginary crease in her deep peach skirt. Her shoulders were slumped as she walked back toward the chaise. Arranging her dress to her satisfaction, Mary Ann lay back and watched Rosemary roam around the room restlessly. "My dear, you will wear yourself out,'' she finally said. "Come. Sit here beside me.''

"Why? So you can point out how hopeless my situation is?'' the girl asked bitterly. She still walked across the room and sat down. "Everything is so complicated,'' she said weakly, her eyes filled with tears.

"I know, my dear. I know,'' Mary Ann said soothingly, putting her arms around her. For some time Rosemary cried until she had no more tears. She sniffed. Mary Ann handed her a handkerchief and then brushed the silver-gilt curls out of the girl's face. She held her close until even her dry sobs had ceased. Then she asked, "Will you answer a question?'' Rosemary nodded. "Do you love Stephen?''

"Yes!'' Rosemary sat up straight, her face mottled from crying but still proud. "I love him so much. How will I ever let him go?''

"If you love him, why did you say you would not marry him?''

"He says he loves me now. What if he grows tired of my failures, what if I destroy his chances for a title? Will he love me then?'' Rosemary got up again and began to walk aimlessly around the room, her face sad.

"I think the question is not whether he loves you. He said he would give up any chance for a title in order to marry you. I think the question is whether you love him enough to do whatever is necessary to make him happy." She walked toward the door. "I will have someone bring you supper on a tray," she said quietly, as though she had not just stuck a dagger into Rosemary's heart.

For minutes Rosemary stared at the door, frozen into silence. "Do I love him enough?" she whispered.

12

THE NEXT MORNING there was a note from Stephen on the tray with Rosemary's chocolate. "Meet me in the hayloft at eleven," it said. She stared at it, not certain she wanted to return to the scene of her embarrassment. Had she but known it, Stephen was also uncomfortable with their meeting place. But he had given much thought to where they would meet. Every alternative he had considered seemed too filled with bad memories or was too impersonal, every one but the hayloft.

When eleven arrived, she was there. Stephen had arrived before her and he was sitting playing with the kittens, which the mother cat had returned as soon as the humans had left the day before. As Rosemary climbed stiffly into the loft, he sat where he was, making no attempt to help her. She winced, wondering if he had changed his mind, if he regretted his offer of the day before. She sat down, the skirts of one of her most fashionable morning dresses puffing around her. The aqua of her gown turned her eyes a blue-green. The mother cat got up and inspected her, rubbing against the sleeve of her pelisse, which was made of velvet a shade darker than her dress. Rosemary kept her eyes on her clasped hands, afraid of what she might see if she looked up into Stephen's eyes. However, she could not resist stealing glances at him. He was dressed in a chocolate-brown riding jacket that hugged his shoulders so tightly that she could see his muscles ripple when he breathed.

He cleared his throat. His heart was pounding so hard he

was certain she could see his chest move. "Rosemary," he began, and heard his voice crack. He started again. "I am sorry for the confusion yesterday afternoon." He cleared his throat again.

"That was not your fault," she said in a whisper, relieved that he did not tell her he was sorry for asking her to marry him. "Most of it was mine."

"Can we simply agree that was a disaster and go on from there?" he asked with a nervous laugh. He ran his fingers around his neck, wondering why he had tied his cravat so tight that morning.

"Yes." Rosemary braced herself for what she was certain was coming. When a few minutes of silence had gone by, she looked up to see him staring at her, a hopeless expression on his face. She lowered her head again to hide the tears that welled up in her eyes. "Stephen . . ."

"Rosemary . . ." Both paused, waiting for the other to speak. Finally Stephen gathered his determination and said, "Rosemary, change your mind. Say you will marry me!" He reached out and took her hand. "I will withdraw my petition. We will not go to London. Please."

Her hand jerked in his. He gulped, certain that she was going to run away from him. "Stephen." Her voice was so low he could hardly hear it. "I do not want . . ." He held his breath as she stumbled over the next words. "You must not withdraw the petition." His shoulders sagged; he was certain she was refusing him again. "Do you love me?" she asked shyly.

"Yes!" he shouted, startling the horse in the stall below.

She looked up, her eyes sparkling as much from fear as from happiness. "Then I will marry you and go to London with you." When he reached for her, she pulled away. "Stephen, please realize that I will do my very best, but it may not be good enough," she said, her face serious. "I only know I love you; I want to be with you always; I want what is best for you."

"Are you certain?" he asked, all the exhaustion of a sleepless night rolling away. "I could not bear it if you changed your mind once more. Please realize that we do not have to go to London. I can withdraw."

"Never! If I let you do that for me, I would always be afraid that someday you would regret it." She smiled up at him.

"And how do you think I will feel if you are unhappy because you think you are not pleasing me?" he asked sharply.

"As long as you are there, nothing can be too bad. With the help of your family and mine, I should be able to manage," she assured him with more confidence than she actually felt. But she had spent hours the night before thinking about the situation and knew her decision was for the best.

"Being without you is terrible," he told her. "Come here." He wrapped his arms around her and pulled her close.

"Is this not what caused the problem?" she asked, her eyes sparkling.

"Problem? Getting enough of your kisses is the only problem I have today," he assured her. He lowered his head and kissed her. The next few minutes erased all the pain of the day before.

From the moment they made their announcement at dinner, both Stephen and Rosemary felt they had gone on board a boat traveling over massive rapids. Each new day brought new rocks to bump against. The few moments they were allowed alone each day refreshed them for a new struggle. The hardest part came when they had to say good-bye for a few days. Stephen had to return to his estate. Rosemary and Lady Longworth remained at Long Meadow. Their trip to Bath had been canceled when one of London's leading modistes had agreed to bring her seamstresses, her fabric, and her fashion plates to Long Meadow. With the city largely empty of the *ton*, the offer was too enticing for her to refuse.

The evening before Stephen was to leave, he and Rosemary walked through his brother's gardens. The air was crisp and very cool. Even dressed as warmly as was fashionable, Rosemary shivered. Stephen wrapped her Kashmir shawl more closely around her. ''You will be ill if we stay out here too long,'' he said, turning her around to lead her back to the house.

''No, not yet.'' The twins were enjoying a weekly treat, an evening meal with the rest of the family. As much as she enjoyed the mischievous pair, she could not concentrate on Stephen when they were around. The twins demanded the full attention of everyone around them—at least Julia did. ''I wish you did not have to go,'' she said wistfully. Even the knowledge that the trip was a necessity did not make the idea of separation any easier. She stopped and turned toward him, the sparkle of a tear trembling in her eyes.

''Please do not cry. I will never be able to leave you if you do,'' Stephen said as he reached out and drew her close to him. Her scent enfolded him as he wrapped his arms around her. ''I love you so much,'' he whispered, his mouth close to her ear. She shivered, this time from passion, not from cold. ''Come, let us walk to the house,'' he said quietly, taking a step back. ''You are cold.''

''No, I am not.'' She followed him, her arms locked tight around his neck. ''Just a little longer,'' she begged.

''I am not going to be very long. When I return, your parents will have returned. I promise I will be back before the first week in November is over.'' He kissed her, letting his lips comfort her as his words could not.

Slightly breathless, she finally stepped back. ''You had better be back before November 8, or I will leave you waiting in the church,'' she threatened.

''Nothing could keep me from you,'' he promised.

As one thing after another went wrong, Stephen began to wonder in earnest whether or not he would arrive in time for the wedding. A workman slipped off the roof and broke a leg. The accident would have been worse, but a tree broke the man's fall. The fabric Rosemary had chosen for what would now be her bedroom was sent in the wrong color, a violent puce. Only when he sent his bailiff to London with the fabric and a threat did the company send the correct material. The laundress ruined five of his shirts, including his new fine lawn one that he planned to wear at the wedding. By the time he left for Long Meadow, Stephen was having second thoughts about the importance of owning land. Only the thought that in two days Rosemary would be his made his life joyful. And when a wheel on his carriage broke, he began to wonder if some malevolent spirit was trying to keep them apart.

Rosemary, too, had had to face trials. Her Cousin Hortense arrived two weeks before the ceremony, delighted that her charge was making such an advantageous marriage. That delight was quickly changed to disapproval when she saw some of the gowns that Lady Longworth had insisted Rosemary order. "I cannot believe anyone from my family would wear something so . . . so . . ."

"Lovely?" Lady Longworth asked at her haughty best. She dared Rosemary's cousin to contradict her.

"But what will people say? The girl must avoid scandal at any cost. That is why I was so worried about her," Mrs. Wyatt said in a worried voice. "I told my husband, God rest his soul, that her mother would come to a bad end, and she did. If Rosemary were still in my care, you can be sure I would send those dresses back immediately. We cannot have everyone talking about her, not with that hair of hers." She frowned, looking at the curls that had grown out some, but not to the most fashionable length. "I do not know why you had to cut your hair. At least when it was long you could pull it back and keep it hidden under a bonnet or a cap."

"Why should she want to do a thing like that? Her hair is lovely, very distinctive," Lady Longworth asked. Her tone was quite brusque. Just a little of Rosemary's cousin was more than she would willingly tolerate from anyone else.

Rosemary cringed. Just as she knew the lady would do, Cousin Hortense lost no time in relaying the story of Rosemary's mother's scandalous life and death. "So, you must realize how dangerous it would be for everyone to notice the child. Far better that she court obscurity,'' Cousin Hortense said confidentially.

Looking at her future daughter-in-law, Lady Longworth smiled. ''Perhaps obscurity is acceptable for your family. Mine has always enjoyed being at the center of the social whirl. Besides, Rosemary is far too lovely to be hidden away for long. I quickly discovered that in Bath.'' She waved her fan languidly. ''Then, too, Rosemary will be introduced as a married lady instead of an insipid young miss,'' she reminded the elder lady.

''Oh, my, my,'' Cousin Hortense muttered, frantically reviewing her list of correspondents for one whose plans included visiting London before Christmas. For the next few days she assumed a wistful look whenever London was mentioned, in the hopes that Lady Longworth would extend her an invitation, but Rosemary had told her hostess what to expect. The only invitation that was forthcoming was for a walk around the garden, which Cousin Hortense refused.

As November 8, her wedding day, grew closer and closer and Stephen did not arrive, Rosemary became frantic. Fortunately, Mary Ann and the twins managed to keep her occupied. The twins were to be her only attendants. James had protested, especially when he had to be fitted for the wine-colored knee breeches and coat, but his sister had enjoyed every moment of the fitting for her matching velvet dress. Julia dragged her brother and Rosemary to the chapel once a day to practice their walk down the aisle. Each visit ended with the same words. ''I wish the roses were still blooming. Papa has one just the color of my dress.''

While Julia was worrying about flowers and keeping her governess busy, Mary Ann was enlarging Rosemary's education. When they accompanied Lady Longworth on a visit to the wife of a tenant who had just delivered twins, a boy and a girl, Mary Ann had released the babies from their wrappings, inspected their tiny feet and hands carefully, making certain that Rosemary had a good look at the differences between them. Then she redressed them, using her own pregnancy as reason for her behavior.

That evening she invited Rosemary into her bedroom. Even for someone as naturally outgoing as Mary Ann, introducing the subject was not easy. However, she did not intend for her stepdaughter to go into marriage as ignorant as she had been on the day of her first marriage. "Come. Sit over here so we can talk," she said with a smile, waving at two chairs near the fireplace. "Have you heard anything further from Stephen?" she asked, knowing that Rosemary had been haunting the hallway hoping for a letter when the post was delivered.

"No." Rosemary bit her lip. "You do not think he has changed his mind?"

"Since yesterday? You did receive a letter from him yesterday, did you not?" her stepmother asked her. Her voice was soothing and sympathetic.

"No. It was the day before. He said he would try to leave today or tomorrow. I had hoped for something more definite today," she said with a quivering lip.

"He will be here. If he said he would give up his chance for a title for you, you can be certain he will be here for his wedding day." Mary Ann paused and then added, "And especially for his wedding night."

Rosemary turned the color of the bright red vase sitting on the mantel. She laughed nervously.

"I remember the way I felt right before your father and I married, half-frightened, half-excited. And I had been married before and knew in general what to expect." A soft smile curved her lips as she remembered that the reality had been much more wonderful than she had ever dreamed of. "You must have some questions you would like to ask." She paused, waiting for Rosemary to respond. When she did not, Mary Ann smiled. "Had my mother tried to talk to me before my first marriage, I would probably have been as mute as you." She reached over and patted her stepdaughter's hand comfortingly. "Everything is rather strange at first, but the marriage bed can be a delightful place if you love your husband." A sudden thought crossed her mind and her face. She frowned. "You do love Stephen, do you not?"

"Of course I do," Rosemary hastened to assure her.

"Good. Now tell me what you have heard about what happens between a man and a woman when they marry," she commanded.

Rosemary flushed again, hung her head, and spoke hurriedly, spilling forth a hodgepodge of facts and fiction. "I did visit the women at the Manor. I heard some of their talk," she explained as if afraid Mary Ann would scold her for the knowledge she had gleaned from her observations.

"I am glad you did. It is always easier to discuss a subject if you know something about it. Now think about the babies you saw this afternoon and the ones you have seen before." Step by step, Mary Ann gave her an anatomy lesson and a frank explanation of the enjoyment men and women could find together. By the time Rosemary left the room, her eyes were wide and her mind was racing.

It was a long time before Rosemary went to sleep that evening. She reviewed her conversation with Mary Ann over and over again. Then she thought of the times she had been alone with Stephen. Her face burned with excitement. "But how do husbands and wives face the world when everyone knows what they have been doing?" she asked aloud, trembling with excitement.

The next morning Rosemary found herself noticing the way her father and Mary Ann exchanged glances, the way her father's hand lingered on his wife's shoulder as he helped her to her seat. And were her stepmother's lips always so red? She glanced around to see if Longworth and his mother had noticed the same things she had. They were talking quietly, as if they had noticed nothing different. Had her father and Mary Ann been acting this way each morning? she wondered. Was she the only one who had missed it before?

When breakfast was over, the three ladies met in the morning room to go over the final arrangements. When guests began arriving later that afternoon, everyone wanted the visit to go smoothly.

Just as they were finishing the last list, Cousin Hortense arrived, bustling into the room importantly. Never rising before ten, the elder lady chose to have her breakfast in bed. As Lady Longworth and Mary Ann walked out of the room together after greeting her, Cousin Hortense grabbed Rosemary's arm. "We must talk," she said in a hushed voice that rang of sinister plots and evil deeds. Rosemary nodded, confused. Cousin Hortense led her to a small settee where only moments before Lady Longworth and Mary Ann had sat. "You poor child," she said as she patted Rosemary on the cheek, an action the girl had always disliked. "Since you do not have a mother—"

"I have Mary Ann."

"I mean that your own mother is no longer here. Because of that, I feel that it is my place to tell you what you need to know about marriage." She stopped, looked around nervously, as if afraid someone were listening, and then went on. "About men." She dropped her voice to a whisper. "And the demands they place upon their wives. My dear, you must remember it is your duty no matter how much you dislike it."

"Dislike what?" Rosemary asked, not at all certain she knew what her cousin was talking about.

"The marriage act," Cousin Hortense said in a hushed voice.

"Oh, Mary Ann has already told me what to expect," Rosemary said, her face flushing with the memory.

"She did?" Her cousin's voice rose with indignation.

"Last night."

"She is your stepmother. I suppose it was proper."

"Papa asked her to."

The last statement flustered the elder lady so, she could hardly utter a sound. "Ohh," she moaned softly. She waved her hand rapidly to cool her heated face. She would have died of embarrassment if he had approached her, she thought. ''Ohhh.''

''Are you all right, Cousin Hortense?'' Rosemary asked, helping the old lady to a chair. ''May I get you anything?'' She looked around the room to see if there was any wine nearby.

''If you would ring for my maid,'' Cousin Hortense said weakly. ''I think I will spend the time until luncheon lying down. I am not strong, you know. All this excitement.''

No sooner had Rosemary seen her up the stairs to her room than the sound of a carriage penetrated the house. Rosemary ran to the stairs and peered over the railing. ''Stephen,'' she called as she caught sight of him and raced down the stairs as James was wont to do. He looked up and then watched as she dashed toward him, opening his arms to catch her. ''You are home!'' she said happily. Then, to the delight of the footmen, he kissed her.

Remembering where they were, Stephen stepped back but kept her hand imprisoned in his. ''Did you miss me?'' he asked, a small smile playing about his lips. Rosemary could not take her eyes from him. His hair was windswept, his boots gray with dust, and his neckcloth rumpled. But he was the most wonderful sight she had seen for days.

''Yes,'' she said, the lightest blush staining her cheeks. ''What kept you so long?'' She took his outstretched arm and walked down the hall with him. ''I was wondering if you had changed your mind,'' she asked, only half-teasing.

''Never. I told you that.'' He turned and grabbed her shoulders. ''You have not changed yours, have you?'' he asked nervously. His face, ruddy from the wind, grew pale.

''No.'' She touched his face with her hand.

''Come here.'' He opened the door to his brother's office, stuck his head in, and then pulled her in after him. As soon as the door closed behind him, he pulled her to him as though he were afraid she might escape. ''Oh, I have missed you.'' He held her close, reveling in the feel of her hands around his neck, her breasts against his chest. He buried his face in her silver-gilt curls, content for the moment merely to hold her.

Rosemary, too, enjoyed the embrace. The memory of her anatomy lesson the evening before crept into her mind as she stood there close to him, her body separated from his by only a few flimsy pieces of cloth. She moved even closer, running her hands over his shoulders as if afraid he would vanish from her hold.

Soon the embrace was not enough for either of them. Rosemary reached up and pulled his head toward hers, her lips ready for his kisses. Locked together, they did not hear the door swing open. They did, however, hear Lord Longworth say, "Sorry, Stephen. I did not know you were here."

They sprang apart. Stephen laughed ruefully. "This is getting to be a habit, David. Are you alone?"

"Unfortunately not." His brother laughed. "Rosemary's father is here too. History seems to be repeating itself."

"At least we were not in a hayloft this time," Stephen said, laughing. Rosemary, who had closed her eyes the moment she heard her future brother-in-law's voice, opened them cautiously. Noting the smile on her father's face, she did not say a word, but merely smiled at him. His smile grew broader.

"I will see you in church tomorrow, won't I?" Daniel asked Stephen sternly. For a moment the thought of giving his daughter to this man made him nervous.

"You could not keep me away," Stephen promised, looking down at the smiling girl in his arms.

13

THE NEXT DAY dawned bright and clear as only crisp fall days can be. Rosemary awoke early, her excitement driving her from her bed to the window. Stephen, although also awake early, chose to stay in bed thinking of that evening. The younger members of the household were awake so early that the maid had not yet made up the fire in the nursery suite. Slipping away from their nurse, they made their way to Rosemary's room, but Mary Ann was quicker than they. "Your father is downstairs looking for you," she said mendaciously. "Perhaps you should see what he wants." She watched with satisfaction as they ran toward the stairs.

"Very good, my dear. I predict you will have an excellent career as a mother," Lady Longworth said as she walked slowly from her room. Although she had seen the children, she had chosen not to become embroiled in their affairs that morning. "Have you seen our bride this morning?" she asked.

"Not yet. I told her maid to let her sleep as late as she could. I do not want her to spend too much time worrying about the details of the day." Mary Ann sighed. "I hope everything goes well." She looked at her cousin. "Can you think of anything we have forgotten?"

"No. And frankly, my dear, if we forgot it, it probably was not important anyway," the elder lady said as she walked toward the stairs. "Do you wish to go with me to inspect the dining room where the wedding breakfast will be held?"

While Mary Ann and Lady Longworth gave their approval

to the fall flowers and leaves that decorated the dining room, Rosemary wandered about her room, not exactly certain what she was feeling. All she was certain of was that she loved Stephen. She thought of him and her cheeks grew hot. She closed her eyes and could feel his arms wrapped tightly around her, holding her close. Then she thought of walking down the aisle toward him, of giving herself to him forever in front of all those witnesses, and she shivered with excitement. Today she would commit her life to Stephen's care. And tonight he would have the right to . . . She put her hands over her crimson cheeks and tried to think of something other than Stephen's smile, his lips, his arms, and his hard body. Poor Cousin Hortense, she thought. Her cousin had not had the kind of marriage that Mary Ann had described. Rosemary glanced at the clock and thought about the ceremony. Although she would have preferred a private wedding, Rosemary told herself this was a test. If this day went well, then perhaps she could manage London.

As strong as her love for Stephen was, the fear of failing him was always in Rosemary's mind. Deliberately she had avoided the thought during the last few weeks, telling herself to deal with one frightening situation at a time. Following Stephen's request, no one else had mentioned the Little Season either. This morning, though, she had no choice; in a few hours she would say the words that gave her future into Stephen's care. As she looked out the window at the blue sky and bright sunshine, she wondered if she had made the right decision. Remembering the way his kiss had made her heart race the evening before and the desolation she had felt when she thought she had to reject him, she smiled wryly, realizing she really had not had a choice at all. She turned back to her bedroom, noting that only a few of her belongings remained. The clock on the mantel chimed just as the door opened.

"I wondered if you were up," Mary Ann said. "No one answered the door." She glanced around the room. "Have you had something to eat?" she asked practically, remembering how her stomach had growled embarrassingly during her first wedding.

"Before I had my bath," Rosemary said quietly. Then she noticed what Mary Ann was wearing. "You are already dressed! Am I late?"

"Not at all. I hurried this morning so that I would have time to help you," her stepmother said reassuringly. "Where is your maid?"

"Gone to press an imaginary wrinkle from my gown. She is far more particular about my clothes than I am."

When she arrived at the church some time later, Rosemary was looking her best. Mary Ann and Lady Longworth had persuaded her to order a new dress for the wedding. A soft, unusual wool, it was the color of Devonshire cream. Like the muslin she had originally planned to wear, it had a pelisse and a ruff about the neck. The sleeveless pelisse was made of a matching velvet woven with a hint of gold thread through it. Two bands of matching velvet encircled her skirt; the second, wider than the first, formed the dress's border. Other bands of fabric occurred under the bust and around the tight, long sleeves. Her bonnet, a confection fashioned from the same velvet, allowed her curls to show. In her hands she carried a small, ivory Bible covered in flowers, a gift from Lady Longworth.

After taking one last look at her stepdaughter, Mary Ann kissed her cheek. She then glanced at her husband. His lips were set in a straight line. Reaching for his hand, she squeezed it as she leaned foward to whisper in his ear. He smiled and held out his arm to his daughter. Quickly Mary Ann took her place at the front of the church.

From the moment the doors opened in front of her, all Rosemary saw was Stephen, dressed formally in his favorite dark blue that complemented his eyes. Sapphires gleamed in the folds of his neckcloth and on his hand. His eyes found hers. She forgot about the others, about her fears. He was waiting for her. She did not notice when James decided to sit with his father and Julia pulled him back into place. The words the minister spoke penetrated, but only because Stephen was repeating them. She made her own vows in a low, soft voice, speaking only to the man she loved. Only the feel of her hand in his, of his placing the wedding ring on her finger, seemed real. The ceremony concluded, she let Stephen hand her into the waiting carriage.

His arms and kisses added to the magic of the moment. The journey to Long Meadow was all too short for the bride and groom. The wedding breakfast with its many removes was all too long. As small as the wedding was, the toasts lasted for hours. Although the immediate reason for the wedding was not forgotten—too many of the ladies had long memories—everyone agreed that Stephen and Rosemary had made an excellent match.

Finally Rosemary slipped away to change into her traveling gown. When she and Mary Ann returned, they found only their immediate families gathered in the hall to bid them good-bye.

"Be happy, sweetheart," Daniel said as he hugged his daughter tightly and gave her a kiss. He shook Stephen's hand firmly.

Both James and Julia, exhausted from the excitement of the day, waited next to their father to say their own farewells. "Will you come to see us again?" Julia asked wistfully as she held up her arms to Rosemary for a hug.

"Anytime your Uncle Stephen does," Rosemary promised, glancing at her husband. She blushed.

"Can we call you Aunt Rosemary now?" James wanted to know.

"Of course you can. Here, give me a hug, too," Stephen told him. The little boy came running, his face beaming.

Everyone tried to keep the farewells light, but a few tears crept in. "We will see you in London in only two weeks, Mama," Stephen reminded Lady Longworth, laughing at her tears.

"You will understand when you have a child, do you not agree, Daniel?" She wiped her eyes and smiled up at her son.

Daniel cleared his throat so that he could speak. "Completely, Cousin Sarah."

The thought of children had made Rosemary's face turn crimson. In the confusion of the moment, as everyone tried to give the departing couple one last hug, no one commented on it. Finally Stephen clasped his brother's hand. During the last few months they had grown closer than they had ever been before. They looked at each other. "Remember what I said, brother," Longworth said quietly.

"I will," Stephen replied, his face solemn. "We will see all of you in London." In spite of the chill in the air, everyone stood on the steps and waved until the coach pulled out of sight.

When the couch turned the first bend in the road, Rosemary sat back, letting the flap down over the window. She sighed.

"Are you tired?" Stephen asked, leaning over to untie her bonnet strings. She had chosen a soft blue wool for her traveling gown. Her cloak edged in gray fur was a shade darker and made her eyes seem almost blue.

"Just a little," she admitted. Alone with him at last, she was shy and uncertain. Her heart raced. Her eyes sparkled as she smiled up at him, willing him to kiss her.

He did. Unlike the kisses they had shared earlier that day, these began with the merest brush of lips against lips. His fingers smoothed her eyebrow, played with her curls. The knowledge that no one would separate them—and the talk that he had had with his brother the evening before—kept Stephen's kisses light. When Rosemary's arms drew him closer, he yielded for a moment and then sat back. She pouted, disappointed. He kissed her again and then said regretfully. "No more now. I have no more control." He put her firmly into the opposite corner and moved as far away as he could.

Confused, Rosemary looked at him, hurt in her eyes. "Have you decided you no longer want me?" she asked in her soft voice.

"Want you?" Stephen laughed. "My dear, the only reason

I moved was so that your first experience as a wife would
not be in a jolting carriage. Silly goose.'' He reached out
and pulled her closer to him. This time when he kissed her,
she had no doubts of his desire.

"Ohhh," she breathed when she was once again able to
do so. Embarrassed by her feelings, she looked down at his
hand holding hers tightly. She looked up immediately, her
face even redder.

"What is the matter?" Stephen asked. He too glanced
down. Understanding lit his face. "Sweetheart, did Mary
Ann or my mother talk to you?" he asked. If his brother
had not reminded him how little information most young
ladies going into marriage had, he would never have thought
to ask himself.

"For the last four weeks it seems we have talked
constantly."

"More specifically." She made no response. He nuzzled
her ear, enjoying the feel of her soft curls on his face. His
lips against her ear sending wonderful tingles through her,
he asked, "About marriage? The roles of a husband and a
wife?"

She gulped and blushed once more. She nodded, her throat
too tight to speak. She wanted to turn her head, to demand
a kiss on her lips instead of on her neck, but she was too shy.

"Good." A silence fell over the carriage. Reassured yet
disappointed that he would not make any more demands of
her at that moment, Rosemary relaxed even more. She
nestled against him and closed her eyes. Soon she was asleep,
exhausted by the emotional upheaval in her life. His arms
pulled her even closer to him. His blood raced, but he kept
a firm rein on his control. The knowledge that she was his,
that no one could keep them apart helped him tamp down
his emotions.

They arrived at their destination, a small estate owned by
Longworth, about four that afternoon. Stephen had chosen
it for many reasons. The house was small, and they would
need few servants. It was also relatively close to Long

Meadow. He escorted Rosemary to her room and then checked with the butler to make certain his instructions had been carried out. Then he went back to their suite.

When he heard Rosemary's maid leave, he dismissed his valet. Then, taking a deep breath, he walked to the door that connected his room to his wife's. He knocked. He heard the footsteps on the other side of the door stop. He knocked again. Now the footsteps came closer. The door opened. Rosemary stood there, her heart pounding so hard that he could see the pulse in her neck throbbing. "May I come in?" he asked. She stepped back. He closed the door behind him. She began to breathe faster. "Is the room comfortable?" he asked. Then he laughed silently at his own ineptness.

"Yes," she mumbled. Her eyes were on him. He was here in her room. And no matter what he wanted to do, no one would stop him. He was her husband. Her heart raced again. Something was different about him, but at first she did not know what. He stepped toward her. She stepped toward him. Then she was in his arms, her body plastered against his as each tried to absorb the other's hunger, passion. Then, she was never sure how, they were on the chaise by the window, late-afternoon sunlight streaming in on them. Somehow he was wearing only his pantaloons and she was in her petticoats.

The first time he touched her breast, she pulled away, her eyes wide. He pulled her back and kissed her again, his tongue playing tag with hers. When he untied her zona and put his hand against the bare flesh of her breast, she caught her breath and moved closer, moaning softly. With all the concentration he possessed, he introduced her to the pleasures of her body, pulling back occasionally to regain his own control. When her breasts were tingling with his caresses, he moved his hands lower. She moved against him restlessly, trying to escape yet imprisoned by her own desires.

When he was certain she would not pull away from him, Stephen loosened the rest of her clothes and pulled her to her feet. Her clothes formed a pool of white around them.

He lifted her face and set her down again in front of him. One hand caressed her while the other loosened the buttons on his pantaloons. He stripped them off. Her eyes grew wide as she saw him nude for the first time. The afternoon sun still lit the chamber with enough light that she could see clearly. Startled and a little afraid, she stepped back, tripping over her own clothes. He caught her, preventing her from falling, and pulled her hard against him. Her hands reached out to grab him. Her eyes grew wide as they slid down to his hips, feeling his taut muscles rippling under her hands. His hands on her waist, he lifted her off the floor and kissed her. Her lips opened hungrily. His tongue took immediate advantage. He shifted one of his hands to give her further support and nudged her legs apart with one of his. She gasped and wiggled against him, trying to get close.

"Wait," he said as he lifted her more, guiding one of her legs around him. He walked over to the high bed, each step sending ripples of desire through both of them. The maid had turned the bed back earlier, and he laid her on the crisp white sheets that smelled of lavender and roses. Before she had a chance to miss him, he was beside her once more. Although he had been quiet before, now he touched her intimately, praising her beauty, her response to him. Soon she had lost the last of her embarrassment, her uneasiness. She moaned his name and whispered her pleasure as he caressed her. When he finally moved over her and made them one, she cried out, but when he would have moved away, she held him closer.

When she awoke sometime later, the room was almost totally dark, only the low flickering flames from the fireplace sending out any light. She moved. Stephen's arms tightened around her. "Are you all right?" he asked softly. She nodded. He grew hard against her again. Then he rolled away and got up, pulling his dressing gown from the pile of clothes on the floor.

"Are you leaving me?" she asked, turning on her side

to watch him, disappointed that he was covering himself.

"No." Stephen walked around to the side of the bed where she was. "You will never be able to get rid of me," he promised. He kissed her. She wound her hands around his neck and tried to pull him into bed with her. "Later," he promised with a laugh. "Now it is time for food. I am hungry even if you are not, Madam Wife."

She laughed and sat up. Swinging her legs off the bed, she stifled a groan as she felt a twinge of pain. Stephen, who had been watching her carefully for just such a reaction, swung her back on the bed. "Stay there," he told her. He went into his room for a moment and came back with a small bowl of warm water and a cloth. "This is the best I can do for now," he told her apologetically.

"I can do that," she told him, her face flaming. She tried to push him away, but he would not go.

"I know that. But I want to. May I?" She looked at him and could deny him nothing. She nodded. Soon she was in a dressing gown and in his bedroom, where the servants had left a cold collation. Allowing her husband to pamper her, Rosemary put her feet up on the settee, and Stephen sat beside her, feeding her. Eating off one plate and drinking from one glass, they whispered words of love and paused for kisses.

When they had eaten their fill and were ready to appease another appetite, Stephen led Rosemary back to her room. To her surprise, he took her cloak from her clothes press. Pulling his dressing gown about him, he wrapped her in her cloak and put her slippers on her. He led her to the door. She resisted, trying to pull him back to bed. "Not yet. Come with me."

"Where?"

"It is a surprise, the main reason I wanted to come here," he told her. He kissed her again. "Come." She took the hand he held out and followed him from the room. Silently he led her down the stairs. Except for his valet and her maid, all the servants lived in small cottages about the grounds, and

he knew no one would disturb them. They went down two
flights of stairs, one of which was narrow and hidden in an
alcove near the rear of the house.

"Are you taking me to the kitchens?" she asked in a
whisper.

"Not quite." He paused before a door, took a key out of
his dressing gown, and opened the door. A wave of warm
air rushed toward her. He walked in. She followed him
slowly.

"What is this place?" she asked, looking about her
curiously. Lit only by the fireplace built against the
outside wall and several candles, the room was warm and
damp. She could see trees and bushes around three sides
but could not recognize them. "How do you keep it so
warm?"

He led her to the corner of the room, where low marble
benches surrounded a tiled pool. He took her cloak, untied
her dressing gown and removed it in spite of her protests,
and put them, along with his clothing, on one of the benches.
Shy once more, she looked anywhere but at him and his
naked body. Glancing around, she noticed the pile of towels
on the end of the other marble bench. "What is this
place?"

He ignored her question. "Come with me." He picked
her up and carried her into the water, ignoring her embarrassed protests. Suddenly fascinated by the pictures inlaid
in the tiles, she arched her neck, trying to see every side.
Then Stephen stepped into deeper water.

"It is warm!" she exclaimed happily. "How do you
manage to get enough hot water to fill one pool?" She relaxed
as she felt the warmth seep into her. She wrapped an arm
around his neck and tried to sit up so that she could look
around further.

He laughed and put her feet down. Then he guided her
to one of the underwater benches. "It is a family secret,"
he teased. She glared at him. He leaned over and kissed her.
"Since you are now part of the family, I can tell you, but

you must promise never to talk about it. We do not want sightseers gawking at us. Promise?''

''Yes. Tell me.''

''One of our ancestors built this house for his mistress.'' Rosemary frowned. ''Do not judge him until you hear the story,'' Stephen said firmly. ''His family forced him to marry a neighboring heiress even though he was in love with another woman. The woman he was in love with had no family, no money. She was so much in love with him that when he told her what plans his family had for his future, she offered to become his mistress, reminding him when he protested that she was giving up nothing but her reputation. To retain his love, that was a small enough price to pay.''

''Poor girl.'' Rosemary sighed. Stephen kissed her. Just when his kisses grew more demanding, she pulled away. ''Finish the story.''

''Now?''

''Now.''

''The estate had been in the family for a long time even then. I think that his aunt had lived here. Anyway, he was looking for a house not far from Long Meadow. He did not want to be too far from his love. Then he remembered this place. The house, really more of a cottage, that was here then needed more repairs than it was worth. He pulled it down and began a new one. As they were digging the foundations, they uncovered this pool, and he created a special room for his love. She was a gardener. She could have plants around her always, even in winter. And they could enjoy the luxury of hot baths whenever they wished.''

''He did not make these pictures out of the tiles?'' Stephen shook his head. ''Then who did?''

''From what they could discover, it was probably built by a Roman. The hot water is from a spring and is always the same.'' He moved closer to her. He pulled her into his arms.

She put her hands on his shoulders to hold him away. ''What happened to the lady, the mistress?'' she asked, her face thoughtful.

"When my ancestor's wife died in childbirth a few years later, he waited the customary year, and then he married her."

"And they lived together happily?"

"As far as I know. They had seven children, most of whom owed their existence to this very room," he said. He lowered his head and took one of her nipples in his mouth.

By concentrating on the story, Rosemary had managed to ignore his closeness. Even before he touched her, his words made her blush again. Then he touched her. Fire flashed through her veins, reviving the emotions she had felt such a short time before. She reached out to pull him closer. By the time he pulled her from the pool, she was limp from the aftermath of passion and from the warmth. Their arms wrapped around each other, they walked up to their suite. Falling asleep in each other's arms, they slept to wake to love again.

During their two weeks alone, they returned to the garden room often. Rosemary was fascinated by the pictures she could see on the bottom and around the sides. Carefully she sketched likenesses, complaining all the while about her inability to draw. They cataloged the trees and plants in the room, marking some so the gardener could send Mary Ann cuttings. When it rained one day, they prowled the library and discovered a collection of information about the Roman occupation of Britain that included detailed drawings of the pool. "I could have saved my time," Rosemary complained. "Not that mine are very good anyway."

"Yours are not bad. These must have been done by someone who had an interest in building. Look at these spots."

"That is where repair work has been done, I am sure of it," Rosemary said excitedly. "Let us go see!"

"Certainly," he said enthusiastically. They walked down the stairs, Rosemary tugging him when he seemed to slow. By the time she reached the pool, she was almost running.

She lay down on her stomach, her head sticking out above the warm water. "Can you see the repairs?"

"Not from here. Perhaps we should disrobe and go closer."

She smiled at him, her hand on one of the ties of her dress. "In the spirit of scientific reason only?" she asked, the corners of her mouth tilting upward.

"I would not want to limit the possibilities," he said quietly, his voice a slow drawl. His eyes twinkled, the gold flecks dancing. "Would you?"

As usual Rosemary felt her stomach tighten; her legs seemed too weak to hold her up. She put her hands on his shoulders and smiled up at him. "I am in favor of exploring any opportunity." He lifted her and held her over the pool. "Stephen, no. Put me down," she begged as she threw her arms tightly around his neck. "If I go in, so do you," she threatened.

"That was my plan." He put her down on the edge and turned her around. "Why do you always wear dresses with so many hooks, buttons, or ties?" he complained.

"They are the fashion. You do want me to be fashionable?"

"You can be as fashionable as you like when we return to London." He felt her body tighten with tension. "But right now I like you best with no clothes at all."

"Stephen!" At times she was still shocked by her reaction to him, and he knew exactly how to make her blush. When Mary Ann had explained lovemaking to her, Rosemary had had no idea that a man and a woman could respond so openly to each other, could tease each other, could find a world of excitement in the other. Her stepmother had tried to tell her, but Rosemary was certain that the joys she described were experienced by only a few lucky ladies. To her surprise, she was one of the lucky ones. Although she never initiated their lovemaking, she responded fully. When Stephen unhooked her dress and slid his hands inside, she felt her knees grow weak with desire.

They whiled away the afternoon with love and with a careful inspection of the tile, noting each missing or loose piece. "You will have someone repair it, won't you?" Rosemary begged. "You cannot let it fall into disrepair."

"And lose one of the most memorable places of our life together? As soon as we see my brother, I will tell him." Stephen's face grew somber. "Or maybe I should take care of it myself."

"Why?"

"My brother and his wife spent a brief holiday alone here just weeks before her death. He has not been back since. I think he would have sold the place except for the entail."

Rosemary's face was as somber as his. "Someday he will be able to return," she said quietly. "We must make certain it is here for him then." Then she laughed. "Can you imagine the reaction James and Julia would have if they were to see this?" She looked down at the scene of a faun chasing woodland nymphs. "Maybe we should wait until they are adults before we show them," she said thoughtfully, remembering her own blushes the first time she had had a chance to study the pictures carefully.

"You may be right. Besides, if they discover the place, we will never be able to come here on our own." She made a face at him and pulled her dress over her shoulders. He sighed. "Come here. I suppose you insist that I hook you back into this thing?"

"It is not a thing. It is one of my newest afternoon frocks." She glanced down at her crumpled skirts. "My maid will threaten to leave me soon if I am not more careful with my gowns." She wrinkled her brow. "I suppose I could tell her you are to blame."

Stephen laughed and pulled his shirt over his head. "My dear, she already knows that."

"Stephen, she does not gossip about us, does she?" Rosemary asked, horrified. "Does everyone know what we are doing in here?" She put her hands to her cheeks in an effort to cool them.

"Rosemary, we are a newly wedded couple. We spend hours by ourselves. Of course people know what we have been doing," he said. "They regard it as natural, which it is." He took her hands in his and pulled her over in front of him. He put a finger under her chin and forced her to look up. "Do you regret marrying me?"

"No. But, Stephen, how will I ever be able to look at these people ever again? I am so embarrassed." She pulled away and walked toward the trees.

"That feeling will go away, I promise you. People have been making love for thousands of years, and no one ever died of embarrassment because of it, at least I never heard they did." Coaxing and prodding her, he managed to lead her back to their suite. Leaving his wife in her maid's capable hands, he went into his own bedroom. Just before he closed the door behind him, he turned. "Remember what I said," he reminded her. She blushed and nodded. When she was freshly dressed, she gathered her courage and glanced into her maid's face. Instead of the speculation she thought she would see, her maid wore a wistful smile. Rosemary lowered her eyes again, her face thoughtful.

That night after the evening meal, her enjoyment of her marriage slipped. Their two weeks alone were almost over. It was time for them to leave for London.

"Are you certain you want to do this, Rosemary?" Stephen asked doubtfully. "If you are doubtful . . ."

"Of course I am uncertain." He opened his mouth, but she cut him off before he could speak. "But we are going to London. Nothing you can say will get me to change my mind." She thought for a moment and then added, "And if you think your mother would allow that to happen, you do not know her very well. She would find some way to get us there." She laughed softly at the picture in her mind.

He laughed ruefully. "You are probably right." He put his arms around her and pulled her down to his lap. "I think we should leave the day after tomorrow. That will put us in London before Sunday."

She nestled close to him, her face tucked under his chin. He could feel her soft breath on his neck. She sighed. "You had better tell me what to expect," she said quietly.

"We will be expected to give a ball; I am certain Mama already has that well in hand. And you will need to be presented."

"Presented? Why? We are not peers of the realm."

"Not yet. But my brother is. Mother tells me that a bride's presentation is much less demanding than a young lady's. You will have to make your bow to the queen in front of only a few people."

"The queen!" She sighed. "I will do my best."

He kissed her, his lips offering both passion and comfort. Then he pulled back. "Because we are so recently wedded, no one will expect us to stay very long at any entertainment." He smiled wickedly, anticipating her reaction.

"Stephen! You are teasing me!"

"No, I am not," he promised, laughing. "Ask Mary Ann if you do not believe me."

"I will." Her face grew more serious. She sighed again. "Are you certain we must leave here so soon?" Her voice was wistful. She looked up at him, her eyes wide.

"Yes." His arms closed around her hungrily. "But it is not time to leave yet."

14

WHEN THEY ARRIVED in London, they found everyone waiting for them. Lady Longworth had been in town for more than a week, and everyone else had arrived the day before. Although London was still thin of company, the day the knocker had gone up on the door invitations began to appear. By the time Stephen and Rosemary arrived their calendar was full.

In spite of her fears, Rosemary found that life in town caused less stress than she had imagined. Accompanied by Lady Longworth and Mary Ann, she made afternoon visits, renewing her friendships with the members of the *ton* she had met in Bath. She was usually the center of attention at these gatherings, a fact which made her rather nervous, but everyone was kind. All of Lady Longworth's friends declared that they had predicted the wedding as soon as they had seen Rosemary and Stephen together. Only the matchmaking mamas who had already selected Stephen for their daughters made snide remarks. The gentleman who had proclaimed their devotion to her when they showered her with bouquets in Bath still worshiped at her feet. As one said to another, it was much safer to be in love with a married woman.

"Have you seen her husband watching you?" his friend asked. He glanced in Stephen's direction. "I would not want him angry with me." Stephen frowned, his eyes dark with displeasure. The other gentleman looked over his shoulder. He turned back around hastily. In a few minutes he made his excuses and disappeared.

The limited number of people Rosemary came in contact with on afternoon calls did not prepare her for the attention she received when they entered Lady Jersey's ballroom. As their names were announced, Rosemary began to feel uneasy. As they made their way slowly down the receiving line, Stephen felt Rosemary's hand begin to tremble on his arm. He put his hand over hers protectively. She took a deep breath and forced a smile back on her lips, trying to master her fear as she met one stranger after another. Only the knowledge that the viscount was on one side of her and her husband on the other kept her moving along the line.

When she reached her hostess, Rosemary was amazed when Lady Jersey took her hand and held it so that she could not move on. "So you are the reason that Mr. Huntington left London so early," she said coquettishly. She turned to Stephen. "Now that you have won your prize, I hope to see you more often. You are not to follow your brother's example and rusticate for most of the year. I will not have it." She glanced back at Rosemary, still standing before her. "She is lovely. A good background too. Would a married couple like you enjoy our little dances at Almack's?"

"Surely you jest, my lady," Stephen said swiftly before Rosemary lost her startled look. "Is there anyone anywhere who would refuse such an offer?" His wife's hand tightened on his arm. "We would be honored to attend." He bowed, and Rosemary made a curtsy. Releasing Rosemary's hand, their hostess nodded and watched them move further into the ballroom.

"Congratulations, Rosemary," her brother-in-law said. "You can count yourself a success."

"So kind of her," Lady Longworth murmured.

Mary Ann and Daniel, who had been behind them, walked up at that moment. "How fortunate that Lady Jersey was impressed with you, Rosemary," her stepmother said. "You will discover that the few words she spoke to you will open doors for you."

"I hope they mean that the king will give Stephen a title."

"Lady Jersey is powerful, but she does not have that kind of influence—not with the king, at least," Daniel said. "If you had asked the Prince . . ." He looked around the crowd. "Shall we join one of the sets that is forming?"

Reluctantly Rosemary let Stephen lead her out onto the floor for the first country dance. Her father and Mary Ann joined them. Rosemary shifted uneasily from foot to foot. In Bath she had known everyone in the set. Here she would have to dance occasionally with strangers. The music began for the first figures. She stiffened her back. Looking down at her, Stephen smiled proudly. From the tip of her silver-gilt curls to the toes of her white slippers, she sparkled. Her dress was white silk shot with silver. Diamonds, his wedding gift to her, sparkled in her hair and around her neck and wrists.

By keeping her eyes on her husband as much as she could, given the complicated figures of the dance, Rosemary managed to keep her panic at bay. When the dance ended, she breathed a sigh of relief. They walked over to join the rest of their family party. "Dance with me, Rosemary," her brother-in-law said firmly. "Let Stephen take care of the duty dances." Glancing back over her shoulder at her husband, Rosemary, more reluctantly than before, allowed Longworth to lead her onto the floor.

This time the dance seemed to last for hours; each turn brought new faces. Although she tried to control it, Rosemary could feel her panic rising. Her breath began to speed up. Stephen, looking over the shoulder of his partner, saw a white line forming about her mouth. He frowned and stumbled. As soon as the dance was over, he apologized to his partner and hurried toward his wife.

"I think it is time we left," he suggested.

"But you have not had a chance to talk to anyone. Let me sit beside Mary Ann or your mother for a while," his wife protested. But he would not listen.

"Mother, we are leaving," he said quietly. "Do you wish to accompany us?"

"Now? You are leaving now?" She looked from her son to his wife and said no more. "No. I will leave with your brother or Daniel and Mary Ann. Do you go home or to another party?"

"Home, I think," Stephen said, smiling as he realized that he would have his wife to himself for the rest of the evening.

Until they reached the carriage, Rosemary protested their leaving. "I could have stayed," she said, trying once more to convince him they should return. He did not listen but handed her into the carriage.

She frowned at him, pulling her white velvet evening cloak more carefully around her. The evening air was crisp and cold, and the flaps at the windows of the coach did little to keep out the damp. The door swung closed behind them. "You are sitting too far away," he protested, putting an arm around her to pull her closer.

She hesitated. "Stephen, I do not understand you. At Long Meadow you said it was important that we attend the social events. Now, at the first sign of my discomfort, you rush me away. I told you I would manage."

"Rosemary, the length of time we spend there is not important. We were there. No one expects a recently married couple, especially one who made a love match, to spend their evening dancing until dawn. They usually have more interesting things to do." Once more he put his arm around her. This time she did not try to resist. "I would rather be holding you like this than dancing," he told her just before he kissed her.

"Oh, so would I!"

The kisses in the carriage were preludes to a more delightful encounter. Walking into her bedroom with her, Stephen dismissed her waiting maid. Rosemary frowned at him. "Would you prefer her to undress you?" he asked, one eyebrow raised and one end of his mouth tilting upward.

"No." She whirled around, showing him her back, wishing that her blushes did not give her away so often.

"Another line of hooks," he complained as he stared at

the back of her dress. "I wonder why they do not make ladies' gowns more simple." He pulled his neckcloth off and reached for the first hook.

"Then what would husbands have to complain about?" his wife asked tartly. "Are you going to finish unhooking me?"

Piece by piece their clothes fell to the floor. They came together in a rush of passion. Timid and shy in public, Rosemary became an outgoing, giving woman in Stephen's arms. As usual when their passion was spent and she lay sleeping in those arms, he lay awake, wondering about the contradictions that made up his wife. He was convinced that something in her past had caused her fear. She fought to overcome it. She was willing; she tried, but whenever she went out into society, she was never completely comfortable. Maybe Dr. Mesmer *was* the answer.

The next few days were nerve-wracking for everyone. As the time of her presentation grew closer, Rosemary grew quieter. She practiced her curtsy wearing both the heavy old-fashioned dress and the ostrich plumes in her hair. "Everyone who is presented has to wear this costume?" she asked for the twentieth time after she had stumbled once more.

"Everyone," Lady Longworth and Mary Ann said together. "Try this again. You can do it," her mother-in-law added.

"And Stephen complains about my usual dresses," Rosemary mumbled to herself. "Wait until he tries to get me out of this."

"What?" Lady Longworth asked.

Mary Ann, who had heard her more clearly since she was closer to her, laughed. "He will manage. There has never been a dress made that could foil a determined man."

Rosemary blushed a deep crimson. She had not realized that she was speaking loudly enough to be heard. Before anyone could say anything else, she made another curtsy, this time perfectly.

"Once more for luck," Lady Longworth commanded.

"Then I must talk to the housekeeper. She has found a small problem in our plans for the ball. Nothing important, she assures me," she added quickly as she saw the frown on Mary Ann's face. "Something about the punch, I believe."

"If there is anything I can do to help, please let me know," Mary Ann said quickly. By the time they had arrived in London, Lady Longworth had taken care of most of the details. Rosemary nodded.

"There is really nothing more to be done. The servants have finished cleaning the chandeliers and inserting fresh candles." She broke off for a moment and tapped her fingers against her chair. "I wonder if we have ordered enough extra candles. It grows dark so early now, we will need more than during the Season. I shall add that to my list." She smiled. "I do enjoy having a ball once more. I had thought the one we gave for you and Daniel would be the last I arranged for a while," she told Mary Ann, her face glowing with vigor and excitement.

Rosemary sighed, wishing that all this was over, that she and Stephen could return to the country. The days had been so dreary and often rainy that no one wanted to be outside. She missed her walks in the gardens, and riding. And as hard as she tried to hide her uneasiness from everyone, she knew she was not succeeding. She sighed again.

"Try one more, Rosemary," Mary Ann said encouragingly. "Then you can change. We are receiving this afternoon," she reminded her. Like Rosemary, Mary Ann too wished for the country, but not for the same reason. Exhausted by their social obligations and unwilling to let anyone know, she longed for the quiet life at the Manor. She smothered a yawn—she always seemed to be sleepy—and longed for her bed.

Rosemary glanced up from her curtsy just in time to see her trying to hide it behind her hand. "Go upstairs and rest, Mary Ann. Cousin Sarah, tell her that we will manage quite well on our own this afternoon."

"Of course we will." She smiled indulgently. "I had

forgotten how sleepy I always felt when I was in an interesting condition. You must take care of yourself. If you do not, I will have to speak with Daniel.''

"Please, no. He has wrapped me in cotton wool as it is,'' Mary Ann said. "He would worry so.''

"It is your decision. Now, hurry upstairs and rest. Rosemary is right. We will do nicely without you,'' her cousin said indulgently. "And you, daughter, find that son of mine and tell him I will expect his presence this afternoon. Maybe we should have Daniel and David, as well as Stephen,'' she said thoughtfully.

"Daniel had some business in the city this morning,'' Mary Ann said apologetically.

"I thought I told you to go upstairs. Hurry along, now. You too.'' She waved her hands much as Rosemary had seen women do when they were trying to get chickens to move. The two younger ladies looked at each other and did as she asked. "Be back here before three, Rosemary.''

"Who invented these afternoon calls?'' her daughter-in-law complained as she walked up the stairs with her stepmother. "We see almost the same people day after day.''

"Yes, but you see them for only a short time. If we did not have this custom, ladies would come for the entire afternoon. Now they cannot, not if they want to be accepted by society. A half-hour is much better. Even the biggest bore or the worst gossip can be endured for that period.''

"I wish family had to abide by those rules.''

"Whom do you mean?''

"Clarissa and her mother.''

"My dear, relatives are a cross you must bear. Just be grateful that you can blame your husband for them. If they were your own, think how much longer you would have known them.'' They both laughed. Mary Ann put her hand on the latch of her door. "Seriously, though. You must expect animosity from that quarter. Clarissa had set her sights on your husband. And she is in a precarious position. This will be her third Season. If she does not marry soon, she will be on the shelf. For one who has been feted as she has, that must be terrifying. And her mama does not help.''

''You are right, of course.'' Rosemary sighed and then smiled. ''If it had not been for her mischief-making, Stephen and I would not have married so quickly.'' Then she frowned. ''It is her fault too that I am in London.''

''Not totally. You know what your father planned for you,'' Mary Ann reminded her. She yawned again. ''Ask yourself which you prefer: London with Stephen or London alone.''

''With Stephen, naturally. Now, go to sleep. If you are still sleepy this evening, stay in bed. We are scheduled to go to some musical presentation.''

''I may. We shall see.'' Mary Ann yawned again, her eyes feeling very heavy. She opened her door and slipped inside.

When Rosemary reached her room, her maid helped her from the court dress and took the feathers from her hair. When she would have helped her dress again, Rosemary waved her away. Pulling on a dressing gown, she walked over to the window and stared out into the gray day. Picking up a book from a small table, she stared at it for a moment and then dropped it, jumping as it hit the table with a loud thud.

''Rosemary, is that you?'' her husband called from his bedroom. He opened the door and peered in. ''Ummm. I like this new fashion you are wearing.'' He walked over to her, put his hands on her waist, and turned her slowly around.

''I am glad you approve.'' She had chosen the dressing gown earlier that week with him in mind.

''Has Mama allowed you to escspe her clutches?'' he asked.

''Do not make fun of her, Stephen. She is only trying to help,'' Rosemary said seriously. Though at times over-whelmed by her mother-in-law's enthusiasm, Rosemary was grateful for her support.

''I know, love.'' He pulled her close and kissed her. ''I

needed that," he said as he nuzzled her ear. He tried to lead her to the bed, but she resisted.

"Stephen, we do not have time for that now. Your mother wants you to receive guests with us this afternoon." He mumbled something softly. "I do not know why you should complain. You manage to escape most of the time. I am the one who has to see most of them. And I did not even want to come to London," she reminded him indignantly.

"I know, love. I know." He took her in his arms again and kissed her slowly, sending tremors of desire through her.

"When will we be able to go home?" she asked, her breath soft on his neck.

"Soon. We cannot leave before our presentation and the ball, but Canning assures me that the king will give my petition careful consideration. As soon as he makes his decision, we will leave. Is the *ton* too much for you? I could still withdraw."

"No. Really I am doing quite well. You will have to forgive me if I slip backward now and then," she said quietly, her hands smoothing imaginary wrinkles on his shoulders. "If I had to do this alone . . ." She paused and shuddered. "I just wish that I could be as comfortable in company as Mary Ann and your mother."

He led her to the chaise, noting how the soft pale blue of the sheer dressing gown gave her eyes the faintest hint of blue. "Do we have time just to talk?" he asked.

"A little. " They sat down, sharing the chaise, their legs entwined. For a few minutes Stephen simply held her. Rosemary felt the tension of the morning slipping away.

He looked down at her, her head resting just below his chin. If only they could stay like this, he wished, knowing that was an impossibility. He shifted. She moved with him. "Rosemary?"

"Hmmm," she answered sleepily.

He glanced down, unwilling to disturb her. Then he forced himself to continue. She had insisted on coming to London with him. It was his responsibility to make her stay as easy as possible. No matter what it took to get her to that point, he reminded himself. "What is the earliest thing you remember about your life?"

He could feel her stiffen as she always did when anyone asked her questions. She tried to draw away from him, but he would not let her go. "What do you mean?"

"Oh, some day that stands out. For me it was my third or fourth birthday. My father gave me a pony, a bay with four white stockings." He smiled as the details came flooding back. "David teased me, telling me my present was useless because I did not know how to ride." He felt her relax again.

"I remember riding in a carriage with my mother. The sun was shining. Every once in a while we would stop, and she would talk to someone." She frowned, trying to recapture the details. "There were trees and people, people walking, riding in carriages or on horseback. I was so proud of my new dress. It matched my mother's. I even had a little hat like hers.' Rosemary's voice grew dreamy as she went on. "Sometimes someone would get into the carriage with us and ride for a while. I did not like that."

"Why? Were you afraid?" he asked quietly, hoping he was close to the answer he sought.

His wife thought for a while, her face wrinkled into a frown. Then she smiled. "No. No, I was not! I simply did not want to share my mother's attention. Although I am not sure she was watching or listening to me even when we were alone," she added thoughtfully. "She always seemed to be looking for someone."

"Perhaps your father," he suggested, glancing at the clock on the mantel to be sure they had enough time to dress before afternoon calls began.

"No, I am certain he was not the one. In fact, I am not even sure Papa was in town with us then."

"You were in London?" he asked in surprise. "I did not know you had been here before you came for your father's wedding."

Once again Rosemary grew still in his arms, her face set in thought. "I must have forgotten. Mama came to London each spring and brought me with her," she said thoughtfully. "We had a house . . ."

"Where?"

"I do not know. I will ask Papa if it is important." She hesitated. "Is that what you want me to do?"

"I just wondered if we lived near each other then," he said quickly. Rather than disturb her further, he would ask her father himself. "What else do you remember about growing up?"

She thought for a moment again. "How strange. I remember being in town. Then I remember being at home with Papa."

He looked at the clock on the mantel one more time. "Do not worry yourself, my dear." He kissed her again. "If we do not want to be in Mama's bad graces, we must hurry. It is a quarter past two."

She pulled away from him and jumped up. "Your mother will never forgive us," she said. "Hurry!" She rushed to the bell rope and gave it a frantic tug. Her maid must have been nearby because she was there only moments later. "Quick! Find me an afternoon gown. Oh, Stephen, you have mussed my hair!"

He sauntered to the door into his bedroom. "I refuse to apologize, madam," he said cavalierly. "Besides, you do not hear me complaining about the wrinkles in my coat."

She blushed and tried to ignore him. "It will take only a moment to smooth your hair, Mrs. Huntington," her maid assured her. The affection between her mistress and her husband may not have been usual among married couples of their class, but their servants took pride in it, not above telling their friends in confidence the way the couple acted when they thought they were alone. Only the highest sticklers among the upper servants did not enjoy hearing of the romance secondhand.

By the time Stephen returned, dressed this time in a coat

of hunter green and wearing an emerald in his neckcloth, her maid was tying the last of the ribbons on Rosemary's dress. "We have time to spare," Stephen assured her. He held out his arm. "Did Mama say why we needed to be present?"

"No. As far as I know, there is nothing special planned. But Mary Ann will not be there. Maybe she felt I needed your support," his wife said, biting her lip in vexation as she realized that if that were the case, her mother-in-law had read her feelings all to well.

"Is Mary Ann all right?" Stephen asked anxiously.

"She is tired. All this racketing around has worn her out. I do not know how anyone keeps this pace up for long. And your mother said the Season is worse." Before they entered the salon where Lady Longworth waited, Rosemary stopped before a pier table to check her skirts. Satisfied they were still immaculate, she took his arm again and let him lead her into the room.

"I was ready to send a footman to find you," Lady Longworth said sharply. "George Canning said he would be here sometime this afternoon. He is bringing someone to meet you, Rosemary."

"Canning at an at-home? You must be joking," Stephen said.

"I have his note right here."

"Me? He is bringing someone to meet me?" Rosemary stammered, feeling her heart begin to pound.

"It may be one of the queen's ladies," Lady Longworth said, trying to comfort her. That thought set Rosemary shaking.

"Or it could be someone who knew you when you were a child," Stephen said hastily. "Whatever happens, I will be here with you," he promised. "Are you expecting anyone else?"

"No. But you know the way at-homes work. I may have one or a hundred guests." She fanned herself, wishing that there were some way to maintain an even heat in the room.

If the fireplace were kept blazing in order to heat the farthest reaches of the room, then those closest to it were often too warm.

"A hundred? Mama, I think you exaggerate," he said laughingly. And you are frightening my wife even further, he wanted to add. "Rosemary, have you ever seen that many people here in the afternoon?"

She took a deep breath, trying to take control of her emotions. She smiled. It wavered, but it was a smile. "I never counted," she said in a soft voice that was almost a whisper.

"You ladies always protect each other," her husband complained. "These afternoon calls are simply a way to make certain that you know what is going on."

His mother took the wind from his sails when she agreed. "Think how dull it would be if we had nothing to discuss. No one would ever go anywhere. Come sit here beside me, Rosemary. Stephen can go stand in a corner if he likes." Knowing the temperature of the salon, both ladies were dressed in muslins with Kashmir shawls. Rosemary's dress was a pale blue with a white underskirt, and Lady Longworth wore lavender. "Do you think the music this evening will be better than that we heard in Bath?"

Before Rosemary could answer, the butler announced the first guest. Although no one stayed longer than the correct half-hour, by the end of the first hour Rosemary was certain that Lady Longworth had not exaggerated the possibilities. At one time they had so many people in the room that only the elder ladies had a place to sit. Reluctantly, one after another left, regretting the strict rules that governed behavior on calls.

When Canning arrived a few minutes after four, the crowd had dwindled to only four guests. At the sight of the lady on his arm, everyone stood. She was tiny, barely five feet tall even with the plume that decorated the turban she wore around her head. Her skin, once flawless, was now wrinkled with age. Her bright blue eyes still twinkled with mischief.

"We are honored to have you as our guest, Lady Babbington," Lady Longworth said as she made her curtsy. Although only a distant cousin of the present king, this lady was royalty. "My daughter-in-law, Rosemary Wyatt Huntington."

The tiny lady looked down at Rosemary's head. "They are right," she said in amazement. Rosemary rose, her face showing her confusion. Lady Babbington simply smiled.

When she and Canning left a short time later, everyone still remaining began talking:

"But she rarely leaves her home."

"Did you hear what she said to Mrs. Huntington?"

"I wonder what she wanted."

Lady Longworth wished she had the answers. "Have you ever seen her before?" she asked Rosemary. "She made it very plain that it was you she had come to see."

"No. Surely I would remember her if I had." Her father walked into the room then. "Papa, do we know Lady Babbington?"

"Babbington? Is she still alive?" he asked, astonished. "She was old when I was a child."

"Is she a family connection, then?" Lady Longworth asked.

"No. Unless you could count her flirtation with my father," he said with a laugh. "They raised a few eyebrows in their time. Made my mother angry. He was younger than Lady Babbington."

"Maybe that is why she wanted to see you," Stephen told his wife. "While you were talking with her, Canning told me that she had promised to speak with the queen. You may receive extra attention when you are presented."

Rosemary blanched. Lady Longworth hastened to her side. "I will be there. And you have already met Lady Babbington. You will manage beautifully. I have every faith in you," she assured her. During the time she had known Rosemary, Lady Longworth had grown very fond of her. "I suppose we should send Lady Babbington a card for our ball."

"Yes. Canning said her support will be very helpful."

"I will send it immediately." She took a deep breath. "I had no idea that life could be so exciting. Maybe we should attend the Little Season every year."

"We, Mama? Please do not count on us. Rosemary and I will be very happy to return home," her son replied.

Daniel Wyatt looked at him with more favor than he usually did. Although his daughter looked happy, he was still not certain that Stephen was good enough for Rosemary, no matter what his daughter had said. Since they had arrived in town, he had tried to stifle his resentment against the man who had taken his daughter from him, but it still crept up on him occasionally.

Rosemary sat quietly, trying to make sense of what had happened that afternoon.

15

WHEN LADY BABBINGTON arrived at the musical entertainment that evening a few minutes after they did, both Stephen and Rosemary were startled. So was their hostess. Rushing forward, she greeted the elderly lady with every courtesy. Normally a recluse, Lady Babbington regularly surprised one or two hostesses a year by attending their gatherings. Those who were so honored glowed, knowing that their reputations as hostesses had been made.

As soon as she had finished the required greetings, the elderly lady swept the room with her eyes. When she found Rosemary seated against the wall in the back of the room, she frowned. She made her way toward her, leaning heavily on a silver-topped cane instead of her escort's arm. The young man, a grandson or cousin—Rosemary was never sure which—followed her, his face set in sulky lines. The moment he caught sight of Rosemary, he smiled.

"What are you doing back here, child?" Lady Babbington asked Rosemary. Then she turned her attention on Stephen. "I would have thought you would have little trouble finding her a more suitable seat near the front, young man. Back here the music will be spoiled by all those hens' twittering voices." She punctuated her remarks with a thump of her cane.

"My wife prefers this location, Lady Babbington," Stephen said quietly. "I will be happy to find you a seat as close to the front as possible if you wish."

The elderly lady leaned forward, searching Rosemary's

face carefully. "No. I will sit with you." Stephen and Rosemary exchanged surprised glances. They stood until the young man had seated Lady Babbington, found a stool for her feet, and arranged her shawl around her once more. "Go on, now." She waved the boy away. "Promised to turn the pages for some chit. Thinks he is in love." She laughed. "Salad love, most likely. At least back here I will not need to see him gawking at her."

Rosemary took her seat again, taking deep breaths to calm herself. Stephen started to take his seat beside her, when Lady Babbington motioned him closer to her. "Sit beside me until the interval. I have some questions for you."

Ruefully Stephen did as she asked. Rosemary nodded her understanding. As they waited for the music to begin, their threesome attracted much attention. Latecomers stopped to pay their respects, and those who had arrived early found some reason to walk to the back of the room. When the music began, everyone turned his attention to the soloists.

"Good. Now maybe we can have a little private conversation. Do not look at me that way, young man. I know that were your wife not a lover of music you would have found a thousand reasons for avoiding this crowd tonight." She leaned closer. "Well, so would I," she said confidently. "Not one of these infants has any talent to speak of." Rosemary glanced at them curiously, the murmur of their voices so low that it did not interfere with the music. She was curious about what they were discussing.

Stephen was just as curious as she. "I would like to thank you for your attention, Lady Babbington," he said quietly.

"No need to thank me, young man. I did it for her." She pointed her cane at Rosemary.

"Because her grandfather was a flirt of yours?"

"What? Where did you hear that? What is her family name?"

"Wyatt. Her father said you and his father were the center of some gossip when he was younger."

"Wyatt." She laughed heartily, not bothering to muffle

the sound. "I had not thought of that man in years. Yes, yes, we were. His wife did not know how to conduct herself, and spread the rumors everywhere. I did not mind. I was always the center of controversy. Made it hard for her, though. I believe she had to rusticate for a Season or two."

Stephen waited for her to explain further. When she just sat quietly tapping her cane in time to the sprightly air being played at the time, he leaned closer. "Why are you interested in my wife?" he asked.

"Knew her as a child. When someone described her to me recently, I decided to find out how she turned out. Very pretty, but seems a trifle skittish." She frowned.

"My wife is uncomfortable in company, Lady Babbington," Stephen said. For some reason he knew it was important to disclose everything to her. "Strangers and crowds make her very nervous."

"It did not seem to bother her this afternoon when I popped in. She was very gracious."

"My mother and I both were there. As long as she has someone that she knows and trusts very close at hand, she can manage unless she finds herself surrounded." He glanced at his wife and then added, "But she is always very nervous."

"Must have good bottom, then, to go through the drawing room," Lady Babbington said softly. "Good bottom." Stephen nodded. As the performance ended and everyone began to clap politely, the elderly lady leaned over to Rosemary. "Did your grandfather ever tell you about me?" she asked.

"He died when I was very small. In fact, I hardly remember him," Rosemary said softly.

"Neither do I," Lady Babbington said confidentially. "Only thing really remarkable about him was his hair. Just like yours. My, did the *ton* talk when they saw us together." She smiled, mischief dancing in her eyes. "Now that I am old, almost everyone has forgotten how I was always the center of a storm of gossip. Why, some of the leading

hostesses refused to have me in their homes. I had my
revenge, though. If I did not get an invitation, their husbands
usually forgot to attend also.'' She laughed wickedly, reliving
those moments.

Her eyes wide with astonishment as she listened to the tiny
lady talk, Rosemary focused only on one fact. "My grandfather had hair like mine. I thought my hair was like my
mother's."

"It was. Only yours was lighter, prettier. Oh, people were
fascinated when they saw you and your mother together.
Thought that was why she did it. Never knew why your father
let her get away with it.''

"With what?'' Rosemary asked. She had long since lost
interest in the music. Stephen too leaned forward so that he
could her their low-voiced conversation.

"Why, using you to attract the men who hung around her
like flies. She would have your nurse dress you in your
prettiest clothes and take you out for a drive. By the time
she returned, she had lured another poor fool into her
clutches. Though she had the face of an angel, she had the
cunning of a shrew. I always thought she kept you with her
simply to attract attention. You two were the talk of the town
the season before she disappeared. Some artist painted the
pair of you.'' Lady Babbington leaned back, her face somber.

"I never saw a painting of the two of us,'' Rosemary
protested.

"Do not think it was ever finished, at least not in London.
Talk was that the artist was the man she ran away with. Think
they took it with them. Could ask your father, I suppose.''

Rosemary looked at her husband. He nodded. The rest of
the evening passed quickly, with Lady Babbington's comments keeping them listening carefully.

When they were in their rooms that night, Stephen asked
his wife, "Can you remember more of your dreams now
that we have returned to London?''

"No. It is almost as though there is a blank in my mind,''

she said after a few minutes. "I am not certain I want to know any more."

"Knowledge is power, my dear." He began to explain. Then he looked into her terror-filled eyes, and decided to wait. He would talk with Lady Babbington again. "Come. Let us go to bed."

The next day he sought out Daniel Wyatt. "Tell me about your first wife," he suggested. His face was grave.

"Why?" Daniel demanded, his face set in harsh lines.

"Lady Babbington was talking to Rosemary last night. She raised some questions we need answers for."

"Gad, will I be haunted for the rest of my life by that woman? She did her best to ruin me while she was alive. Is she now reaching back from the grave to pull me down?" He got up and began to pace about the room angrily.

Mary Ann walked in, her face rosy from her morning walk in the garden. She looked at her husband and ran to him anxiously. "Daniel, what is wrong? Has something happened to Rosemary?"

Gradually he got himself under control. "Rosemary is fine. But she is the only good thing that came from that marriage," he said angrily.

"Why are you talking about that time?"

"Stephen asked."

Mary Ann turned to glare at her cousin. "Why are you upsetting my husband?" she demanded. Without conscious thought she placed herself between the two men.

"Because Lady Babbington has been upsetting Rosemary. Daniel, I beg you to give me an honest answer." Mary Ann looked from one to the other.

Daniel took her hand and led her to the settee, taking a seat beside her. "Sit down, Stephen. I will try to tell you what I know." His voice was as dull as spent coals. Mary Ann put her arm through his and clasped his hand. Stephen took a chair opposite them so he could watch Daniel's face. His heart told him to stop, to let Daniel keep his secrets, but his mind told him that his wife had a right to know and she had asked him to find out.

"Were you in town with her when she left?"

"No! If I had been, do you think I would have allowed her to take Rosemary away?" Daniel asked angrily. Mary Ann tightened her grip on his hand. During the month they had spent together after the wedding, they had discussed their previous marriages, but both had agreed that some things were too painful to relive. "We had gone our own ways for years. As long as she did not bring open scandal to my name, I did not care what she did. Most of the time she lived in London and I stayed in the country. She would make visits from time to time—repairing leases, I believed. Then she would take Rosemary with her everywhere. At most other times she would ignore her. Until that last Season. She asked me to let her take Rosemary to town for several months." He ran his hands through his hair as if he could comb that memory from his mind.

Stephen and Mary Ann waited for him to continue. "I began receiving letters, anonymous ones, telling me that my marriage was in danger, that my wife and my daughter had been seen where no woman of reputation would dare to appear. At first I thought they were from my wife in an attempt to get me to raise her allowance. Then I thought of Rosemary and grew worried—I left for town within two days of receiving the first one; I do not know if I would have been able to do anything even if I had left that first day." His face was full of pain.

"That is all right, my darling. Everything is all right," Mary Ann said soothingly, putting her arms around him. Stephen said nothing, his face set in stark lines.

"When I arrived in London, Rosemary was missing and so was my wife. Later that day, Rosemary was delivered to the door. The household was at sixes and sevens. No one got a good look at the coach she came home in. The butler thought there was a crest on the door, but he could not be sure. There was a note on plain paper pinned to her dress."

"What did it say?" Stephen asked.

"That she had been found wandering near the park. The author of the note had had her examined by her doctor. As soon as she discovered who she was, she sent her home."

"Did you question Rosemary?"

"Of course I did. All she could remember was that she had been frightened, that Mama had not come back, but a nice lady had taken her home with her. Soon after that I noticed that she began to shy away from strangers. She always wanted to know where I was. She did not like changes. And she began to have nightmares."

"And what did your wife say about this?"

"She never knew. She disappeared. Until someone sent me the notice of her death he had seen in an English-language newspaper in Italy, I did not know where she was, nor did I care," he said bitterly.

"How much of this does Rosemary know?" Stephen asked quietly. He sympathized with his father-in-law, but his first concern was for his wife.

"None of it. She did not remember anything, and I did not want to revive bad memories," Daniel said. "I would advise you to keep it from her too."

"She already remembers some," Stephen told him. "And Lady Babbington's questions have made her very curious. May I tell Rosemary what you have told me?"

"Everything? Even about how I ignored the warnings?" Daniel asked, despair in his face and in his voice. "She may think I did not love her."

"Stephen, please. Consider carefully what you tell her. Do not destroy her love for her father," Mary Ann pleaded. Her arms were around her husband, holding him tight, as though she could protect him from the hurts the world had given him.

"Daniel, you are my wife's father. I will do nothing to destroy your relationship. She loves you. All I want to discuss with her is the day you arrived in London," Stephen said earnestly. He crossed the room to put his hand on Daniel's shoulder. The older man grasped it eagerly. "Do you want to be there when I tell her?" he asked.

"No." He shuddered. "But I will be if you think it will help her."

Quickly Stephen declined his offer. He made his way to Rosemary's and his suite. Although her maid was there, Rosemary was not. "Do you know where Mrs. Huntington is?" he asked.

"With the children."

Climbing the stairs to the next floor, Stephen thought about what he must tell his wife. He stiffened his shoulders, put a smile on his face, and opened the nursery door. "Uncle Stephen!" James shouted. "Come see the game Aunt Rosemary brought us."

Stephen took his place on the floor with the three of them. "Who is winning?" he asked Julia.

Her face carefully uncaring, she said, "James. Aunt Rosemary brought me paints. Would you like me to paint you a picture, Uncle Stephen?" Her voice revealed her excitement.

"More than anything," he assured her. "No, it does not have to be right now. I actually came to take Rosemary away with me," he admitted. "But we will return soon," he promised. Although their faces were gloomy, the children were too well behaved to make much of a protest.

As soon as they had returned to their suite, Stephen told Rosemary what her father had said. "Do you remember anything, anything at all about that day?" he asked.

"I have told you that everything is a blank after the carriage ride. Then I remember being home at the Manor with Papa." Her voice shook with her repressed emotions. Her nerves quivered. She kept trying to swallow, but her throat was so tight it was impossible.

Stephen put his arms around her. "It is all right," he said soothingly. "Everything will be all right." Once again he wondered about communicating with one of Dr. Mesmer's pupils. Since he had been in London, he had investigated several of them. Though most were charlatans, one had had great success with patients who could not remember. He sighed and decided to postpone any decision until after their presentations.

Before Rosemary felt she was ready, the day of her presentation dawned. Stephen, who was attending a levee held by the king, was ready first. He then invaded Rosemary's dressing room and began teasing her. Nervous as she was, before long both she and her maid were ready to throw something at him. Picking up a large bottle of scent, Rosemary raised it over her head threateningly. "If you do not leave immediately, sir, you will need to change your clothing," she promised.

He drew himself up indignantly. "I was only trying to help," he protested. He inched his way toward the door.

"Well, you did not succeed. If I am to be ready on time, you must leave." The maid nodded vigorously.

At that moment his mother walked in. She took one look at Rosemary and let out a gasp. "You are not ready!"

"Your son keeps interfering," her daughter-in-law told her. She gave Stephen a look very much like the one Julia wore just before she said, "Now you are going to be in trouble."

"Get out!" His mother held the door open. "You may wait for us downstairs." Stephen glanced at his wife, who was now laughing. He shrugged his shoulders and left the room.

Less than fifteen minutes later Rosemary walked down the stairs, carefully maneuvering her wide skirts. "How did people ever manage when they had to wear these every day?" she asked.

"We were used to them. Somehow it was easier when you wore them all the time," Lady Longworth told her. "Let me see you curtsy." Willingly Rosemary sank to the floor. "And for the princesses if they are present?" Once again

Rosemary made her bow. "Good." She checked her plumes one more time. "It is time to leave."

When they returned home that afternoon, Lady Longworth was in alt. "So gracious, Daniel. The queen put her hand on Rosemary's head and murmured a few words. I was stunned. Absolutely enthralled," she continued. "Mary Ann, I wish you could have been there to see it. Three of the princesses nodded to her. It must have been Lady Babbington's doing. Or perhaps Canning's."

Rosemary had stiffened when she heard Lady Babbington's name. Soon she relaxed again. She smiled at her father, relieving his fears that she would blame him for what had happened to her as a child.

"Although she was nervous in the carriage, as soon as we arrived, no one would have suspected anything was wrong. She smiled at the right time. Her curtsy was so graceful that I saw one mother nod her appreciation." She smiled and sighed. "I told you that you would do well." She glanced around the room and then frowned. "Where is Stephen?"

"He has not returned yet," Daniel said. "Longworth said the king sometimes likes to talk to the gentlemen being presented." Rosemary yawned. Now that the ordeal was over—and no matter what Lady Longworth believed, it had been an ordeal for her—she was ready to retire for several hours' sleep. Daniel looked from her face to that of his wife. "Let us stay home tonight," he suggested. "We can send our regrets."

"If we are promised for dinner, it would be very rude to cancel at this late hour," Mary Ann reminded him.

"We eat at home tonight," Lady Longworth said serenely. "Then we are promised for a ball. If you do not wish to go, I will press Longworth into service as my escort."

"You just want a chance to tell someone about the queen's treatment of Rosemary," Mary Ann teased. The door opened, and the butler walked in. Knowing it was too late for callers, they looked at each other in puzzlement.

"Lord Longworth. Sir Stephen," the butler said proudly, as though the baronetage had been a personal gift for him.

"Stephen!" Rosemary cried, and ran into his arms. He picked her up and swung her about. She laughed and held on.

"Tell me everything!" his mother demanded of her elder son. "Were you there when the elevation was announced? Did the king tell you himself?"

"Let Stephen tell you," his brother told her. "It is his title."

"What happened? How did you find out?"

Stephen put Rosemary down but kept his arm around her. He winked at her. "We arrived a short time before our appointed hour," he began slowly. His mother raised her eyebrows threateningly. "That will not work with me any longer, Mama. I am a baronet, a peer of the realm now."

"A peer." Tears filled her eyes, and she brushed them hastily away. "Your father would have been so proud."

"I know, Mama." He crossed the room and stood beside her, placing a kiss on her cheek.

"Get on with it!" she said impatiently. Mary Ann smiled to see her usually calm cousin in such confusion.

"I was announced first," Longworth said.

"Then it was my turn," Stephen added. "I began to walk into the room when I was given the signal. Then I almost stumbled and fell."

"What happened?"

"I was announced as Sir Stephen Huntington. How I ever made my bow, I will never know."

"You thanked his majesty very nicely, little brother," Longworth said. "I was proud of you."

"No wonder the queen was so kind to Rosemary. Do you suppose she knew?" Mary Ann asked breathlessly.

"Without a doubt," Lady Longworth said firmly. "Longworth, have you any plans for this evening? I need your

escort. My usual companions are too exhausted. And I refuse
to stay at home on such a glorious evening.''

Delighted by the opportunity to spend the time alone with
his wife, Stephen smiled at her.

Already making plans for leaving London, Daniel asked,
''How much longer must we stay in town now that Stephen
has his title?''

''You make us sound as though we are holding you for
ransom, Daniel. Are you so willing to leave us?'' Lady
Longworth asked.

''Not the company. Just the place. There are many things
I must check for myself. We have been away from home
for quite some time now,'' he told her. ''Besides, I promised
Mary Ann we would spend Christmas with you. And I think
she needs some rest before another family gathering.''

''So do I,'' Stephen murmured so low that only Rosemary
could hear. She poked him in the ribs to keep him quiet.
''Your daughter is mistreating me,'' he complained to
Daniel.

''You have the right idea, little sister,'' Longworth said
with a smile. ''Julia does the same thing to James.''

Her tone more serious than the others, Lady Longworth
said, ''No one will leave before the ball. And unlike a ball
that may end at midnight or earlier in the country, this one
may last until dawn. Two days after the ball—that should
be early enough for all of us.''

Later that night Stephen lay beside his wife, turned on his
side so that he could see her face. He bent and kissed her,
resisting the impulse to make love with her again. She smiled
at him. ''Lady Rosemary,'' he said caressingly. Her smile
grew wider. So did his. Then he lay back and drew her close
to him. ''Are you interested in scientific experiments?'' he
asked, running his finger down her side.

Not quite certain if he were teasing, she asked, ''What
kind?'' She put her head on his shoulder.

''Have you ever heard of Dr. Mesmer?''

"Who has not? Some of your mother's friends who live in Bath believe he has the cure for everything." Then she stiffened. She pulled away from him, as far away as she could get and still be on the bed. She sat up straight. "Stephen, what are you suggesting?"

"That we witness an experiment with his techniques. One of his followers has had remarkable luck with reducing pain. One man had his tooth pulled without feeling a single twinge."

Rosemary relaxed a trifle. "I do not think I want to witness a tooth-drawing."

"He does not allow witnesses for things like that. If I promise you there will be no blood, nothing extracted, will you go with me?" He lay still, waiting for her answer.

"I suppose. As long as there is nothing painful."

The next morning he reminded her of her promise. "I have already sent him word to expect us," he told her. "Are you still willing to go?"

"Yes. But what does one wear to a scientific experiment? Have you asked Papa and Mary Ann? They may want to go too."

"This first time we will go alone. If we decide to return, they can go with us then."

Rosemary had already begun to have second thoughts when they got out of the carriage in front of a modest house. "Are you certain this is the place?" she asked.

"Dr. Walsh sent me the address himself," he assured her.

"He is a doctor?" She turned to walk back to the carriage.

"You promised," he reminded her, taking her arm and leading her up to the front door. He knocked.

A few moments later the door opened. "Good, you are right on time," a short man said heartily. His face and body reminded Rosemary of a ball because they were so round. "I am Dr. Walsh. The others are waiting in my study." He led the way down the short hall. "I think you will be very interested in my results."

The mention of others made Rosemary breathe easier, a

rather startling fact when she thought about it. What was happening to her fear of strangers?

They took their places around a table. Dr. Walsh quickly told them the background of his patient, a young woman whose dress and accent marked her as one of the lower classes. Offered a job she needed badly, that of a laundress, she could not take it because she had a fear of water. Rosemary's eyes grew wide. She had never come in contact with anyone who had a fear like hers.

Gradually, using a sparkling object he kept in front of his subject's eyes, Dr. Walsh put the girl to sleep. His voice, low and calm, soothed her. Then he began to question her. "Learning the cause of a fear can sometimes help a person overcome it," he told them. Gradually he led the girl to the day when her fear of water began. The story was a tragic one. When the girl had been little more than a toddler herself, the mother had left her in charge of her younger brother. Just beginning to stand, he had pulled himself up by using the side of a wooden bucket. When his legs gave out, he tumbled forward into the water. The girl had tried to pull him out, but she had not been strong enough.

"Her mother was to blame. Leaving a child that small alone. It is criminal," said one of the elder ladies who were also there as observers.

"But she does not know that. Her mother and father blamed her. I wonder if they would have beaten the boy had the situation been reversed?" the doctor said.

"Surely you are jesting?"

"No, madam, I am not. A boy can be sent out to work. Unless a girl from a poor family goes on the streets, there is not much for her to do. That is why this job is so vital to the girl."

"Can you do anything?" Stephen asked. Rosemary leaned forward to hear the doctor's answer, interested in spite of herself.

"I can try. Sometimes just remembering the incident is enough. Other times, I must see the patient several times."

Turning to his patient, he talked to her, soothing her, telling her how brave she was to try to save her brother. He also suggested that as she worked with water her fear would disappear. Awakening her, he had her go to a bowl in the corner of the room. There he had her stretch out her hands. He began to pour water over them. Although she flinched, she no longer screamed as though she were being burned.

"It will take longer with this one. Her fear has a deep hold on her," the doctor said patiently. One by one the observers left, until only Stephen and Rosemary remained. He had started to get up, but she stopped him. "What else do you wish to know?" Doctor Walsh said. He was not certain their interest was genuine.

"Like that poor girl, I have a fear, a fear of crowds and of strangers. Can you help me?" Rosemary asked, her pretty face serious and just a little sad.

"With your husband's permission, I can try. You must know I can promise nothing. With pain I am usually successful. With fears less so."

"I do not expect you to make it go away," Rosemary explained. "I simply must know why I have it." The doctor glanced at Stephen. He nodded.

"I would be happier if we did this at my brother's home," Stephen said firmly. "I will give you the address. Can you come soon?"

The doctor consulted a list in his pocket. "Will this afternoon at two be too soon?"

When he arrived that afternoon, he was shown into the library, a place Stephen had chosen because it was most like the doctor's own study. Deciding to keep their own counsel until the doctor had made his attempt, Stephen and Rosemary had said nothing to the others.

The two hours that the doctor worked with them were the longest of Stephen's life. He held Rosemary's hand until it went limp. Then he listened while a little girl, dressed in her finest, prettiest clothes, her silvery blond curls sparkling in the sunlight, called to her mother. Then she screamed.

Quickly the doctor calmed her, telling her she was safe. When she was quiet once more, Dr. Walsh turned to Stephen. "If I try to get her to remember more today, she might react more violently. She has hidden this experience within her for so long, I will need several sessions with her in order to bring it to the surface." Stephen nodded. "I believe she will respond. We will simply have to proceed slowly."

Dr. Walsh returned each afternoon at the same time. Each afternoon, Rosemary, her face set, lived through that day in her childhood. Each night she had nightmares. But finally they were able to piece together a picture of Rosemary's last afternoon with her mother.

Slipping away from her nurse, Rosemary had hidden in her mother's carriage parked in front of the door, planning to surprise her. She grew cold and drew the carriage blanket over herself, going to sleep in its warmth.

When she awoke, she climbed down carefully, making certain the coachman, who was very gruff, did not see her. She stared in perplexity at the luggage on top of the coach and turned to go into the house. It was not hers. But she knew it. She had been there several times when her mother had visited the artist. Rosemary's forehead creased as she tried to remember his name, but it escaped her.

Before she had gotten the courage to go inside, she heard a noise. Knowing her mother would be angry if she thought Rosemary was spying on her, she slipped across the street. Then the door opened. Her mother and the artist came out, their faces shining with excitement. They climbed into the coach and drove away. Rosemary ran after them, begging her mother to stop, to wait for her. At the edge of the park in a section not favored by the smart set, Rosemary stumbled and fell.

Frightened, she began crying. Her outcry drew a crowd of working people. For a few minutes they simply stared at her. Her crumpled dress and slippers were finer than anything in their lives. Her hair, as tousled and sweaty as it was, gleamed in the late-afternoon sunlight. More than one person crowded close to her to touch it and finger the lace on her dress.

Before a few enterprising souls had done more than consider the profit they could make from her clothing and from the child herself, a coach stopped. Slowly the crowd around her drew back, intimidated by the grooms and coachman who walked toward them, their whips in their hands.

"Lady Babbington," Rosemary whispered. "Lady Babbington."

"What do you mean, Rosemary?"

"It was Lady Babbington's coach. She had heard me scream and seen my dress."

"Lady Babbington? What was she doing there?" Stephen asked, not expecting an answer.

"She said sometimes good came out of sin, she supposed." The men exchanged glances. "So tired. Lady Babbington will take care of me," she mumbled.

Quickly, before she fell asleep, Dr. Walsh told her that when she awoke she would remember everything, especially that Lady Babbington had rescued her and that she did not have to be afraid.

"Whether that will be enough, Sir Stephen, I do not know," the doctor said, stretching. "She will wake refreshed. Do you know the lady of whom she spoke?"

"She is a recent acquaintance."

"I would suggest that you encourage your wife to visit her, talk with her perhaps."

"We are to leave for the country soon."

"Encourage a correspondence, then. Make certain she remembers the lady," the doctor said. Stephen nodded. Crossing to the desk, he pulled out a bag of coins he had left there and handed them to the doctor. "This is too much, Sir Stephen, too much!" the doctor exclaimed, weighing the bag in his hand.

"Not for what you just helped us to discover. Thank you."

Still protesting, the doctor walked to the door.

When Rosemary woke up a short time later, her face glowed with happiness. Then it clouded over. "Why did my mother leave me?" she wondered.

"Maybe she knew her new life would not suit you," Stephen suggested. He had wondered the same thing but was not willing to explain his own theory that the lady did not care for anyone but herself.

Although she was not sure that what he had said was the truth, Rosemary was not willing to discount the idea either. She stretched lazily. "I want to see Lady Babbington again," she said quietly. Even though she would always have her doubts about her mother, now that she knew why she was afraid of people, she was ready to face her fear. And thanking Lady Babbington would be her first step.

"She has sent her acceptance for the ball," he reminded her. "No one will think it strange if you sit out one or two dances to talk with her."

"I would be willing to sit them all out."

"Not mine. I want to dance with you. At least let me have the supper dance."

"Do not beg. It is not befitting a baronet."

"Come upstairs with me, Lady Rosemary. Tell me how a baronet should behave." He pulled her up and stood holding her for a moment.

"My husband's wish is my command," she said, lowering her eyelashes and then sweeping them up again.

"Then I wish I had all your dances tomorrow night."

"Stephen!"

When the time for the ball arrived, Rosemary was as nervous as she usually was. Only the realization that she could not let the family down made her leave her room. Looking her best, she wore a white silk gown figured in blue. Stephen had given her a pearl set with sapphire clasps for the occasion. She carried a new fan from her father and Mary Ann and flowers from the twins and their father. She had refused to allow Stephen to escort her downstairs. She had wanted to do this herself. She took a deep breath and opened the door.

"I hate doing this," her father muttered under his breath as he stood in the receiving line beside his daughter and his wife a short while later.

"Hush, Papa. Someone will hear you."

"Well, they probably hate it too."

Rosemary felt her husband's shoulder shake and wanted to hit him. Instead she smiled and said a few words to the lady in front of her. She was not certain why, but standing here was not the ordeal she had expected it to be.

"Here she comes," Stephen whispered. "I see her in the doorway."

"Who?"

"Lady Babbington."

Rosemary rehearsed the few words she had planned one more time. Then the lady was before her. "Lady Babbington, would you honor me by letting me speak with you later this evening? Perhaps during the second country dance?"

"Anytime you like. I am here merely as a spectator, my dear. You are the one who should be dancing," the lady said. This evening her cane was gold to match the trim on her rich purple gown. Rosemary smiled at her.

As guests of honor at the ball, she and Stephen led out the first set of figures of the first dance. Never giving her audience a thought, she smiled at him and performed flawlessly. They separated. When they came back together, Stephen was beaming in delight.

"You are talking to your partners," he said quietly. Her eyes widened. "No, do not try to gawk at them. Your father and my brother were two of them. The other five you did not know."

"Stephen, it is working." They separated again. "But I still was frightened," she said when they came together again.

"Remember. Dr. Walsh said that fear could not be erased instantly for some people. Give yourself time. Talk with Lady Babbington."

When he escorted his wife to the settee beside the window leading to the balcony, his bow was deeper than normal. "You do me much honor, sir," the lady protested, her smile showing just a hint of disapproval.

"Never too much for someone who did me so great a service," he protested.

"Lady Babbington, I have just remembered where we first met," Rosemary explained.

"You have? Rumor had it that you had forgotten all about that episode."

"I want to thank you."

"Nonsense, child. You helped me put a dangerous relationship behind me. Had it not been for rescuing you, I might have been in serious trouble. No, do not ask me more. I cannot tell you." She smiled and leaned forward. "I told you that I had led a scandalous life, but I always had a place in society. You, perhaps, kept me from losing that place for all time," she said seriously.

Mary Ann and Daniel walked up at that moment to add their thanks, but Lady Babbington brushed them aside. "Lady Huntington's curls reminded me of my childhood. Never did like the habit of wearing a wig and powder. Always preferred men who wore their own hair. Wore my own, too, until it fell out." She tapped Daniel on the arm. "Never told the man, but I liked your grandfather because we could have been a matched pair. Both of us blond and neither liked powder, filthy habit." She smiled. "Now, dance. Always liked to see pretty girls and handsome men twirl about the floor."

When the evening was over, Stephen yawned and headed upstairs beside his wife. "This is the first ball we have attended where we are among the last to leave."

"Your mother would have been heartbroken if we had left

early. She was ecstatic. Everyone will envy her for weeks, maybe longer. Her ball was a crush." She smiled up at him.

"And what did you enjoy the most?"

"Now." Then she added quickly, "And talking to Lady Babbington and dancing with you. I am so happy you encouraged me to come to London and to see Dr. Walsh. If you had not . . ." She shuddered.

"Do not think about things that did not happen," he told her. He pulled her close to him. "You are safe, and I plan to keep you safe for the rest of my life." He glanced at her serious face and smiled wickedly. "At least you will be safe from everyone but me."

She laughed softly and took his hand, pulling him up the staricase toward their room. "Do you promise?" she asked mischievously. Her soft laughter echoed up and down the stairs until they were surrounded by sounds of happiness, a happiness they shared for the rest of their lives.